Big Bright Land

By ENID JOHNSON and
ANNE MERRIMAN PECK

Big Bright
Land

GROSSET & DUNLAP, *Publisher*

NEW YORK

CONTENTS

Big Bright Land

Chapter I

"WESTWARD HO!"

JEAN MERRYWEATHER TRAMPED ALONG THE VILLAGE street, head down against the wind and rain of a late September storm. Yellow leaves whirled by and clung to the wet sidewalk underfoot. Ugh! This storm was a warning that winter was on the way.

"How will Dad get through the cold weather?" Jean thought anxiously. That was the question which had overshadowed everything for her and her twin brother, John, ever since the doctor had warned them that the bleak New England winter would be extremely dangerous for their father, weakened by a severe attack of pneumonia during the last year.

As though it were not enough to have this anxiety

gnawing at her heart on such a gloomy day, Jean had just been to the station to see her two best friends off to college. Jean and John had graduated from high school in June, but there had been no money to send them to college. Their father's illness had drained his resources and since then he had been too weak to go on with his work as an architect. Jean knew that she would not have left her father anyway in his present ill health.

She pushed open the gate in the picket fence enclosing their dooryard and hurried up the steps to the comfortable, solid white house. She looked in the open door of her father's study. He was lying back in his comfortable chair by the reading lamp, absorbed in a book. How white and hollow-eyed he looked, and how listless the long thin hand resting on the chair arm!

"Cup of tea, Dad?" she asked brightly.

He looked up with the warm, affectionate smile which was Jean's reward for everything she did for him.

"Lovely, dear, if you will join me," he answered.

Jean quickly prepared the tea tray and brought it to the study.

"Your favorite ginger snaps, Daddy," she announced, offering him the cookies. While they sipped their tea, Jean chatted lightly, hoping that her father would not ask her where she had been, but he did.

"What took you out in the rain this afternoon?" he wanted to know.

"Oh, Ruth and Dottie started for college today and the gang went to the station to see them off," she replied casually.

A look of dejection crossed her father's face.

"Ah, Jeanie," he sighed, "you and John should have been going, too."

"It doesn't matter a bit, Dad," Jean assured him. "Seventeen isn't such a great age—there's plenty of time for us to go to college when the family ship comes in and you're well. Neither John nor I have any burning desire for careers—not yet, anyway. We'll get along this winter with post-graduate courses at the high, and there are plenty of the crowd left here to have a good time with."

She carried away the tea things, then went into the living room. Leaning against the window she listened to the rain beating on the glass. The weight of responsibility for her father seemed very heavy at the moment. She had, as well, a forlorn feeling of having been left behind by her friends. She would not admit to her father or brother that she minded being unable to start college with them, but it was hard, nevertheless, to give up the exciting new experiences to which she had looked forward. John didn't seem to care—she thought—he was so easy-going and not particularly ambitious.

Jean's thoughts went back to the agonizing days last winter when their father hovered between life and death. The twins' fear had been made more poignant by the fact that two years before they had lost their mother. In that time of grief and bewilderment fifteen-year-old Jean had determined to keep the home going and to look after her father and brother. She had done it, too, although it had been difficult to combine home-making with her high school work. She knew that both her father and brother depended on her, and that knowledge gave a motherly quality to her affection for them.

"Heavens, I'm in the dumps!" Jean thought to herself.

She turned on the light and went to survey herself in the mirror. Shining, honey-colored hair waved softly about her face. Steady gray eyes looked back at her.

"Buck up, now," she told her reflection and brought a smile to her drooping mouth. "John and I will find a way to send Dad somewhere to a warm climate. Maybe there will be a letter from Uncle George tonight."

This almost mythical uncle, unlike their quiet, scholarly father, had always been a wanderer. Over the years letters had come from him, telling of mining in the Andes, of adventures in the Australian bush and in South Africa. A few years ago Uncle George had written that he had bought a ranch in southern Arizona and settled down to be a cattleman.

In their desperate search for some means to get their father away from a New England winter, the twins had written to the unknown uncle telling him of his brother's illness, and asking that he invite their father to spend the winter on his ranch. So far, no answer had come, although they watched for it eagerly each day.

The front door slammed and a gust of cold wind accompanied brisk footsteps down the hall. "Hi-ya, Sis," came John's clear hail.

He tramped into the living room and stood, hands in pockets, grinning at her, while his raincoat dripped on the rug.

"John, for heaven's sake, put your wet raincoat in the kitchen," Jean ordered. "It's making a regular pool on the rug!"

"Okay, Bossy," answered John, as he hurried into the kitchen. Jean smiled after him, indulgently. Dear John, what a kid he was—so lean and long and sprawly, his boyish face lighted by dancing gray eyes, matching her own in color, and a humorous mouth. His blond hair stood up in a curly mop.

"Guess what I've got in my pocket, Jeanie," he grinned when he returned to the room. As her face lit up, he went on, "Yes, a letter from Arizona. You wouldn't have been so fussy about a little rain dripping on your precious rug if you'd known that, would you?"

"Oh, John, let's take it to Dad, quick!"

"Funny thing, though," John went on, studying the envelope, "this has the address typed and I never knew Uncle George to use a typewriter."

They went together to the study and John said, "Here, Dad, you've a letter from Uncle George, and we're both busting to know what he's up to now."

Mr. Merryweather read the letter slowly, with a look of increasing concern and distress. Then he looked up at the twins.

"This is quite a shock," he said gravely. "It is from George's lawyer in Tucson, telling me that my brother died last week of a heart attack!"

The twins looked at each other in dismay. They could not feel personal grief for an uncle they had never known, but now there would be no Arizona for their father that winter.

"I'm sorry about Uncle George, Daddy," said Jean, softly.

"Yes," said Mr. Merryweather with a deep sigh, "I shall

miss George although I haven't seen him for years. He was a fine man and we were fond of each other, in spite of the fact that we were very different. There is startling news of another sort in that letter, too," he went on. "The lawyer writes that George has left me his ranch and asks for my instructions about the property."

"Jiminy crickets!" shouted John. "That is what I call providential. An Arizona ranch is just what we needed in this family. Why don't we go out there and spend the winter in the sunshine? I believe that is what Arizona has plenty of."

"Nonsense," said his father. "You know that is impossible, when our funds are so low. Here you have worked all summer in the supply company just to help keep the family going until I could get back into business. I shall have to ask the lawyer to place the ranch for sale with some real estate firm. If we could get a good price for it, our finances would be much improved."

"Well, let's discuss it as soon as we've had supper," suggested Jean. "I'll go make some waffles, and you, John, please build a fire in the fireplace. It's so chilly and dreary tonight."

During supper the twins kept up a constant speculation about their newly acquired ranch, asking their father everything he could remember about the country and Uncle George's place.

"It's in the desert, but it is good cattle range, George once said," Mr. Merryweather told them. "He said, too, that the country is beautiful."

"Now, Dad, can't you just see yourself basking out there in the sunshine this winter instead of staying here and shivering with cold and probably getting sick again?" John pleaded.

Mr. Merryweather smiled, and the eager watchers saw that his resistance was weakening. But he shook his head. "It sounds very alluring," he said, "but land and cattle don't mean ready money, you know. We can't afford to go out there, and I must try to get back to my business here. The town is ready to give me the job of designing the new high school building as soon as I am strong enough."

"Put your conscience to sleep, Mr. Merryweather," begged Jean. "We are going to hold a family council as soon as John and I have done the dishes."

Soon the three were gathered in front of the blazing log fire in the living room. Jean sat on a footstool, leaning against her father's knee. John sprawled on the hearthrug, playing with Timmie, their pet Scottie. Mr. Merryweather looked at his two tall, slim children with deep pride and affection. How he wanted for them the best the world could give!

"You know," he said, "how much it has distressed me that I couldn't send you both on to college this fall. But it has been a comfort that you were going to take special courses at the high school, so that you could enter college in the sophomore year when there were available funds. Now, even if we had money to go junketing off to Arizona, I couldn't bear to have you give up your studies."

"Listen, Daddy," said Jean. "The family Merryweather is a co-operative organization, isn't it—each for all and all for each. And up to now the junior members of the firm have had the best of it. Now it is time for the senior member to have his innings. When you are well again, designing country homes for rich New Yorkers, John and I will go zipping off to college like a shot. Are you with me, John?"

"A hundred per cent!" said John, briefly but convincingly.

"There, you see, you're outvoted, Mr. Merryweather," laughed Jean.

"And speaking of rich New Yorkers!" exclaimed John, sitting up and pushing Timmie aside. "I'll bet I have the solution to the money problem. Bill Hanson was telling me the other day that his real estate business is booming. I'm sure Bill could rent this house for enough for us all to live on out West."

"I don't know that I like the idea of letting strangers live in our home. Do you, Jean?"

"Well, no, Dad—I know how you feel. But it could be done if we were very choosey and got nice people."

Both Jean and her father were deeply attached to the dignified old house which had been built by the children's grandfather. Here Mr. Merryweather had brought his bride and here the twins had been born and had grown up. John loved it, too, but he did not have as strong a feeling for family tradition as the other two.

"I say we rent it if we can find the right people," said Jean stoutly, after a little thought. "It would be worth it to see you well again, Daddy. We'd go just for the winter, or a year at the most, wouldn't we?"

"If we make the move at all I think we should stay a year," said her father. "I must say the prospect of warm sunshine tempts me. Probably while we were out there we could arrange to sell the ranch and the cattle. Then we would return with funds in hand for you two to begin college."

"Uh-huh," said John, without enthusiasm. Already his adventurous fancy pictured the free life on the ranch and he saw himself, in Western attire, rounding up cattle like a regular Gene Autry.

A definite decision had to be postponed until they learned whether they could rent the house. And while the golden October days went by the household buzzed with activity. Jean called in their faithful standby, Mrs. Jenkins, to help her make the house ready to rent. Mrs. Jenkins was a spare, wrinkled village woman who came in once a week to clean and wash for them. She was devoted to the family and made no secret of her conviction that this was a hare-brained adventure.

"Seems a crazy thing to me to leave your good home and all your friends to go traipsin' out to that wild West," she scolded.

"But we'll find friends," Jean replied cheerfully, although she felt that Mrs. Jenkins' forthright remarks expressed her own fears.

The Merryweathers studied Uncle George's few letters from Arizona.

"In the first letter he says he has bought five sections of land and expects to lease six more," announced John. "Let's see, how much is a section? Six hundred and forty acres, isn't it, Dad?"

His father nodded.

"Gee, what a lot of land! Why around here, a forty-acre farm is quite sizable. What was he going to do with it all?"

Further study of the letters disclosed Uncle George's plan to "run" about two hundred head of cattle.

"Whatever that may mean," commented Jean. "I should think a couple of thousand cows could run or walk or even roll on such a huge ranch. And he says the place is called Circle M Ranch, that it is twenty-five miles southwest of Tucson, and has a three room adobe house. What's adobe?"

John had an answer ready for that, having spent his free time studying up on Western matters.

"They make adobe bricks from earth mixed with straw and water and baked hard in the sun," he announced.

"Well, I can't imagine what such a house will look like," said Jean. "And how will we get our supplies, do you suppose?"

"After all," said her father, "we have the station wagon, and Tucson is quite a city, I believe. It is a health resort, you know, and the State university is there."

Jean brightened at that news. "Oh good! Maybe we'll meet some of the students. Probably it's a co-ed college, too."

The lawyer, in his letter, also said that George Merryweather's Mexican cowboy, Pedro, was still at the ranch looking after the cattle, and that he would stay as long as they wished.

"Good," said John. "He can teach me a cowboy's job. I bet I'll have to spend most of every day just riding over the land to see if the cattle are all right."

On the very day that Jean had given the last "lick and polish" to the house, Bill Hanson appeared with an elderly prosperous-looking lawyer from New York, and his kindly, gray-haired wife. Jean showed them around, shyly.

Her heart warmed to the good people when they exclaimed with delight over the simple charm of the house and its furnishings. They would be sure to take good care of the precious place, she thought.

So the die was cast. When Mr. Merryweather came in that evening with the lease and a check for the first month's rent, the three looked it over solemnly, and as solemnly shook hands all round. Now that they were actually going on what was, for that family, a big adventure, Jean and her father were almost as excited as John.

Eagerly they began to plan for departure right after the middle of October. At first they thought that all three could drive out in the family station wagon, affectionately known as Joshua. But Dr. Braman, Mr. Merryweather's physician, would not hear of that.

"Even if you were well and strong that trip would be very tiring," the doctor said. "Let the twins drive out by themselves and get settled and then, after a week or two, you follow by train. Meanwhile Mrs. Braman and I would be delighted to have you stay with us."

"Do you think it's safe for the children to travel alone?" asked their father, in alarm.

"Sure it is, Dad," said John. "We aren't babies, you know."

"I'm sure it is perfectly safe," said the doctor. "Jean and John have lots of good common sense. They mustn't drive too fast, nor pick up strangers on the road, nor drive after dark. The best plan is to stop at any likely looking place you come to a good hour before sunset—not keep on looking for a better place."

The twins beamed at him gratefully. Mr. Merryweather

reluctantly agreed, and a few days later, when he returned from a business trip to New York, he brought back road maps on which the best and quickest route had been marked by a touring bureau. They studied the red-marked highway, as it ran from state to state, while John added up the mileage. To their astonishment, they found that it would probably take them a week to reach Tucson.

"Heavens, what a big country this is!" exclaimed Jean. "It's about time we began to discover it. Look at tiny New England over here in the corner. And we've never been west of the Hudson. Provincial, that's what we are."

"I'll follow, then, in about a week," said Mr. Merryweather.

"No, Daddy," said Jean, "you had better wait two weeks so that we will be all settled by the time you get there."

When it came to packing, each member of the family brought precious volumes from the bookshelves, favorites which must get into the one box of books they were taking. A few rugs and pictures were chosen to make the ranch house look homelike. Jean packed one party frock among her more serviceable clothes.

"Though I'll probably never have a chance to wear it," she thought with a rueful smile.

Jean had had a hard time restraining her impetuous brother from piling up a bill at an expensive sports wear shop in New York, for whose catalogue he had sent as soon as he knew that they were really going West.

"But see here, Jean," he had protested, "I don't want everybody in Arizona to know I'm a tenderfoot in my Eastern clothes. Dad wouldn't mind my buying a few things—you know he wouldn't."

"John Merryweather," his sister had answered severely, "Dad hasn't a penny to spend on this foolishness, and you know it. Besides for the rough ranch work that you will have to do, your old working clothes will be all right. You won't need anything but boots, and we'd best wait until we get there to see what kind of boots real cowboys wear. If you wore the wrong kind of boots, and brand-new at that, they'd be sure to know you were a tender-foot."

"Okay, Bossy, you've got something there," John admitted reluctantly, and threw away the beautiful catalogue, saying no more about it.

On the last afternoon Jean flopped down exhausted on the doorstep. Everything was done. That night the boys and girls of their crowd, who had not gone to college, were giving the twins a farewell party. Then, in the morning, they would be off on the most adventurous journey of their lives.

Sitting tired and relaxed, Jean was sharply aware of how much she loved everything in this dear home place. The last golden leaves floated down from the maples lining the quiet village street. Children, coming home from school, laughed and scuffled among dry leaves, just as Jean had done when she was a little girl. The scent of burning leaves in the cold air was bound up with her happy childhood.

Close to her in the friendly town were neighbors, kindly people as familiar as her own family, people who were always ready to lend a hand, who had helped and comforted them when their mother died and again when their father was so ill.

In the flower borders of the small garden, fringy asters and button chrysanthemums still bloomed bravely. Jean looked at them lovingly. Her mother had taught her the joy of working with growing things and Jean had been proud to keep the garden bright in memory of her.

Whistling merrily, John came up the path and sat down beside her.

"Not moping, are you, Jeanie?" he asked, looking anxiously at her sober face. "Sometimes I'm afraid it will be too lonesome for you out there in Arizona. You are such a popular gal. You'll miss the boy friends."

"Nonsense," scoffed Jean, hiding her own qualms behind a reassuring grin. "I'll have you and Dad, won't I? And I'll be too busy seeing new things and learning how to run a ranch to be lonesome. At that, I may pick up a cowboy for a boy friend, who knows?"

"They'll be eating out of your hand," declared her brother, twinkling at her. "As for me," he went on, "I'm rarin' to go. I have an idea outdoor Western life is going to be just my meat. As I think of it, the best times I've ever had have been on those camping trips in the White Mountains hiking, sleeping on the ground, cooking over a camp fire. That, and horseback rides in the wood paths with you and Dad, and the times I've gone hunting with him."

"Time will tell," laughed Jean.

She looked at her brother searchingly, wondering, as she often did, when he would grow up and take a serious interest in what she called "reality." She could see that his ideas of Western life centered on what a fine figure he would cut, dressed in his cowboy clothes, riding horseback. Did he realize how much monotonous hard work lay before him? Jean wondered. Fond as she was of her twin, she was critical of his lack of ambition and his play-boy attitude toward the business of living.

"Come on," she said at last, "we must have an early supper so we can get all dolled up for the dance. We want to go out in a blaze of glory, you know."

That was a party to be remembered always, the twins told each other as they crept into the house in the small hours, warm with laughter and fun. A few hours of sleep, and then John's call roused the others to tumble out in the chill October dawn, to eat a hurried breakfast and pack the last things.

While her father and brother wrestled with the over-crowded station wagon, Jean made a last tour of the pretty, orderly rooms, and tears sprang to her eyes at the thought of what she was leaving.

"Silly—stop that!" she scolded. "We're coming back, after all. A year isn't so long."

She tied a bright kerchief over her blond head, buttoned her warm coat and ran down the path with Timmie at her heels. The little dog was beside himself with joy at the signs of a trip.

"Hi, Jean," called her brother. "I hope you brought along a shoe horn to help you get aboard. We've sure got a load. How about leaving Timmie behind?"

"No you don't," cried Jean, picking up the little dog. "I couldn't live without Timmie!"

Before she climbed aboard, she turned to her father, who put his arms around her. "Good-bye, my darling," he said softly. "Please be careful—and remember your promise— don't let John drive too fast; don't try to drive too far any one day, stop before dark, I mean, and above all, don't give any stranger a lift."

"Please don't worry about us, Daddy," she answered. "We'll send you a wire to Dr. Braman's house every night."

"Good!" said her father. "Take care of your sister, son," he said to John.

"I will, sir," answered the boy, shaking his father's hand, heartily. "Good-bye."

"Well, then, Westward Ho! Merryweather, Incorporated," said their father.

The clock on the steeple struck six, as John started the engine. Just then gay shouts were heard and down the street pelted a group of boys and girls.

"Surprise, surprise!" cried one of the girls, as they surrounded the station wagon. "We just had to see you off, even if we've been up practically all night."

"I wish you had room to take me along," said one of the boys. "I want to be a cowboy, too."

The twins laughed and waved and shouted good-bye as Joshua rattled down the village street.

Jean bit her lip to keep back tears, as John stopped the car at the foot of the hill and turned for a last look.

"Good-bye, old town," said John. "We sure will miss you, but we'll be back sometime, sure."

"Oh, we will, we will!" cried Jean.

Chapter II

THE NEW PASSENGER

"My, it's fun to be gypsies on the road," commented Jean. It was the second morning of their trip and the twins were travelling along the Lee Memorial Highway in Virginia, between the Blue Ridge Mountains and the Alleghenies.

"It's a starved gypsy I am," John returned. "We started so early this morning that I've forgotten I ever had breakfast and I've seen so many barbecue signs that my mouth is watering."

Jean agreed it was high time they sampled the famous barbecued sandwiches of the South, so they stopped before a roadside stand. When they had satisfied their hunger with the savory food, washed down with sweet apple cider, they rolled on down the Shenandoah Valley at a good pace.

Soft autumnal haze veiled the gentle rhythms of the Blue Ridge and the more abrupt masses of the distant Alleghenies. Between the mountains lay the rolling fields and neat orchards of the fertile valley, each farm marked by a capacious red barn and white farmhouse.

When they stopped for gas at a station they were delighted with the attendant's, "Come back and see us again, please Ma'am," as he accepted Jean's money.

"How polite everybody is in this part of the country," said Jean, "and how hospitable!"

"After all this is the South," John reminded her, "the place noted for its good manners and hospitality. We're polite enough in our neck of the woods, but not so—so—"

"Picturesque?" suggested Jean.

"Yeah, that's it," agreed John.

It was late the next afternoon, however, when they were crossing the Cumberland Mountains, looking for a much advertised "tourist court" where they planned to stay for the night, that something happened to shake their faith in the hospitality of the South.

They had just passed a little village when they came upon a group of men on horseback gathered around a shabbily dressed young man with a very pale face and dark, frightened eyes. The leader of these men was apparently the sheriff, for he had a star pinned on his coat and a holster with a revolver strapped around his ample waist.

"You git out of this town and stay out," he was saying, as John stopped the station wagon to listen. "We've got no room in our town for bums and deadbeats."

"Yes," put in one of the men, shaking his fist at the youth, "don't ever let me catch you pussyfooting around my place again asking my wife for victuals. We can't feed all the hoboes that come to town—especially one like you, just out of jail!"

"But—but, please," the young man said in a pleading tone. "I wasn't doing any harm, sir. I offered to work for a meal at your house. I haven't had anything to eat since yesterday noon—"

"John," whispered Jean, "can't we do something for him?"

John jumped out of the car and impulsively walked up to the group of men.

"You're a heck of a bunch of guys," he cried to the men who were too surprised to answer him. Taking the young fellow by the arm, he said, "Say, chum, we lost you back there. Come on in the car." He gave the startled young man a broad wink and hustled him into the station wagon, abruptly stepped on the gas and drove quickly away.

"It's okay, Timmie," John said to the little dog who sniffed at the stranger. "This is a friend!" Timmie settled down contentedly on the pile of rugs in the rear of the car.

None of them heard the sheriff's parting shot, "Don't you young fools come back crying around me if that sneak thief steals your wallet!"

"Gee, thanks, fella," the young man was saying. "But I don't want to crowd you this-a-way."

"You aren't crowding us," spoke up Jean. "We'll stop at the next town and buy you something to eat while we have supper."

"You're mighty good to a stranger," responded the youth. "I sure thank you, Ma'am."

"That's okay," said John, and, driving as fast as the curving mountain roads permitted, they soon pulled up before a lunch room, and seated themselves at a table.

As the young man ate with evident relish, the Merryweather twins observed him. His face, under a shock of black hair, was homely and thin with high cheek bones. But his eyes, large and dark and fringed with long lashes, were beautiful, Jean thought, but for the look of suspicion and fear in them. There was suspicion, too, in the hunch of his shoulders, as though he was prepared to ward off a blow.

"Poor fellow," thought the girl. "What has the world done to him to make him hate it so?"

When the young man could hold no more food, he began to talk in a slow drawling voice, like the cowboys Jean had heard on the radio. He might be a cowboy, she thought, for he wore high-heeled boots and blue jeans,

"I think I ought to tell you folks that it's true what that man said back there," he told the twins. "I have been in jail. I was accused of stealing a watch and some money from my boss—but I didn't do it. Please believe me."

Jean looked into the deep, honest eyes turned pleadingly toward her.

"I believe you," she spoke up.

A smile lit up his brooding face. "Thank you, Ma'am," he drawled.

"How about telling us the story," suggested John. "Your moniker and all."

"Sure," said the young man. "My name is Nat Barton. I've been working on a ranch in the Texas Panhandle for the past two years. One of the other fellows in the outfit was a bad actor, and he and I had a fight and I licked him, so he had it in for me. Then my boss, the fellow that owned the ranch, got sore at me one day—said I'd mistreated a mare of his. When I denied it, he swore at me and I got mad. I've got a bad temper, I reckon, and I can't stand being yelled at. Anyhow, a few days after our argument, this man's watch and wallet were missing and the fellow who was my enemy told him, the owner, to search my kit. He did, and there he found a pawn ticket for the watch. I swear I don't know how it got there—but I've always believed that fellow who hated me planted it there.

"Well, of course it looked mighty bad for me and my boss was glad to have something on me, anyway, so he had me arrested. Nobody believed I was innocent after they found the pawn ticket. I was just framed, that's all." His mouth twisted, bitterly, "But I didn't do it—I swear it!"

Once more his eyes turned to Jean and she smiled at him and repeated, "I believe you!"

"How did you happen to get mixed up with that sheriff and his gang back there where we picked you up?" John asked.

"Well," went on the young man in his slow, Southern drawl, "after I'd served my sentence they turned me out and told me to git out of the state of Texas. I didn't much care where I went, but I figured I'd light out eastwards and look for a job in a garage—I'm kinda handy around cars. But I didn't strike any luck in the towns I passed and I got down to my last cent. Then I hitched a ride with a truck driver and he was kind to me and fed me along the way.

"I was fool enough to tell him my story, and that was

all he needed, apparently. He didn't believe me, either, and he set me down in that town—said I'd played him for a sucker. How I happened to tell him my troubles was that we got to talking about how unfair things are sometimes in this world. He must have tipped off the sheriff in that town about me."

"The dirty low-life," put in John, hotly.

"You bet," said Nat Barton. "Anyhow I couldn't get anything to eat in the whole place. No matter where I went the ladies who came to the door slammed it in my face. One of them even sicked her dog on me. Then, at the last place I tried, the man called the sheriff while I was talking to his wife at the kitchen door, and the first thing I knew I was being run out of town by that gang with the sheriff at their head. That's all, folks. And thanks a lot for the meal. I guess I'll mosey along now."

"But where will you go?" asked Jean.

"Oh, I'll go back on the road. Someone will give me a lift, and I'll have sense enough now to keep my mouth shut. I'm heading back West, though—that's where I belong. I'll steer clear of Texas, but there's plenty of cow country, and cowpunchin' is my job."

The twins looked at each other. In John's eyes was a question which Jean read. She nodded her head emphatically.

"How about coming along with us, Nat?" suggested John. "We're on our way to a ranch near Tucson in Arizona that my father just inherited from my uncle. I believe there's plenty of cattle country in Arizona and you could look for a job around there somewhere. Come on!"

Nat turned to Jean. "How about you, Ma'am?" he asked diffidently. "Do you want me to do as your brother says?"

Jean spoke up hastily. "Of course I do, Nat."

Nat Barton's face lit up. "You'd be taking an awful chance on me, you two," he said, slowly. "But if you feel like you can, I'll thank you for the rest of my life and I swear I won't let you down. I haven't got a cent, though, so you folks would have to grub stake me until I get a job and can pay you back."

"That's okay," said John. "Now let's get along and find a place to stay for tonight. Gee whiz," he went on, "it's almost dark and we promised Dad we'd stop every afternoon before dark."

The same thought struck both twins simultaneously. They had broken another promise to their father—a very solemn promise—not to pick up any strangers on the road. And here they were, offering to take this stranger clear to Arizona with them! They looked at each other in serious questioning, then Jean said, "It's all right, John. I'm sure Dad would have done the same thing."

"Sure he would," John answered heartily. "Say, Jean," he went on, taking his sister's arm and leading her out of Nat's hearing, "I'll not say anything about our new passenger to Dad in my wire tonight. We can explain all this to him after we get to the ranch and write him."

"I suppose you're right, John. It would only worry him —but I hate—I hate—" his sister hesitated. Her heart was heavy with the realization that, for the first time in her life, she was not keeping a promise to her father. She lulled her conscience to sleep, however, sure that he would only worry about them. After all he hadn't seen what a likable, honest person Nat was. She promised herself that as soon as they had safely arrived in Arizona she would write her father and make a clean breast of this part of their adventure. So John went blithely to the telegraph office and sent their usual wire: "All well. Joshua behaving beautifully. Love. John and Jean."

At the end of the following day, the station wagon had a slight breakdown, and Nat proved he was indeed "kinda handy around cars." When he had skillfully and efficiently made the repair, John remarked, "That job makes us quits for at least two days' food and lodging, Nat."

"Look here," Jean now suggested to Nat. "Why don't you take the wheel awhile?"

"May I, John?" asked Nat.

"Sure thing," answered John heartily.

"Say," said Nat, a flush of embarrassment spreading over his face, "I'd like to tell you two what a swell pair of folks I think you are. Here you pick me up and feed me and now you trust me to drive your car—and you don't know a thing about me except that I'm a jail bird and I might be lying to you about being framed. Gee, I'm—"

"Don't be dumb, fella," broke in John.

"Give us credit for a little sense, Nat," added Jean. "I guess John and I know an honest man when we see one."

Nat's dark eyes met Jean's proudly.

"Okay, Ma'am, thanks," he said.

Chapter III

CIRCLE M RANCH

"HEAVENS, HOW EMPTY IT IS!" COMMENTED JEAN, AS Joshua plodded across the great open spaces of southeastern Texas.

"You know what they say about this country," said Nat with a chuckle. "You can look farther and see less than anywhere else in the world."

"I believe it," said John.

"This is the country where I was raised," Nat went on. "I like it. I hate to be shut up in towns." Then his face darkened. "Some day I'll come back to it, when I've made good somewhere else."

Warmed by their casual friendliness, Nat's reserve had

melted and he had become talkative and humorous. The wary, hunted look in his eyes was less evident.

From Nat's desultory talk John and Jean glimpsed a life utterly different from anything they had known. Nat, an orphan since he was eight years old, when both his parents had been killed in a train wreck, had been brought up by his grandfather, a Texas cattleman. At his grandfather's death, two years before, he had gone to work as a cowhand on the ranch from which he had been railroaded to jail.

And the twins' talk of their tight little New England town was as strange to Nat as his stories of ranch life were to them. He listened to their tales of good times with their "gang" in parties and in summer and winter sports. He looked at them, so confident and carefree—grand kids, he thought, but they don't know a thing about life yet.

Jean and John were eager to learn how people lived in this vast western land.

"What a lot of variety there is to America!" exclaimed Jean. "It's a wonder we all have the same form of government when the country is so different."

When Nat, who was at the wheel late in the afternoon, steered the car along an avenue of cottonwoods leading into El Paso, he announced proudly, "There's the Rio Grande, folks, and on the other side lies Mexico."

"Really!" said Jean. "Are we actually on the border? That sandy-looking thing isn't my idea of the big Rio Grande River."

"You should see it in a spring flood," said Nat.

John poked his head out of the car window to stare at the mountains of Mexico. "I say," he cried. "I have to set foot in Mexico before we leave this place. Can we do it, Nat?"

"Sure thing," Nat answered. "We can cross to Juarez this evening, if you like."

So, after they were settled in a tourist court on the outskirts, the three young people set off to explore the busy metropolitan streets of El Paso, and to cross the bridge over the Rio Grande to Old Mexico. They wandered along the streets, wide-eyed, staring at the brown-faced men in sombreros, the shawled women crouching by their stands of strange foods along the sidewalks. From the open door of a shop came the haunting lilt of a Mexican song.

"Come on in the market," said Nat. "That's something to see."

When they entered the big shedlike building Jean exclaimed with delight. "I never saw anything so gay," she cried. "They've all the colors of the rainbow in these things."

They passed quickly by the stands of fruits and vegetables to investigate the hats, sandals, baskets, pottery and lacquered ware.

"I just have to have one of these big hats," said Jean. "I'll need it for the sun." She picked up a floppy hat, its wide brim edged with cerise and green. "And look at those heavenly baskets!"

"Come, Nat, let's drag her away before she buys out the whole place," said John, seizing his sister by the arm.

Jean captured the hat before she was reluctantly led away to return to the tourist court and to sleep.

They were up at dawn, for that was the last lap of their long journey and the twins were eager to reach their destination. After some hours of riding, the station wagon wound up through a pass and its excited occupants looked down into the state of Arizona, spread out before them. The horizon was rimmed with mountains and the vast desert was a shimmering gray-green plain.

Now the end of the journey must be at hand, they thought. But hour slipped into hour and still they rode. Occasionally they passed a village or small town. Then again the white ribbon of road ran ahead of them across empty plains, or wound up and down through mountains colored red and ochre and purple with the minerals they contained. Although Jean appreciated the beauty of color and form in these strange mountains, the vast emptiness of the landscape terrified her.

"Don't they have any people in this country," she thought to herself.

"I thought a desert was bare and sandy," she said aloud, looking at the rolling land sparsely covered with low scrubby vegetation. "What's that brownish green stuff that's everywhere, Nat?"

"That's greasewood," he replied, "but I don't know much about cactus, except prickly pear, those bushes with big flat leaves. Those great tall things, though, are the giant cactus—the sahuaro."

"The ones without limbs look like big dill pickles standing on end," said John.

Jean stared at the huge angular plants, which lifted gaunt arms against the sky. "And those with limbs look like prehistoric animals—with accordion-pleated hides," she added, as she noticed the fluted green surface of the strange trunks and branches.

Nat said he would leave them in Tucson, to inquire for a job on one of the cattle ranches. Now that the end of the journey was drawing near, he felt choked with a rush of gratitude toward these new friends, but could find no words to express his feeling. He hated to leave them, knowing well the loneliness which would engulf him once more.

The twins, too, were regretting the time when they would have to part with Nat. They looked at each other and John burst out, "See here, fella, why don't you come out to the ranch with us for a couple of days? You can't leave us without at least taking a look at this famous Circle M Ranch we've had dropped in our laps."

"Yes, do come," added Jean. "You will be a big help to us while we get started. John and I don't know the first thing about running a ranch. It will be a place for you to stay while you look around for work, too."

Nat's face lit up with pleasure. "You sure are good to me, you folks," he said gratefully. "I'll never forget how you've staked me all these days and treated me like a friend. I'll admit I was kinda hating for this day to end, knowing I had to leave you. So, if I can help out, I'm glad to come along with you."

"All set, then," cried John, cheerfully, "and I believe I see Tucson away off there in the valley."

Sure enough, as they rolled down the long steep slope of road, they saw the city sprawled in the valley, against a backdrop of moutains which were deep blue in the afternoon light.

It was Saturday afternoon and the streets of Tucson, like other towns which are centers for large country districts, were crowded and busy. Trucks and ancient jalopies mingled with sleek cars in the traffic. Guest ranch station wagons with alluring Spanish names painted on their sides were parked along the curbs. From these cars descended what Nat scornfully termed "male and female dudes" dressed in a Hollywood version of Western clothes, pants, smart leather jackets and big hats.

Jean noted with amusement Nat's disgust at these people. Personally she thought they looked very smart and picturesque in their well-tailored clothes, and she longed to own some, too. But she didn't express her thoughts aloud, although John said, "I think they look swell. Why not dress well even if you are working on a ranch?"

"Working on a ranch!" scoffed Nat. "These here are drug-store cowboys. An honest-to-goodness cowman's got no use for them."

"This doesn't look like the other Western towns we've passed through," commented John, who was trying to keep one eye on the traffic and the other on the sidewalks while he steered Joshua along the streets.

"Too many dudes," answered Nat, scornfully.

They all observed, with interest, the number of dark-skinned people, Mexicans and Indian farmers, among the townsfolk. The copper-brown Indian women were almost like gypsies in their brilliant cerise or purple skirts and black head-shawls. Cowboys, too, in faded blue jeans and high-heeled boots, caught the twins' attention. They lounged along the streets with the rolling gait of men who spend most of their lives on horseback, or squatted on their heels along a sunny wall.

They asked Nat if he approved of them, or if they, too, were "drug-store cowboys."

"Heck, no," Nat responded. "They're the real thing."

Weatherbeaten ranch women were doing their Saturday marketing, stopping with their arms full of bundles to stare at dresses and housefurnishings in shop windows. The children, meanwhile, tugged at their mothers' skirts, begging to see a movie.

Finally John found the office of Mr. Farmington, the lawyer who had written of their uncle's death. He greeted them with the easy familiarity of the West, and warmed their hearts with his friendliness.

"Old Pedro has been looking for you ever since your father wrote that you would come out," said Mr. Farmington, after he had given them directions for finding the ranch. "You will find him a great help in getting started." His eyes rested on Nat, noting the unmistakable earmarks of a cowboy. "It's a good thing you have this young man with you," he said. "Oh, by the way, there are a couple of letters for you here." He handed Jean two thick envelopes, one addressed in their father's writing and the other in Dr. Braman's.

"Excuse me," said Jean, tearing open the envelope from Dr. Braman. "Oh John," she said, in a concerned tone, "Daddy's been sick again. Dr. Braman says he won't be well enough to travel for at least three weeks. He wants us to wire Dad that we are all right and don't need him."

"What does Dad's letter say?" asked John.

"Nothing much about himself. But full of advice to us, and very much concerned because he must leave us 'to get started all alone.' Here, read it," she said, thrusting the letter into her brother's hands.

"I am so sorry, my dear," said the lawyer. "Now see here, you must count on me as a friend. Let me know if I can do anything for you."

"Thanks so much," said Jean, biting her lips to keep back the tears. "First of all, please tell us where to buy provisions."

He told them of a market near his office where they could buy fruit, vegetables, meat and groceries. After they had left he wondered if perhaps he should not have warned them about the primitive ranch house waiting for them, but he, like his callers, had been too concerned with the bad news about their father to think of anything else. Then, too, he thought, that young cowboy they had with them would know what to do, and no doubt George Merryweather had told them about the ranch before he had died.

First Nat and the twins went to the telegraph office where they dispatched their father a reassuring message, after which they went to the market and bought a load of supplies. Then John headed the station wagon south toward their ranch.

"But how far away it is from the city," Jean thought, as they went on and on over the gravel road, looping up and down over big humps, twisting in and out over the desert land, covered with low bushes and thick, oddly shaped cactus plants. The late sunlight picked out some of the bushes with a silvery sheen.

"They look soft and fuzzy," commented Jean.

"I'll bet you would find that fuzz made of the sharpest spines you ever imagined," returned Nat.

"How deserted the country is," Jean kept thinking.

"And how lonely. What if Dad should take sick again all these rough miles away from a doctor?" The news in the letters from home was weighing on her mind. And when she noticed a scowl on her brother's face, she knew that he, too, was worrying about their father.

The road dipped into hollows, "streams of sand," Jean called them, crossed the road and wriggled away between clay banks.

"Those are washes," Nat explained. "In the big summer thunderstorms the water rushes down from the mountains through these gullies, and it's often so deep in the dips that you have to wait for it to go down before you can cross."

"Well, this *is* a weird country!" exclaimed John.

Occasionally they passed squat, unattractive little huts along the way.

"Can't say much for the style of architecture of these houses," said John. "They look as if they were made of mud."

"Well, they are sort of mud," said Nat. "They're made of adobe."

"Adobe!" exclaimed both twins, simultaneously. "That's what our house is made of, Uncle said," said Jean.

"Oh, but our house won't be like these," declared John, loftily. "After all, Uncle George was Dad's brother and he must have had some of Dad's ideas of decent architecture."

"I don't think these houses are so bad," said Nat. "Adobe houses are warm in winter and cool in summer. Besides, they are cheap to build."

"Well, they sure look it," said John.

At length they came to a sign which read "Circle M Ranch."

"Here we are, folks," cried John. " 'Home on the range.' "

As they drove up the road which was little more than two ruts in the sand, they strained their eyes eagerly for a glimpse of the house, their new home. The road twisted and turned and the station wagon struggled through sandy dips and bounced over cattle guards.

"Tomorrow morning I'm going to work on this road," declared John, "or else old Joshua will break a spring one of these days."

"Oh, you get used to roads like these, John," said Nat, "but you'd better go slow and take it in second. This is a regular ranch road—no worse than many others I've ridden on," he added philosophically.

A final turn of the rough track, and there before them was a long adobe building, almost the color of the earth around it. Across the front ran a porch, roofed with slim poles which were supported by weather-beaten crooked tree trunks. Behind the house a windmill showed its gaunt framework above small trees with pale green bark which they learned later were palvo verdes. Large maguey cactus plants lifted their fleshy blue-green leaves in urn-like clusters before the porch, and some feathery tamarisk trees nearby only accented, to Jean's eyes, the bareness of the surroundings.

The house looked like a forlorn shack to the Easterners' eyes, and the twins surveyed it in startled silence. They climbed out of the station wagon and looked around. Behind the house the land sloped upward to low brown mountains dotted with dark green shrubs. Eastward, in the other direction, a vast landscape spread before them,

"What a heck of a dump the house is"

to a valley framed in sharp mountain ranges. In the sunset light, mountains and valley were taking on exquisite hues of purple, rose and blue.

"Well," said John, "the view is okay, anyway." Then he went on, almost angrily, "But what a heck of a dump the house is! How in the name of heaven are we going to live here?"

Nat looked at John in surprise. This didn't sound like the good sport John had proved himself to be on the long trek. Besides, to Nat's eyes, the small adobe building looked first rate—just a usual ranch house. John caught Nat's look and shrugged his shoulders.

"What's the matter, fella?" he asked belligerently. "Do you expect me to say this is a palace?"

"No, of course not, John," answered Nat. "But why not look it over before you blast it?"

John sensed criticism in Nat's tone and he bristled. "He has a heck of a nerve criticizing me," thought John to himself.

He honked the horn and at the sound a lean wiry Mexican came out of the door of a hut near the house. A broad smile lit his leathery-brown face as he came over to the station wagon.

"Howdy, señores and Miss," he greeted them.

"Hello, Pedro," responded John, extending his hand. The Mexican wiped his palm on his jeans, and shook the hand that was extended to him.

"Welcome to Circle M Ranch," he said courteously, as though it were a speech he had learned by heart. "I hope you will all be very happy here." With that he turned on his heel and went back into his hut.

"Like heck we'll be happy in a dump like this," muttered John, and turned to see how Nat took it. Nat started to retort but bit back the words. John saw the older boy's disapproval, however, and was rubbed the wrong way by it.

"Well, let's see if it's any better inside," suggested Jean. They opened the door and stepped into the living room of their new home.

"Oh, it's awful!" exclaimed Jean. "Almost as bad inside as out!"

She glanced around quickly, noting the walls of rough, white plaster, the worn brick floor, the fireplace of adobe brick. A large window, facing the porch, framed the valley view and was, to Jean's mind, the only redeeming feature.

Beyond the living room they found a small bedroom with a cot bed, a dresser and a stand holding a china wash basin and pitcher. The kitchen, on the other side of the living room, was equipped with a wood cook stove and a primitive sink with a pump.

"And this is all," said Jean, mournfully. "No bath room. Why did Dad's brother live here all these years without a bathroom?"

"Lots of ranchers get along without bathrooms, Ma'am," put in Nat, consolingly. "After all, you have running water in your kitchen. When I was a kid we lived in a house without even that!"

John's temper was near the breaking point. He burst out with, "Well, Mr. Pollyanna, it's no wonder you think this place is okay. You've never known anything better. Well, we're used to modern improvements, thank you, and I agree with Jean about this place!"

"Why, John!" Jean exclaimed. "Don't—"

"What does that mean—'Mr. Pollyanna?'" broke in Nat, flushing angrily.

"Pollyanna was a girl who always made the best of everything," explained Jean.

"Well, what's the matter with doing that?" asked Nat.

John smiled at his simplicity. "Nothing, fella," he said, contritely, suddenly ashamed of his bad temper.

"Come on, boys, let's unpack," said Jean, huskily. "By the time we've put up our pictures and spread out our rugs and books this room won't be so bad."

"Good girl," thought Nat. She was certainly making an effort to be of good cheer.

They went to the car to unpack their luggage. Pedro stood in the doorway of his hut, watching them, with Timmie sniffing at his heels. As they worked a big, lean jack rabbit leaped across the road and Timmie gave chase with delight. But no Connecticut dog could possibly catch an Arizona jack rabbit, and soon the little Scottie returned, running on three legs, yelping with distress.

"What's the matter, Timmie?" asked Jean, taking the dog's paw in her hand. "Oh look," she went on, "poor Timmie has some cactus thorns in his foot." She pulled and tugged at the spiny joint caught in the dog's paw.

"You'll have a steady job doing that, Ma'am," said Nat. "Everything on this desert is covered with thorns."

"I repeat," muttered John, "one heck of a place."

Once Timmie was relieved of the thorn he ran all over the place, sniffing and barking. But his excitement over the jack rabbit was as nothing to the uproar he made when a herd of cattle with rough red hides and blank white faces came slowly into the corral, a few hundred feet from the house. They went through the gate of the corral, fenced with intertwined branches fastened together with strong wire and up to a large tank of water.

"How do they look to you, Nat?" asked John.

"Pretty good bunch," said Nat, and added, "And that's no Pollyanna remark, either."

John tried to count the cattle as they passed, and thought there were about seventy-five head.

"Is that all of our herd, Pedro?" he asked the Mexican.

"No, Señor, that's just about half—best half, though. See that bull?" He pointed a brown finger toward a huge creature that was butting some of the steers out of his way. "He very fine bull—he champion. Señor George bought him two weeks before he died. Name's Domingo Third. He very mean bull. Better you and Miss keep away from him."

Timmie, however, did not understand the Mexican's words. He ran to the corral, barking loudly, and made straight for the bull. The animal lowered his head. In a moment the little dog would have been caught on the sharp horns. But Nat sprang to a coiled lasso, hanging on a nail by Pedro's door. He ran back to the corral, swinging the rope around his head. Like a flash it hooked itself around the wicked-looking horns, jerking the bull's head back.

"Boy!" exclaimed John, his voice vibrant with admiration. "What a throw!"

"Here, Timmie, here Timmie," called Jean. She snatched up the little dog, hugging him to her breast, while she looked at Nat, her eyes full of the gratitude she could not speak. Nat, meanwhile, loosened the rope from the bull's horns.

Old Pedro looked at Nat with respect in his eyes, but only said, "You no dude, are you?"

"No, Pedro," John answered. "Nat's a cowboy. He has worked on a ranch all his life. I'm the only dude in this outfit, I guess," he finished, humbly. His irritation with the older boy had vanished in admiration for his skill.

Jean began putting away groceries on the shelves in the kitchen, already growing dusky with twilight. Pedro came in bearing an arm-load of dry branches. "Here firewood," he announced. "This morning I filled lamps."

"To be sure," thought Jean, "there wouldn't be electricity."

She lighted two kerosene lamps and by their ineffectual glow felt her way around the kitchen, trying to assemble supper for the hungry, tired boys.

She thought she would never forget her first struggle with the wood stove. With eyes smarting from the smoke, she attempted to cook that first meal.

"Here," said Nat, who came into the kitchen during her struggles, "you must open the dampers and let the fire breathe. And see here, the ashes are choking it."

He took out the ashes from the bottom of the stove and skillfully laid a new fire which was soon roaring merrily. The kettle began to sing, ham and eggs frizzled in the skillet and the coffee pot gave out its enticing odor.

Jean heaved a sigh of relief. "Nat, you certainly have a way with this horrible stove. Now will you tell John that supper's about ready? And Nat," she went on, gravely, "please forgive John for his bad temper. He was worrying about Dad, you know, that's what was the matter."

"Sure," said Nat. "That's okay. But I reckon I'd better watch my step and not rub him the wrong way."

He went to the doorway of the kitchen and, cupping his hands about his mouth, shouted, "Come and git it!"

John, who was still out looking at the cattle with Pedro, chuckled as he heard that call.

"Here's some warm water to wash your hands in," Jean said, as he entered the kitchen.

"Swell service at this hotel, isn't there, Nat?" John said in a teasing voice. "Yum, but that food smells good, Sis. I could eat a bear!"

They drew up their chairs around the rough kitchen table, over which the oil lamp shed a cheerful glow.

"You wouldn't have had any supper tonight if Nat hadn't shown me how to make that pesky stove work," declared Jean.

"Yep," said John, trying to make up for his treatment of Nat before. "I don't know what we would have done without you, fella."

"Neither do I," said Jean, heartily.

"I wish you never had to find out," said Nat, wistfully.

"Gee, I wish we could afford to give you a job, Nat," said John, and really meaning it. "Old Pedro was just telling me it's too much work for one cowboy—taking care of all our nerd—and I won't be much good for a week or two until I learn the ropes."

"I'd be glad to work for my keep, folks, just to stay on with you," replied Nat, eagerly.

"Oh we couldn't let you do that, Nat," said Jean. "But do stay with us until Dad gets here, then we'll see what he says. Will you?"

"You bet!" said Nat Barton, earnestly.

"Hurray!" cried John. "Say, will you teach me how to throw the lasso, the way you did when you saved Timmie?"

"Sure," answered Nat, "only we call it roping. It's easy when you know how."

"Well, now that's settled, I vote for bed," said Jean.

Dishes were piled in the sink and the boys quickly improvised beds on the living room floor with rugs and blankets. "We'll drive into town on Monday and buy a couple of cots," vowed John.

Before she went to bed Jean took out her five year perennial diary, a Christmas gift from her father. Under October 23rd, she wrote, "We arrived at Circle M Ranch today. It is too awful to describe—but a year from now we will be HOME!" Hastily she turned back to October 15th and wrote under the space for the next year, "Today we leave for HOME! Thank goodness!"

Then she fell into bed, settling Timmie on the floor beside her. She felt lost and frightened in this vast, silent country, but she closed her eyes, telling herself it would be better in the morning. Scarcely had she dropped off to sleep, when she was awakened by a weird, high-pitched cry, followed by staccato yelps.

"What's that?" she cried in alarm.

"Just a coyote," Nat called from the living room. "Go back to sleep, Ma'am. It won't hurt you."

Timmie had heard the coyote, too, and added his barks

to the wailing cries outside. When the commotion had subsided Jean lay and listened to the intense stillness.

"It's as though there were no one left in the world but us in this awful little house," she thought. She felt cut off from the dear nearness of neighbors to which she was accustomed in her old home. Memories of that home swept over her, engulfing her in homesickness. "What if the sunshine won't make up to Dad for all the comforts he is used to?" she thought. Perhaps she should write and urge him not to come.

"I'll talk it over with John in the morning," Jean said to herself. "Oh I hate it, I hate it," she sobbed into her pillow.

Outside, the windmill clanked and an owl hooted solemnly. Then stillness again, only the hollow sound of the night wind. At last Jean buried her head in the blankets and fell asleep.

Chapter IV

FIRST WEEK

RED GOLD FLUSHED THE SKY ABOVE THE DARK SILHOUETTE
of mountains when Jean woke next morning. She dressed
quickly and stole out to watch her first desert sunrise. The
glow behind the mountains touched with light the soft
bands of crimson cloud which stretched across a pale
green sky. Then the sun popped up above the sharp peaks,
radiating a clear light over the desert. No sound broke the
stillness but some bright bird calls.

Jean took a deep breath of the pure dry air. "Oh, it's

44

beautiful!" she said to herself. "And it's not so frightening by daylight—but still it is awfully empty."

When she went in she found that Nat had started the fire and set the kettle on to boil. The boys had rolled up their improvised beds and gone outside. After Jean had cooked a mighty pile of flapjacks and made the coffee, she imitated Nat's call of the night before.

"Come and git it, men," she cried from the doorway.

Nat and John came tramping in, eager and alive. Her brother looked like a happy kid on vacation, Jean thought, as they gathered around the kitchen table.

"There's lots more to our domain than we saw last night," John announced, attacking a plate full of flapjacks. "We found a big shed back there, where Pedro keeps saddles and tools and all sorts of things. There's a pump and sink, and Nat says we can buy a length of hose and rig up a cold water shower."

"Why didn't you ask Pedro to eat breakfast with us?" asked Jean.

"Oh I did, but he wouldn't come. He's got a little gasoline stove in his hut that he cooks on. Now he's gone to catch the horses. Says they usually come up to drink at the water tank early in the morning, but he wants to be sure we see them all. Then he's going to show us the range."

Breakfast over, Nat and the twins went out to see the horses. Nat was surprised to learn that the twins knew how to ride horseback.

"Sure we can ride," said John. "That's one thing you won't have to teach us tenderfeet."

"Oh look," cried Jean. "There they are!"

Pedro, on a pinto cow pony, rode behind a group of horses, which were stalking slowly toward the horse corral. The three young people leaned over the fence of the corral studying the animals as they ambled in. They were sturdy cow ponies, with wise bright eyes.

"Come on," said John. "Let's each pick a favorite. You first, Jean."

Jean had a lump of sugar ready in her hand. She studied the horses and held out the sugar to a gentle-looking white pony. The horse came toward her, nuzzled his nose against her palm and whinnied softly.

"Oh this little beauty is mine," she cried with delight. "Isn't he a darling? What is his name, Pedro?"

"Fritz," answered Pedro. "Señor George liked him best. But best horse on the place is my pinto," he went on, patting his horse's neck. "I raised him from a colt."

Soon Nat had thrown a saddle on a chestnut mare and John was putting a bit into the mouth of a clean-limbed roan.

"The mare is Pepita and the other is named Chico," remarked the Mexican.

"I hope Dad will like this lady," said John, indicating a placid gray mare.

"That's just what Señor George call her—Lady," said Pedro.

"Okay, then," said John, fastening his horse's girth. "All aboard for the range."

Nat lingered behind for a word with Jean. "You won't be too lonesome here by yourself, will you, Ma'am?" he asked. "We may be gone for quite a spell."

As a matter of fact Jean was feeling very forlorn about

being left alone, but she wouldn't have admitted it to Nat for anything.

"Of course not, Nat," she answered huskily. "I've a lot of work to do—it will keep me busy."

"Okay, then," said Nat, smiling at her. "So long!"

Jean stood in the doorway watching him gallop after John and Pedro. The Mexican had given each boy a cake of salt which they placed in their saddle bags for the cattle. When they were out of sight, she turned reluctantly into the living room and looked around. "Men's housekeeping!" she thought scornfully. "This place is filthy."

She tried to sing while she attacked the rooms vigorously with broom and mop, but she had so large a lump in her throat that the song had little chance to come out. "After all," she said to herself, "there's no one to hear me. I don't have to pretend I'm h-h-happy."

Calling Timmie to her, she sat on the hearthstone and gathered the little dog into her arms, snuggling her face against his soft fur. "You're all that's left me of home, Timmie, darling," Jean sobbed, patting the little Scottie's head.

Timmie, hearing his mistress's sobs, whimpered sympathetically, although if he could have talked he would probably have told her that he considered an Arizona desert a wonderfully fascinating place, in spite of the cactus.

Back out of doors she went into the bright sunshine. "Listen, Jean Merryweather," she said to herself sternly, "this sunshine will do Dad tons of good. You've got to figure out a way to make him comfortable and let him come." Then she resolutely returned to her housework.

When everything was scrubbed and polished she spread their rugs on the clean brick floor of the living room. Then she hung their prints on the white plaster walls, and, hands on hips, surveyed the result. "Not too bad," she decided. The large window, framing the gorgeous view of valley and mountains, was like a painting on the wall. When they had a couch in the living room and their books out, it would be better.

"If only I had some way of keeping food cold, and if only we had a bathroom, I guess I could stand it," she said to herself.

On a shelf in the living room were some books which had belonged to her uncle. Jean looked them over curiously. One was a treatise on the raising of Herefords, their stock. "Maybe John might study that," she thought.

There were several books on the history of the Southwest, a dog-eared complete works of Shakespeare, a volume of modern American poetry, and an old Bible that looked as if it had had much use.

She took down another book, written in a hand very like her father's—evidently her uncle's diary, and perching on the arm of a large chair, opened it at random. The first entry made her cheeks burn. "At last I have found peace," she read, "here in this great magnificent land. I suppose there are people—little people—who would be lonely here and prate about the emptiness of the landscape—but for me it is fulfillment, completion—the thing I have been searching for all my life—Peace!"

"Well," said Jean Merryweather, closing the book with a bang, "I'll try to agree with you, my dear uncle, but I'm afraid I'm one of those 'little people' whom you despised so much."

While she waited for the boys to come back from the range, she busied herself making a list for their shopping trip on the morrow. There were so many things they had to buy and their funds were getting low. Although Nat had carefully chosen the cheapest foods on the menus during their trip, still having a third mouth to feed had cut into their finances appreciably. And now they must buy two cots and a really comfortable couch for her father and more blankets.

"I'll have to be careful and not spend too much," she thought, "and I'll surely have to practice forethought, all right, now that I can't run down the street to the stores when I've forgotten something, with twenty-five long rough miles between home and market!"

While Jean was busy organizing the household, John was viewing their land with excited interest and learning some of a cowman's duties. Riding behind Pedro, he and Nat traversed the huge tract of land comprising Circle M Ranch. They rode slowly along the fences to see that they were in order. Occasionally Pedro dismounted, and, taking a pair of pliers from his pocket, fastened two broken strands of wire fencing together. John wanted to go faster. He loved horseback riding, but got bored at the slow pace necessary to examine the fences thoroughly.

"Can't we step on it, Nat?" he asked.

"Sorry, fella," Nat answered good-naturedly, "but a good cowman goes over all his fences every day, if he wants to keep his cattle on his own range."

They inspected the water holes and left the cakes of salt beside them. Here and there they came upon groups of cattle grazing on the sparse, dry grass. The animals lifted blank white faces to stare at the riders, then returned to the business of finding sustenance from desert vegetation. John was surprised to see spiny joints of cactus hanging from some of their mouths.

"Doesn't that hurt them, Pedro?" he asked.

"No, they get used to it," answered Pedro. "That's cholla cactus. He so fierce, we Mexicans say it jumps at people."

They had been riding for several hours when Pedro took his rope from the saddle horn and skillfully threw it over the horns of a big bull calf.

"Why did he do that, Nat?" asked John.

"He's probably going to take it back to the corral to brand it. That little fellow got overlooked at the last round-up, I reckon, and he's too big to be running around without a brand on him."

The sun was directly overhead when Pedro turned his horse, with the young animal following, toward the ranch house. They came to a roadway across which was the most ramshackle gate that John had ever seen. It was made of several heavy tree limbs fastened together with wire. Nat dismounted to open the gate.

"Better take a look at this, John," he suggested. "It's what we call a Texas gate. Kinda hard to fasten unless you learn the trick. And by the way, be sure you always do fasten gates behind you when you ride in cattle country."

As John watched Nat struggle to pull the collapsing gate to the post and anchor it by a loop of wire he secretly thought a Texas gate a very make-shift affair, but he made no comment.

Soon the three horsemen rode into the corral, where Pedro dismounted and shut the gate. His horse braced its feet and stood still, holding the rope taut, while the calf struggled to free itself.

The boys looked on as Pedro built a small fire between some bricks on the ground and put his branding iron into it. When it was hot, he threw the animal on the ground, deftly tying its legs together, then he placed the hot iron on its side. There was a stench of burning hair and flesh, and bellows from the victim as it fought against the iron. For the first time young John Merryweather saw that mark of a circle enclosing the letter M placed on one of his cattle.

Pedro untied the calf, opened the gate, and the creature dashed out of the corral to freedom. The boys unsaddled their horses, turned them loose, and went into the house to dinner.

"Well!" exclaimed Nat, surveying the reorganized living room. "I wouldn't know the place. You sure are a whiz!" He turned to Jean with a grin.

Jean glowed at his praise, and she saw with pleasure the look of pride in her brother's eyes. She knew better than to expect words of praise from her teasing twin, however.

"Don't give her a swelled head, Nat," he warned. "This is the sort of thing she has to do for Dad and me. We expect it of her."

"I expect you boys to unpack the books, when we've decided where to put them," she retorted.

"I'll tell you what," suggested Nat. "When we go into Tucson tomorrow to get those cots and stuff, let's look up a lumber company and buy some boards for shelves for the books. How about it?"

"Good idea, if it won't cost too much," said Jean. "I've made a list as long as your arm already."

"Yep, I've got to have some riding breeches—and I'd like some boots, too," said John.

"You'd better buy blue jeans, John," said Nat. "This work is too rough for fancy riding breeches—also you would have to have them dry-cleaned, and jeans can be washed."

"Okay, Professor," answered John.

"I'm glad I brought my blue jeans along," said Jean.

They had finished dinner when Pedro appeared in the doorway, his arms full. "Here Señor George's things I saved for you," he announced.

John pounced on a beautiful pair of cowboy boots with stitched ornament around the tops. "Hey, here are my boots!" he exclaimed.

He pulled them on and swaggered around the room with pleased satisfaction. He cast longing eyes on a wide-brimmed Stetson hat, but that proved too large for him. He tried stuffing paper under the rim inside the hat, but still it was too large. How he wanted that hat! It looked as handsome to him as the hats he had seen on what Nat called "male dudes" on the streets of Tucson. Finally he reluctantly gave up trying to make it fit, and put the hat and a leather jacket on a shelf in Jean's room to save for his father.

"But I'm going to buy one just like it in Tucson to-morrow," he promised himself.

Pedro held out to Jean a large blanket woven in stripes of rich, warm colors. "This Indian," he said. "Señor George brought it from South America. I think you like it, Miss."

"Oh, what a beautiful thing!" cried Jean, smoothing the firmly woven wool. "When we have cots, Dad's bed can be in the living room, and with this cover on it, it will be a handsome addition to the room. You boys can sleep on the porch."

Later Pedro came up to the house, riding his pinto. He was going to spend Sunday evening with his family.

"I like you all come and see my family," he said, shyly. "It's not far."

"We'd love to, Pedro," said Jean. "Have you boys had enough horseback riding for today? No? Good, then let's go on horseback."

They quickly saddled their horses and set out. Pedro rode ahead of them along a twisting road until they came to a rambling adobe house, some miles farther on. They entered through a yard enclosed in walls of rusty corrugated iron; a yard, which, in John's eyes, looked like a miniature zoo. Chickens scratched and clucked behind the wires of their run, and next to them rabbits were munching on lettuce leaves. Two young wild cats spit and snarled in their cage at the mongrel curs wandering about. From the rafters of a crude porch hung cages of small birds.

The room into which Pedro led them was cluttered with furnishings and its walls were decorated with staring chromos of saints. Bright pink curtains edged with lace were draped at the windows. Half a dozen small brown Mexican children scurried out of the room and peered at the strangers from the doorway.

Pedro introduced his sister, a fat, dark woman, who smiled shyly, but said nothing. "She no speak English," Pedro explained. Then he brought up his nephew, Roberto, a grave polite young man, and Yolanda, his pretty, plump wife. Roberto, they learned, was a builder of adobe houses and a jack-of-all-trades.

The two women were busy in the kitchen, patting balls of dough deftly back and forth from palm to palm, swiftly turning and molding each piece until it was as large and round as a plate and paper-thin. Then it was flipped to the hot stove top to cook.

"*Tortillas*," explained the beaming Pedro.

Nothing would do but that the guests should sample the fresh *tortillas*, and the *frijoles* or Mexican beans which were simmering on the stove in a big pot.

"I say, these are good!" exclaimed John. "Jean, you'd better learn to make *frijoles* and *tortillas*."

"I'm sure you have to be born to the making of *tortillas*," laughed Jean, "but I'll undertake *frijoles*. Will you teach me?" she asked Roberto's wife.

The young woman smiled with pleasure. "Please come any time," she urged. "But my Uncle Pedro can teach you, too. He makes *frijoles* every day."

Before they left she presented them with a pail full of savory hot *tamales*. "For your supper," she said, cordially.

"Oh how good they look and how spicy they smell!" said Jean. "That's awfully nice of you."

The *tamales* tasted as good as they looked and the three young people had what John termed a "royal gorge" before they went to bed that night.

In the morning, armed with their list, they started to town. "We've got to watch our step," Jean warned them. "We haven't very much money left and I hate to ask Dad for more. I know he's hard up, too. I'm afraid I'll be having to feed you baked beans and corn meal mush to fill you up."

While Nat and Jean went to a lumber yard to buy boards for the bookcase, John went off on a mysterious errand of his own, saying he would meet them at a restaurant at lunch time.

They were seated at a table when John swaggered in, resplendent in a plaid shirt, blue jeans, and wearing upon his head a beautiful Stetson hat, which he doffed and made them a low bow. "Please kin I sit with you a spell, Ma'am?" he said to Jean in such a perfect imitation of Nat's voice that the older boy blushed furiously.

"John!" cried Jean. "You look wonderful, but you must have spent a small fortune on that outfit. We can't afford to dress like that," she went on in a kindly tone, seeing the look of disappointment in his eyes. "How much did you pay for that hat?"

John told her reluctantly and Nat gave a low whistle. Jean was near tears. "Why, John Merryweather, you idiot," she said sternly. "I could feed the three of us for a week on that. You will have to march right back to that store and make them give you back your money."

Then Jean broke down and told the boys how little they had left to live on until their father came, and John agreed to try to make the store-keeper from whom he had bought the hat refund his money. "But, gee, how I hate to," he said. "I admit, though, that you're dead right, Bossy," he went on, turning to Jean. "I'm sorry I was such a fool."

John never told the others what a difficult time he had persuading the store-keeper to take back the Stetson. As a matter of fact, he had to leave a deposit, as well as the hat itself, promising to buy it later when he could "afford" it. Afterward Nat took him to a cheap store where he bought a "regular cowboy lid," in Nat's vernacular, which looked well and cost less than a fifth as much.

Homeward bound with their purchases, the twins were very quiet, and Nat's efforts to cheer them fell, apparently, on deaf ears.

"You know, Jean," said John, breaking one of their silences, "we're never really broke as long as you have Great-aunt Hettie's earrings. If the worst comes to the worst we can always pawn them for plenty—like that time —you remember—"

"No, John," Jean interrupted. "We aren't that hard up yet. It has to be a real emergency before I'll pawn those earrings."

Both twins remembered when a "real emergency" had occurred. The doctor had ordered an oxygen tent for their father, and the small hospital in their home town did not possess one—so they had had to have one brought from a larger hospital in a neighboring city. Their funds were so low at the time that Jean had pawned the diamond earrings which Great-aunt Hettie had given their mother for a wedding gift.

Their reveries were broken by Nat's voice, saying, "If it's money for food you're worrying about, why not have Pedro butcher a calf? Then we would have meat enough to last for a long time."

"How would we keep it fresh?" asked Jean.

"Easy," Nat answered. "We could store some of it in a large tin in the water tank, and we could cook up a lot of it and salt down the rest. I can help you with that, Ma'am. Don't worry, we won't starve, and you won't have to ask your father for more dough, either. Pedro has a rifle—and there are plenty of rabbits—cotton-tails, you know—around. And if I do say as hadn't ought, I make a mean rabbit stew."

"Hurray!" said John. "You make my mouth water, fella."

When they got back to the ranch they saw some clothes hanging to dry on a clothes line between Pedro's hut and a palo verde tree.

"Pedro must have been washing his clothes," said John. "That reminds me, Jean, shouldn't we have taken our dirty clothes to the laundry?"

Nat started to speak but Jean got ahead of him.

"I'll have to do the washing around here, John," she said, quietly. "We can't afford to send our things to the laundry."

"But, Jean," protested John, "you haven't any electric washer."

"No," answered his sister, "and I haven't any Mrs. Jenkins, either, worse luck. But if one of you boys will help me fill and empty the wash tub I guess I can manage."

Nat made good his promise to shoot a rabbit and cook it, and the next night the three of them sat down to "as mean a rabbit stew as ever I put in my mouth," as John expressed it.

Jean was trying valiantly to be a good sport about the lack of conveniences of the "awful little dump." She especially wanted Nat to have a good opinion of her, but it was hard work, all the same. She fell into bed at night, utterly worn out. Housekeeping at home had been nothing like this, she thought. When the boys had stopped talking on their cots at night, Jean lay awake in bed, thinking of her old home, longing to be there, but deciding, resolutely, that she would make the best of their life in this great lonesome country, for Dad's sake. Day after day passed and still she did not have the courage to write her father about Nat. Perhaps he would have to go away, anyway, Jean thought, for he and John were often at sword's points. Nat seemed to be growing more and more critical of the younger boy's lack of "stick-to-it," and John resented Nat's manner.

It was a hard nut for the young girl to crack, and she often felt stretched between the two boys, her reason and common sense telling her Nat was right, and her love and loyalty making her stand up for John.

Matters first became acute on the day that Jean had done the washing. The three were seated at the dinner table when Pedro came in with bad news.

"Cattle got loose," he said. "Somebody left gate open —lots of cattle got away."

John looked at his plate, but said nothing.

"What's the matter, cowboy?" asked Nat, scornfully.

"Were you afraid the Texas gate might spoil your pretty little hands?"

"What makes you think John did it, Nat?" asked Jean, quickly.

"I don't have to think; I know," Nat replied. "Honest, Ma'am, I can't stand to see the way you work around here to save money and then your brother lets good cattle get away, just because he's too shiftless to bother to fasten a gate. I came in that way a couple of days ago about half an hour after you did, John, and I saw what a punk job you did of fastening that gate. I told you then you always have to fasten gates right in cattle country."

"Oh John," cried Jean, "why don't you grow up?"

"Well, darn it all," said John, angrily. "I'm sick of living with a dictator and a know-it-all. Come on, Pedro, we'll go and look for the cattle."

"Okay," said Pedro, "we'll try to find them."

"Wait," said Nat. "I'll go, too."

Jean stood watching them ride off, her heart heavy with worry over the bad feeling between Nat Barton and her twin. She well remembered the evening when Nat had come in and gently protested to John about the latter's having left the gate open.

"Okay, Professor," John had said blithely. "I'll never do it again." But he had, and now they had lost several valuable head of cattle.

Later when the three men returned, their long faces told her the bad news.

"How many head got away, Pedro?" she asked the Mexican.

"Don't know for sure, Miss," Pedro answered. "Mebbe

ten or twelve, mebbe more. I'll try to count in the morning how many are left."

"Oh John," said Jean, sorrowfully.

"Well, heck, don't rub it in," answered her brother. "I'm sorry and I'll never leave that darn gate open again—what more can I say? I guess I'll go for a ride and get out of here." Before Jean could protest he mounted Chico and galloped across the desert.

"He oughtn't to ride so fast in the desert," said Nat. "The ground is full of kangaroo rat mounds covering their holes. He might break his horse's leg if it should step in one."

"Well, don't tell him about it tonight, Nat, please," answered Jean in a worried tone. "He's had all the scolding he can bear today."

John's punishment was self-inflicted, however. A little later Nat and Jean watched him riding full speed back toward the house. His horse stumbled and John was thrown over its head and landed in what looked at that distance like a large cholla cactus bush. In spite of themselves they burst out laughing, and John, when he had at last managed to extract himself from the thorny cactus, found them howling with mirth, when he arrived limping at the house.

"Go ahead and laugh," he said, morosely, "but while you do, for Pete's sake, somebody pick these cactus spines out of my back."

All evening long while John lay moaning on the couch, Nat and Jean, with Jean's tweezers, pulled out the sharp cactus spines from John's back.

In spite of her mirth Jean sympathized with John's discomfort. It seemed to her that she never walked out more than a few feet from the house without one of the cholla cactus "jumping" at her. And she was everlastingly taking spines out of poor little Timmie's paws, often transferring the cactus from the dog's foot to her own fingers in the process.

"I guess I had this coming to me," said John Merryweather, after his sister and Nat had removed every thorn.

Poor John, thought Jean. He sounded so humble and contrite. If only he wouldn't be so changeable—if only he were more thoughtful and considerate—if only he would try harder, or rather not give up so easily when things were hard or annoying—if only he were more like Nat, she found herself wishing, and then blushed at the thought. She mustn't be disloyal to John, even in her thoughts, but what a kid he was—what a shiftless, heedless kid!

And what was she to do about the mounting discord between the two boys? Should she tell Nat to go? Oh, she couldn't do that! He was such a fine person—and besides, what would they do without him? He was so helpful in every way. In spite of John's boast that he would learn to be a cowboy in two or three weeks his twin knew better. How she wished she had a kind older person to confide in, Jean thought, longing acutely for her father. It had occurred to her to consult that nice Mr. Farmington. They had called in at his office when they went to Tucson and he had been so friendly and helpful. But her fear that he might criticize Nat and her loyalty to John prevented her from telling Mr. Farmington of their troubles.

It was their first Saturday night at the ranch when things came to a head. John was sullen and quiet all through supper. Nat tried to make conversation with Jean's feeble help.

"Well," Jean said, "we've been here a week tonight. It seems more like a year, though."

"I'm sorry you don't like it better, Ma'am," answered Nat.

"Oh, for Pete's sake, stop calling her 'Ma'am!'" John spoke angrily. "It makes you sound like a servant. Is that what you've been?"

"John Merryweather," said his sister, "you apologize to Nat for talking that way."

"We Texans aren't anybody's servants," Nat replied, hotly. "But in our neck of the woods we have respect for ladies—that's why we call 'em 'Ma'am.'"

John rose from his chair and kicked it against the table. He went out to the shed where he and Nat kept their clothes and changed his soiled shirt for a clean one. He fastened a silk kerchief around his neck, put on his jacket, combed his hair and placed his new hat at a jaunty angle on his head.

Jean stood in the kitchen doorway, waiting for him, wondering what was in his mind. He came out of the shed, and without a word to his sister, started toward the station wagon.

"John," Jean called after him, "where are you going?"

"Out," answered her brother sullenly.

"Where, John?" she persisted.

"Oh heck," answered John, "do you expect me to stay

around this dump night after night playing tiddle-de-winks? I'm going to town to have some fun!"

Without waiting for a reply, he stepped on the gas and sent Joshua roaring down the road.

Jean and Nat sat in the living room, trying to read. Every now and then one or the other of them would look up and catch the other's eyes—then they would make a pathetic effort to smile at each other—efforts far from successful. At length Jean said, huskily, "Guess we'd better go to bed."

"Okay, Ma'am," said Nat. "I mean Jean. Say, do you feel the way John does about my calling you 'Ma'am'?"

"No, of course I don't—that is, I didn't at first. But now that we are friends, why don't you always call me Jean?" the girl answered kindly.

"I will, Jean, thanks," Nat replied. "And honestly I wish you didn't hate this place so much. I love being here with you. It's more like a home than I've had since my ma and pa died when I was a kid."

"Well, if you and John could only get along better, it wouldn't be so bad," said Jean. "But I never know when he's going to get provoked at something you say—and I go around all the time as if I were walking on eggs. What's the matter with you two, anyway?"

"John just won't take telling, that's all," Nat answered. "At first he wanted me to show him everything that a cowboy has to do, but now, if I try to help him, he says 'Okay, Professor,' and walks away. Maybe I didn't handle him right. Or maybe he just hasn't the patience it takes to learn to be a cowboy. You remember what he said that first night—that it might take him two or three weeks to learn how. Well, I wanted to tell him right then that it would take him a heck of a longer time than that if he was going to be any good, but I kept my mouth shut. But you see, Jean, if John can't learn a thing right away, he gives up. Take roping, for instance. That takes practice and John only tried a few times this week, and couldn't get the hang of it, so he says 'What the heck!' and gives up."

"I know, Nat," said Jean sadly. "He's always done only the things that were easy for him. He's never worked hard. Even that job he had all summer in the supply store was easy—he just drove a light truck around all day delivering produce. He's a good swimmer, and he was a football hero in high school—but when it comes to something that's hard to learn—he—he gives up." Jean tried to keep the tears back, but without success. Nat sat on the arm of her chair and awkwardly patted her back.

"Don't cry, Jeanie," he said gently. "Maybe this country out here will make a man of him."

"Oh, if it only would I wouldn't hate it so," Jean said through her tears.

"Please try not to hate it, Jean. Think how much good the hot sunshine is going to do your father."

"Nat, that's one thing that's worrying me," said Jean. "Daddy is used to so many things we don't have here. I'm afraid he'll be too uncomfortable."

"Look here, Jean," Nat said earnestly. "He'll have all the necessary things. Your good cooking, a comfortable bed to sleep on, the hot sunshine to lie in, and his own Jean to wait on him. Don't tell me those things won't make up for doing without a bathtub!"

Jean smiled at Nat's earnestness. "Okay, fella, as John

would say. You've made me feel better already. Nat,"
she went on, "where do you suppose John went tonight?"

"Oh I reckon he is at some joint dancing to a juke box,"
Nat answered. "He got all dolled up, you know. Maybe
he met some guys from dude ranches to fool around with."

"Just a drug-store cowboy, isn't he, Nat?" Jean said
with a sad little smile. "Well, I guess we'd better not wait
up for him any longer. Good night, Nat."

"Good night, Jean," Nat said softly.

Jean lay awake hour after hour waiting to hear the
sound of the station wagon. It was nearly dawn when she
heard John stumble into bed. Nat's voice spoke to her
twin sleepily. John muttered a reply, then she heard the
heavy breathing of both boys, and soon fell asleep herself.

In the morning it was a heavy-eyed John Merryweather
who morosely answered his sister's cheery, "Good morning, Twin."

"Did you have a good time?" Jean asked.

"Who wants to know?" her brother replied, sourly.

"Well, anyway, tell me what you did with the station
wagon. I heard you come in but not a word out of Joshua.
He isn't usually that considerate."

"I had a blow-out about five miles away from here and
the car skidded off the road and landed in a barbed wire
fence. I couldn't get out, so I walked all the way home."

"Oh John," protested Jean, before she thought. "It will
probably cost a lot of money to get it fixed. Why aren't
you more careful?"

" 'Oh, John,' " her brother mimicked her. "I suppose I
could help having a blow-out. Well, Bossy, you'd better

lay off picking on me. I've had enough of you and the Professor, here, bossing me around all day long."

"See here, John," spoke up Nat, "that's no way to talk to your sister. It's bad enough your staying out all night worrying her to death."

"Yeah, put in your two cents' worth, Professor," John told him angrily.

"John, stop it," said Jean. "You mustn't talk to Nat that way."

"What is this—a conspiracy?" asked John, belligerently. "Well, darn the two of you."

Nat's temper was rising. "Take that back, John," he said in a sharp tone.

"Who says so?" demanded John, hotly.

"I do," answered Nat. "You don't insult a lady in my presence and get away with it."

"Who's going to make me?" asked John, doubling his fists.

"Come outside and I'll show you who," Nat answered, his face red with anger.

"Boys, boys, for heaven's sakes don't act like a couple of children," pleaded Jean, but they paid no attention to her.

Right outside the kitchen door the two raised their fists and lunged at each other. Pedro stood in the doorway of his hut, silently watching them.

"Pedro," shouted Jean. "Stop them!"

"No, Miss," answered the Mexican. "Better to let them fight it out."

For a while each boy seemed to be giving as good as he got, but soon it became apparent that Nat was getting the best of it, in spite of a rapidly closing eye. Then, in a flash, he landed a blow on John's chin which knocked the younger boy flat on the ground. He did not move and Jean rushed to him.

"John," she cried. "Are you hurt? Speak to me, John."

"Guess he's knocked out," said Nat, contritely. "I'm sorry, Jean."

"Well, you ought to be," answered the girl, trembling with anger. "Of all the uncivilized performances I ever saw. What do you two think you are, anyway?"

"Here," said Nat, "let me help him onto the couch. Then we'd better bring him to with some cold water." Together they picked up the battered boy from the ground, and, with Pedro's help, carried him into the house. Jean bathed her brother's head with cold water.

"I guess I'd better go away, Jean," said Nat Barton, humbly.

"Yes, I guess you should," Jean answered without looking up.

John stirred. "Nothing doing, Nat," he said. "Don't you dare leave now. I had it coming to me. Shake, fella!"

And to Jean's utter amazement the two boys grinned at each other sheepishly and solemnly shook hands!

Chapter V

NOW WE ARE FOUR

"Better put some raw meat on that shiner I gave you, Nat," said John a little later. "Good thing that Pedro butchered a calf yesterday. Just in time, eh?"

"Sure was," Nat answered. "After a bit when you feel better, let's ride down the road and bring back the station wagon."

"Okay," said John. "Thanks. I guess I feel well enough to go now."

He got up from the couch, went outside with Nat, and the two boys saddled their horses and went off down the road, talking and laughing like the best of friends.

Amazed, Jean watched them go. "Men!" she said to

68

herself. "Don't anybody ever expect me to understand them."

Even so, she was delighted at the outcome of that fight, for now, perhaps, John and Nat would get along better. Then, too, now Nat could stay, at least until their father came. She must write to him at once about Nat.

She took pen and paper and sat at the little folding shelf Nat had made for a makeshift desk when he had built the bookcases. "Dearest Daddy," she wrote, "John and I have a confession to make to you. On our trip we broke a very important promise to you—we picked up a stranger on the road and gave him a lift clear to Arizona. Please don't be angry with us—you would have done the same thing if you had seen how badly he was treated by the sheriff who was running him out of that little Southern town because he was a jail bird—" She broke off and read what she had written. "Oh that will never do," she sighed. "I guess I'll have to wait until Daddy gets here and then John and I can tell him face to face and he will meet Nat right away and see what a grand person he is."

So once again Jean procrastinated and again lulled her conscience to sleep with the comforting thought that she was saving her father unnecessary worry. She tore up the letter and began again, telling him that the sun was shining, that she and John were getting along all right, that Pedro had butchered a calf so that they had plenty of fresh meat, and that they hoped he was better and would soon be able to come. Not a word about the discomforts she was enduring, not a word about needing money—and most particularly, not a word about how she feared the great, empty, lonely country, despite its moments of great beauty.

"If this isn't deceiving Dad about the true state of affairs," she said to herself as she sealed the envelope, "I don't know what is. But it's all in a good cause, and I'll never, *never* let him know I hate this country until next October 15th, when we start for home."

For several days after their fight John and Nat were as good friends as they had been on the long trip.

"That kock-down drag-out battle John and I had was just what we needed," Nat confided to Jean.

Not once had John called the older boy "Professor," nor had he resented Nat's suggestions. "I hope it will last," Jean prayed.

There had been a near call when Nat came into the kitchen while John was pumping water to get a cold drink —letting the water run down the waste pipe.

"Hey, John, that's like throwing away gold, what you are doing," Nat had protested.

"How come?" John had demanded.

"Gee, fella, this is desert country. You can't waste water like that. Suppose the well goes dry—then you and the stock will be in a fix, sure."

"But I want a cold drink," John had said. "What do you expect me to do—drink lukewarm water?"

"No, but fill up every pot and pail in the house with that water you're pumping away," Nat had advised.

John, Jean remembered, had started to say, "The heck with that," but instead he said, "All right, Nat, I guess you know what you're talking about." And Jean was so pleased with her brother that she wanted to hug him.

As a matter of fact, they did get a taste of what Nat meant, when, for several days, there was no wind, and the windmill didn't pump any water into the tank. Then Pedro showed them some empty five gallon cans in the shed and advised Nat and John to take them in the station wagon to be filled at the well belonging to the storekeeper down in the valley. Poor Jean, it wasn't enough that she had to cook on a measly little wood stove, that her ingenuity was taxed to the utmost to fill up those two boys with nourishing but cheap food—now she had to be sparing of water, too!

After a few days the wind began to blow, and blew steadily for several days. The windmill turned and filled the water tank, but the Merryweather twins had learned a lesson the hard way, and never again wasted water.

When the next letter came from their father it contained a small check, most of which had to be spent for new tires for the station wagon. John's collision with the barbed wire fence had ripped one tire beyond repair, and the tire that had been blown out, as well.

Both Jean and Nat had been careful to say nothing to John that he could resent about the car. In fact, the three of them had apparently agreed to let bygones be bygones, and never mentioned that first terrible Saturday night. For a few days afterwards John made a real attempt to learn the difficult art of roping, but somehow couldn't get the hang of it, and gave up in his usual heedless manner. Even so, neither "Bossy" nor the "Professor" scolded him for it, nor did they mention the fact that if he was ever going to be a real cowboy he must learn to rope cattle.

They had been at the ranch about three weeks when one day Jean returned from the mail box with a letter from her father.

"Boys," she called to Nat and John, who had just come in from riding the range, "Dad arrives day after tomorrow."

"Hurray!" cried John.

"By the way, Jean," said Nat. "What did your father say about me being here?"

"Why—why," Jean blushed with confusion. "I've never told him about you yet, Nat," she confessed.

"Gee whiz, Sis," said John, "neither have I. You see," he went on hurriedly, seeing the concern on Nat's face, "we promised Dad before we left that we wouldn't pick up any stranger on the road—but say, it will be all right. When Dad meets you he will know that Jean and I have been darn lucky to have had you here."

"Of course he will, Nat," Jean added. But Nat heard the note of uncertainty in her voice, and was troubled by it.

"See here," he said. "If you two think it best, I'll pull out before your Dad gets here. How's about it?"

"Oh no, Nat," the twins spoke together. "I'm sure Dad will understand," added Jean.

"Besides, we couldn't get along without you," said John emphatically. "Please stay until Dad has a chance to see how much we need you. Of course," he went on, "I don't know whether or not Dad will be able to pay you any wages. So maybe we shouldn't stand in the way of your getting a decent job."

"Don't worry about that part of it, John," said Nat. Then he turned to Jean and added, "I told you before that I'd be willing to work for my keep, and I haven't changed about that."

"You're a swell egg, Nat Barton," said John impulsively. "I'm sure Dad will want you as much as Jean and I do."

"Okay, then," said Nat. "But I'll tell you what, when your Dad gets here, you give me the high sign, and if he doesn't want me to stay, I'll vamoose pronto."

All the way into Tucson to meet their father the twins rehearsed how they would break the news to him about Nat. But when he got off the train, they were so glad to see him, that they forgot the words they had planned to use. As Joshua plunged along over the rough miles to the ranch, they told him about their trip until they came to the part about picking up Nat on the road.

John took a long breath and plunged into a description of the scene in the little town, with the sheriff and the group of indignant citizens. He told in elaborate detail how mean the men were to Nat—how pale and drawn the boy looked, and what he had said about being hungry and having no place to go.

"Poor fellow," said Mr. Merryweather. "You two must have hated not to interfere."

"We did interfere, Daddy," said Jean. "John jumped out of the car and took him right from under the noses of those horrible men—and we brought him all the way to Arizona with us!"

"My dears!" exclaimed their father in alarm. "You two were taking an awful chance! Why, you know nothing of this young chap except that he was a self-confessed jail-bird. Great Heavens!" he went on, as the full import of what they had been saying struck him, "he might have robbed the two of you and ridden off with the car. I'm afraid you let your sympathy run away with your common sense."

The twins were silent, apprehensive about what their father would say when he learned that Nat was still with them.

At last he said, "Well, apparently no harm was done because you both are here, safe and well. So it turned out all right, anyway." Then he asked, suddenly, "Where is the young fellow now?"

"He is living at the Ranch with us, Daddy," said Jean. Then together, interrupting each other in their eagerness to have their father want Nat to stay, they confessed the whole episode, omitting nothing of the story of what a great help Nat had been to them, getting settled, and how much they both liked and depended on him. But of course, neither twin told him of the great "knock-down and drag-out battle," that Nat and John had that first Saturday night.

"But why didn't you write and tell me about this?" demanded their father.

"We were afraid it might worry you, Daddy," said Jean. "After all, you hadn't seen Nat—you didn't know how splendid he is—"

"I see," said Mr. Merryweather, quietly. "Well, if he is what you say, all that I can say is that you two have been extremely lucky—more lucky than wise."

"Don't be angry with us, Daddy," begged Jean. "If you had been there in that little town and seen those terrible men—and Nat's white, scared face, I'm sure you would have acted as John and I did."

"Perhaps," agreed her father, "but taking him to the

next town and buying him a meal is a long way from keeping him with you all this time. And what about his wages? Has he done all this work as you tell me, with no pay?"

John and Jean hastened to explain Nat's saying that he would gladly stay with them for his keep.

"Wait until you see him, Daddy," said Jean. "I'm sure you will like him, too."

"We'll see," answered Mr. Merryweather, "but even if I do, I wouldn't let him stay on those terms. It wouldn't be fair."

"But he wants to, Daddy," said Jean. "He told me one night—when John was out, that he hadn't ever had a home since he was eight years old when he lost both his parents. He loves being with us. Please let him stay."

"Well," said her father, "we'll see. But George's lawyer wrote me that Pedro gets sixty dollars a month. If Nat boards with us, mind you, that is if I agree with your estimate of the young man, he surely should be paid forty dollars a month at least, and I just haven't that much money to spare."

"How are you going to afford to pay Pedro, Dad?" asked John.

"Mr. Farmington suggested that Pedro's wages can be paid after the round-up in the Spring when we can sell some of our cattle. He wrote that George often paid him that way," their father replied.

"Well, then, Dad," cried John, happily, "why can't we pay Nat the same way?"

"Perhaps, we shall see."

No more was said about Nat Barton during the rest of

their drive to the ranch. In answer to their questions, Mr. Merryweather told them all about their many friends in the old home town, until Jean grew so homesick she was afraid she would disgrace herself by bursting into tears. Every now and then, however, he would interrupt his account of the activities of their friends to comment on the beauty of the country through which they were passing. And he grew more and more enthusiastic over the translucent atmosphere, and the delicate blues and mauves of the sharply cut out mountain masses which rose one beyond the other as they advanced.

"It is so vast," he said, "and so satisfyingly beautiful, isn't it, my dears?"

"Yes, Daddy, of course," said Jean, making a valiant effort to sound enthusiastic, herself.

"Oh sure," added John. They thought they had reassured their father, but he knew them too well to be deceived.

"We ought to warn you, Dad," spoke up John, shortly before they turned into the roadway of their own land, "that the house is a dump."

"I gathered from your letters that there aren't many creature comforts," said their father with a chuckle. "All that worries me on that score is lest it mean too much hard work for my Jeanie. I shan't mind roughing it—if I can have this glorious sunshine and the two of you."

When he saw the ranch house he noticed not its lacks, but its simple, well-planned lines.

Jean and John introduced him to Pedro, who shook hands heartily and called him "Boss." But where was Nat? Then Jean spied a note on the mantelpiece. Tearing open the envelope she read, "Dear Jean, I shot a rabbit and it is on the stove stewing for dinner. I am down at Roberto's house. Thought it would be easier for you and John if I got out from under. Regards, N. Barton."

"Silly boy," she said to herself. She showed the note to her father and John. "Jump into the station wagon, John," said her father, "and go down and bring Nat home."

"Bless you, Daddy," said Jean, hugging her father close.

That night at a dinner of Nat's stewed rabbit and Jean's baking powder biscuits, Mr. Merryweather took stock of the young man. He liked what he saw. Apparently his impetuous twins had been right in their estimate of this youth. How fortunate they had been! Thinking how differently this adventure might have turned out for them, he groaned inwardly. But the fellow seemed straightforward and honest, quiet and unassuming. Perhaps it would be well to keep him, since the twins so much wished it.

After dinner, he noticed how, as a matter of course, Nat cleared the table, took water from the stove and filled the dishpan and called to John, "Come on, fella. Let's give Jean a vacation from dishes tonight."

"Aw heck," said John. Then, catching his father's eye upon him, he hastily said, "Okay, sure," and went back into the kitchen.

"See, Daddy," said Jean, settling herself on the arm of her father's chair, "how helpful Nat is?" Then, in a low tone, she added, "He's a good example for our John, don't you think?"

"Yes, dear," answered her father. "And it looks as if you and John have acquired a fine addition to our ranch family."

"Goody!" said Jean, happily. "I knew you'd appreciate Nat when you saw him."

When Nat and John came into the living room, Nat suggested that he build a fire in the fireplace to take the chill off. When the four were seated around the fire of blazing mesquite logs, Mr. Merriweather said, "Nat, Jean and John have told me that you would like to stay on here and help John learn to be a cowboy. Is that true?"

"Yes, sir, it sure is," answered Nat, earnestly.

"But you see, my boy, I haven't any money to pay your wages," said the older man.

"Well, sir," said Nat, "I've told both Jean and John that I'd be glad to stay for my keep in order to be with you all. It's a home for me, sir—something I've never had since I was a small kid."

"That's very generous of you, I'm sure, Nat," said Mr. Merryweather, "but I can't accept such a sacrifice. How will this do, suppose I give you an I.O.U. for forty dollars every month. And I will pay you what I can when we sell the cattle after the spring round-up. That is my plan for paying Pedro, too."

"That's fine, sir," said Nat eagerly. "But you don't need to pay me that much."

"Indeed I do, Nat," answered Mr. Merryweather, with a smile.

"Well, thanks ever so much, sir," said Nat, happily.

Next morning while the boys were riding the range and Jean tidied up the house, her father went out to sit in the bright, warm sunshine. She stole a look at him every now and then, as he sat, utterly relaxed, gazing contentedly at the landscape. "How white he is," she thought, anxiously.

Soon she joined him. "Getting rested, Daddy?" she asked, tenderly.

"Yes, darling," Mr. Merryweather replied. "I feel this wonderful sun penetrating right to my bones. I shall pick up strength here in no time. And the peace of this place and the quiet! I feel the weight of worries lifting already!"

His words reminded Jean of what her Uncle had written in his diary. Would her father feel the same way about this big empty country? Would he, perhaps, like her Uncle, want to stay here the rest of his life? The thought made Jean's heart constrict! But surely, no. Her father belonged back home in Connecticut just as she and John did. They would all be ready to go back next October— but what a long, weary way off next October was!

"Look at the clear pure line of those blue mountains against the delicate sky," he father was saying. "It is like the backgrounds in the paintings of the Renaissance Italians. It reminds me of my student tour in Italy. I'd like to get out my watercolors."

"That's just grand," exclaimed Jean. "You will have a chance now to do lots of lovely work you've never had time for these last years."

"Did I ever tell you, darling," her father asked, "that I started out thinking I was going to be an artist? But I got side-tracked into architecture. This landscape makes me want to try to paint again."

"Oh, do, Daddy," Jean responded, eagerly.

"Maybe I shall," said her father.

That afternoon Mr. Merryweather with the twins and Pedro, looked over the whole "estate." Pedro did not realize how the twins regarded the buildings, and, indeed, they were surprised to hear their father's pleased comments.

"By the way, Pedro" said Mr. Merryweather "this morning as I was resting outside, I noticed the thin poles that make the roof of the porch and are used in the ceiling in the living room above the beams. What are they?"

"Those come from inside big sahuaro cactus when he dead," replied the Mexican. "Señor George and I ride all over desert hunting for them. He liked Mexican building. We call porch a *ramada*."

"That's a pretty name," said Jean.

As they strolled about the ranch, studying the buildings, Mr. Merryweather had an idea.

"It would be nice to have a few chickens to provide us with fresh eggs," he suggested. "Do you suppose you could take care of them, Jean? We might even raise a few more than we would need for our own use and you could sell eggs and earn some pin money for yourself. Would you like to try it?"

"Of course, Daddy," she said. "That's a good plan."

Pedro spoke up, saying that Mrs. Dawson, their "next door neighbor," who lived seven miles down the road, had chickens and would probably sell some.

"Let's go and see her this afternoon, and get some," proposed John.

Pedro gave them directions and all four piled into the station wagon.

The sign on the roadway said "Lottie D Rancho" and John turned the car down the winding track to the ranch house. A high woven fence enclosed the house and yard, where green grass and borders of gay calendulas were growing. Jean's eyes noted with joy the graceful pepper trees before the porch.

"I'm going to get something like this growing around our place," she resolved, "then our house won't look so stark and bare."

As they opened the gate a woman's voice boomed out at them, "Howdy, strangers!" They looked up to see a tall, raw-boned woman with a head of frizzy, blond hair. She wore high-heeled boots and blue jeans and a cowboy's plaid shirt. Although she walked with the lithe grace of a girl, Jean noticed that her face was a mass of wrinkles under liberal layers of powder and rouge.

"How do you do, Madam," said Mr. Merryweather, bowing over her outstretched hand. "I am John Merryweather, the brother of your old neighbor, George Merryweather, and these are my son and daughter, John, junior, and Jean, and our young friend, Nat Barton."

"Well, land sakes, I'm sure pleased to meecha," said Lottie Dawson, shaking each one firmly by the hand. "I thought a whole heap of your brother, Mr. Merryweather. He was one fine *hombre*, as the Mexicans say. How are you making out up at his place. But say, come on in!"

They followed her across a porch cluttered with saddles and bridles, boots and spurs, riding crops and coiled ropes. The living room beyond was dominated by a huge stone fireplace, its hearthstone one large slab of rock. On the mantel were pictures of white-faced bulls, one of them decorated with a blue ribbon. Old calendars and announcements of cattle shows and rodeos of past years covered the walls.

Lottie Dawson noticed Jean's interested glances around the room.

"Come and see my bedroom," she suggested, and led the way into the adjoining room. What a contrast it was to the rest of the house! At the windows were dainty dimity curtains with tie-backs of baby blue ribbon. The bed was covered with a dimity spread edged with lace. This revelation of femininity explained Lottie's frizzled hair and the awkward attempts at make-up on her weather-beaten face.

The owner of the room stood, hands on hips, looking pleased and proud.

"It's perfectly lovely," Jean said. "And is that a bath-room in there? Yes? Oh, how I envy you. I've been wishing for a bathroom ever since we got here."

"Well," said Lottie, "if you have a good year with your cattle, you can get your Dad to put in a bathroom."

"It would hardly be worth while to put in a bathroom for such a short time. We are going home next October."

"Going home?" repeated Lottie in surprise. "How come?"

"We just came out for a year for Daddy to get well, you see," Jean explained.

"What are you going to do with your ranch when you go back East?"

"Sell it, we hope," answered Jean.

"You'll be able to catch a dude easier, if you have a bathroom," said Lottie, then, seeing Jean's bewilderment she explained, "That's what us ranchers call selling a ranch to an Easterner. Besides, for your own sakes, you'd better have one for hot weather."

"I've been worrying about the hot summer and keeping food cool," said Jean. "It's bad enough now."

"Lady, you ain't seen nothing yet," commented Lottie.

"Maybe we could have an icebox if we sold lots of cattle," said Jean.

"As for an ice box," said Lottie, "come out on the *ramada* and I'll show you what us ranchers use to keep food cold."

"This here is a desert cooler," she went on, indicating a tall, narrow cupboard made of burlap stretched on a wooden framework. Above the cupboard was suspended a deep saucepan with a spigot inserted in the bottom. Drops of water from the spigot dripped down the sides, keeping the burlap wet. Lottie opened the door of the contraption, revealing food stored on the shelves within.

"Put your hand inside of there," she ordered Jean. When the girl did so, she was surprised to find that it was indeed cold inside.

"Nat, Dad, do come here," she called. "Look at this thing."

"That certainly is ingenious," Mr. Merryweather declared.

Jean, meanwhile, had noticed a large earthenware vessel hanging from the rafters of the *ramada*.

"What is that, Mrs. Dawson?" she asked.

"That's an olla and the Indians make 'em. You see, this clay jar is porous and when the wind blows on it, it sweats and keeps the water cold inside. You can buy them at the Indian reservation on the way to town." Lottie lifted a tin lid from the top of the olla and dipped out a gourd full of water for Jean. It was delightfully cool.

"What a lot I'm learning about how to get along in this iceless place," Jean commented.

"Don't forget why we came to see Mrs. Dawson, Jean," Nat reminded her.

"I've been so interested in seeing your place and all your things that I almost did forget. We wonder if you would sell us some chickens?"

"Why sure, I will," Lottie answered in her deep voice. "Come on down to my run and pick out the ones you want."

They followed her to the chicken yard.

"These white leghorns are the best layers," she said, indicating a flock of stream-lined chickens busily pecking at some grains of corn.

"All right," said Jean. "We'll come back and get them as soon as John and Nat have built a run for them. How many do you think I should have to start with?"

"About a dozen hens and a cock," said Mrs. Dawson. "These hens are all laying now. Pretty soon you can set some and have baby chicks."

The price was arranged and the family prepared to leave, but hospitable Lottie would not have it so.

"Now, folks, let me give you a cup of coffee before you go," she boomed. "I'm right glad to have a visit with you."

They could not resist her urging and so they sat around the living room drinking coffee, while she regaled them with bits of information about the neighborhood.

"You know," said Jean, "I do love the Spanish names that are used so much here and the Mexican ways of doing things. It's so different from our part of the country. As for Pedro and his family, they are just darlings."

"Yes, the Mexicans are fine folks, although, of course, some of them are shiftless and lazy," answered Lottie. "They don't always get a square deal from the ranchers or in the town, but they ought to. Their children go to the public schools and make good Americans."

"Yes," commented Mr. Merryweather, "the blending of other races with the American makes our country richer."

"That's right, Mr. Merryweather," Lottie replied, looking much impressed. "Your brother used to talk that way. He'd knocked around all over the world and known all sorts of people, and I never knew a finer fellow for getting along with Mexicans, Indians and Americans and having a good word to say about all of them, too."

She accompanied her guests to the station wagon when they left, saying with hearty friendliness, "Now, folks, I'm your neighbor and I want to help you all I can. Don't forget to call upon me for anything I can do."

"That's very kind of you, indeed, Mrs. Dawson," replied Mr. Merryweather, gratefully.

"Looky, folks," she cut in, "the name is Lottie. To tell you the truth I've had so many last names—bin married five times—that I don't rightly recognize my current last name when I hear it. But ever sence I was born, I bin answering to Lottie."

They laughed and said goodbye. "Well, we've certainly found a friend," said Mr. Merryweather as they drove home.

Next day, Nat built the desert cooler, and the cold repository for food did much to lighten Jean's housekeeping problems.

Pedro took the station wagon and returned from a trip over desert tracks with a huge load of branches of the ocotillo bush to make a fence for the chicken run. The branches were thin and hard, lined to their tips with big thorns as sharp as wild cat claws and hard as iron.

"No animal can get through those," Pedro explained, as he helped the boys plant the branches firmly in the earth and bind them together with lengths of barbed wire. Then the chickens were brought from Lottie Dawson's ranch and installed. Jean took over her new job, turning to Pedro for advice as to food and care for the providers of fresh eggs. Pedro, indeed, was always on hand, his wrinkled brown face alive with interest, ready to help with labor and information. He was very proud of his new Boss and the family, especially Jean.

"It very nice to have a lady here," he commented.

Her father's presence did much to lessen the friction between Nat and John, Jean saw. Also, although John did often give up trying, when a task seemed difficult, he was proving a little more adaptable. She often watched the boys as they rode about on their horses, Nat teaching John "to know as much as the horse," in John's phrase. She liked the sure grace with which Nat whirled and threw the rope, wishing, always, that her twin could learn that trick, too. And on horseback, she thought, Nat was wonderful. He and his mount seemed one creature.

"You are really very patient with us tenderfeet, Nat," said Mr. Merryweather one evening, when he had been questioning him about some fundamental facts on cattle raising. "You never look down your nose at us when we display our abysmal ignorance."

John turned to wink at Nat, who was saying, "Look at all the things you folks know that I don't. Why you, sir, are a regular walking encyclopedia, and the twins know lots more than I do when it comes to books. I always liked books, but haven't had much chance at them."

"Dad's right, though, Nat," said Jean, smiling at him. "You are patient with us tenderfeet."

Nat thought, looking at her, it was no wonder her father and brother depended so much on this girl. Slim and pretty as a picture she was in those blue jeans, but there was no nonsense about her. She had seemed more contented with the ranch since her father had come. Maybe, Nat dared hope, she wasn't hating it so much anymore.

To celebrate the night that marked the end of the first week their father had been there, Jean gave them an extra fine supper. Afterwards he sat over his book in the living room, listening to the gay chatter in the kitchen where the young folks were clearing up. They had been right about Nat Barton, he thought, his dear, impetuous twins. He smiled as he heard Nat and John singing lustily while they dried the dishes for Jean.

"Home, home on the range
Where the deer and the antelope play.
Where there seldom is heard a discouraging word
And the skies are not cloudy all day."

Chapter VI

NEW FRIENDS

"WHEN YOU AND JOHN GO TO TOWN FOR PROVISIONS," Jean said to her father at breakfast one morning, "why don't you stop off at the Indian reservation and see if you can get an olla like that one of Lottie Dawson's."

"Good enough," answered her father. "As a matter of fact, I have wanted to get a close look at the old Spanish mission church on the reservation ever since I came. It looks beautiful from a distance."

"From far away on the highway," said Jean, "it looks

like two sails on the blue sea of the desert. You have to get fairly close before those sails turn into church towers."

It was late in the afternoon before her father and John returned proudly bearing the clay olla. Jean had been alarmed about them. That night John explained why they had been so long.

"We sure got lost on that old Reservation," he said. "On the way, we passed an Indian driving a wagon-load of firewood into town and asked him where we could buy an olla. He was pretty discouraging—said nobody had 'em for sale in the winter. Dad persisted, though, and finally this Indian admitted that an old woman who lived next to him (Maria Garcia, her name is) made them in summers. So we got directions from him and we did our best to follow them—but honest, each road looked like every other one and all Indian huts look alike. Boy, I thought we never would find the place. As a giver of instructions," John continued, "that Indian is a fine cook!"

"I didn't mind being lost," said his father, "I was so interested in seeing those primitive Indian houses close at hand. And, Jeanie, we must take you to see the mission and the great cottonwood trees which line many of the roads. The leaves are still tinged with the deep gold of autumn colors, even though it is early December."

"Did you get close enough to see the mission?" Jean asked.

"Yes, indeed we did, and it is beautiful." He described the worn stone carving of the façade, pale creamy brown against the white of the towers, and the carved wooden balconies before the tower windows. "I am going back there some day soon and make a thorough study of tha beautiful old church, inside and out. No, I didn't mind being lost at all."

"You minded when we got stuck in the sand in one of those crazy washes, Dad," his son reminded him.

"Oh," said Jean, "how did you manage to get out?"

"John walked around until he found some Indians who came and hauled us out with a team of horses," answered her father with a chuckle. "We were pretty discouraged, but finally we persuaded one of them to go with us to Maria Garcia's house. We found it at last with their help."

"It took about half the population of the Reservation to explain to her what we were after," volunteered John, grinning broadly. "They all looked at us as if we were nuts. I guess buying an olla in the winter just isn't done in the best Indian circles."

"But how did you finally get it?" asked Jean.

"Oh, Dad was poking around the place and spied it, and we managed to get her to name a price and made the deal. The whole thing had taken us five hours."

"Well, you must have felt as if you'd carried the message to Garcia," said Jean.

"We did at that," replied John, "only here we call it 'Gar-see-a.' "

After supper Mr. Merryweather showed Jean some sketches he had made at the Reservation that day. He never went anywhere, Jean noticed, without taking his sketch book along. And every few days he sat out in front of the house before his easel painting the desert rimmed with mountains.

Jean was pleased with the jar of cold water always at

hand, and soon she thought of another acquisition that would add to their comfort.

"What we need is a cow that gives milk," she said one day. "Here we have all these cattle, yet we have to use canned milk."

"By Jove, Jean, you've got something there," her brother agreed, enthusiastically. "Let's try to buy a Jersey cow and I will sell all the milk we don't need for ourselves."

"We'd better ask Lottie Dawson's advice about where to get it," suggested Nat.

"You know, Jean," said Lottie, when they went to ask her advice, "I've had the same idea as you about needing an honest-to-goodness milk cow. But you beat me to it— so I'll tell you what—I'll buy milk from you if you do get a cow, and I know where you can get a good one. There's a big dairy down near Nogales run by a friend of mine. He will sell you one of his Jerseys at a decent price. But say, can any of you milk a cow?"

"I can," said Nat. "I'll take on the milking as my job. John can deliver the milk in the station wagon and Jean can wash the bottles, or maybe I could, if you're too busy, Jean."

"Hold your horses, Nat," said John. "You said a decent price, Lottie. How much do you mean?"

"I reckon a good Jersey will cost about a hundred dollars." Then, seeing the look of disappointment on their faces, Lottie went on, "What's the matter, kids, haven't you got that much to spare?" Receiving confirmation from them she said, "Well, see here, it's just providential that you need a hundred dollars, for I've my eye on two of your heifers. As a matter of fact I was just making a deal with your Uncle shortly before he died. Their calves will have been sired by Domingo Third, you know. I'll pay you fifty dollars apiece for them if you will sell them right away—and then you can take the money and go down to Nogales to buy the cow. And I bet Joe Smith would buy your extra milk in his store. Let's go ask him right now."

Putting action to her words was Lottie Dawson's long suit, and soon they were spinning along the road to Joe Smith's store. Before they reached it they crossed the dry bed of a river. John pointed to a sign fastened to a post near the absolutely waterless expanse of sand and stones, "Danger. Floods. Cross at your own risk."

"That sign always hands me a laugh," he said. "Floods, my eye!"

"You'll laugh out of the other side of your face one of these days, my fine fellow, when the river is running," said Lottie.

"How you tell me!" answered John, incredulously. It was impossible to believe that they would ever see enough water in that dry bed to make crossing dangerous.

"Joe's storekeeping is a joke," Lottie confided to them before they entered his store. "He has such a soft heart, he just can't say no. He gives credit to all the Oakies and Arkies that come to pick cotton in the irrigated fields in the valley. We all get mighty provoked at him, but he's so kind that we can't help but love him."

"It would be a good idea if someone cleaned up his store once in a while," said Nat. "I've watched him try to find something a customer asks for. He never seems to know where anything but the big stuff is."

Lottie chuckled. "Joe has a sister in Tucson who comes out for a month every year and cleans up his house and store both. That old place fairly shines after she's been to work on it. She won't allow any credit, either, except to the ranch owners in the neighborhood. When she's here Joe's affairs take a turn for the better. But a few days after she's gone he is up to his old tricks again and his store looks as messy as ever."

Joe's father and mother had been pioneers in Arizona, Lottie told them, and Joe had inherited a large tract of land, most of which he had lost, bit by bit, through bad management.

The storekeeper welcomed the delegation with cordial good humor. He was a plump little old man with a kindly red face and watery blue eyes.

"Sure, I'll buy your milk," he said in answer to John's query. "I'll give you ten cents a quart for it and sell it for twelve—fair enough? But of course, if you can get customers nearer home it will pay you better. But I'll take all you have left over."

"That's awfully kind of you, Mr. Smith," said Jean.

"Not at all, not at all," Joe replied, beaming all over his ruddy face.

"Well, that settles the problem of disposing of our produce," remarked John happily, as they returned to the station wagon. "Now let's go up to our ranch and you pick out the heifers you want, Lottie. Then maybe tomorrow we can go to Nogales to get the cow."

"We can go to Nogales this afternoon," said Lottie.

"Never mind about the heifers. Tomorrow will do all right for them. I've got a trailer at the ranch we can bring the cow home in. But say, don't you think we had better speak to your father first about selling me the heifers?"

"If Uncle George had promised them to you, Dad will agree, I know that," said John. "But we'd best go and tell him where we're going."

"Maybe he'd like to come along," suggested Lottie.

Mr. Merryweather, however, said he would help Pedro get a cowpen ready while the rest of them went for its occupant. They drove off, leaving him and Pedro busily constructing a cow corral.

On the way down the Nogales highway, they noticed the long lines of cottonwoods following the river in the valley. Jean pointed to the ruins of a Spanish church, its mellow old walls and domes shining in the sun against a back drop of purple mountains. "What's that?" she asked.

"That's the old mission of Tumacacori—the ruins, I mean," Lottie answered. "It's a National Monument now. There's a museum in that nice neat little building beside it."

"We ought to tell Dad about this place, John," said his sister. "You know how excited he was about the church on the Reservation. He'd like this, too."

"Better bring him down here some day," said Lottie. "Father Kino founded this mission for the Indians hundreds of years ago, although he didn't build this church. He was a great old guy—that padre—he taught the Indians all kinds of useful things about irrigating and stock raising and so forth. He didn't take it all out in prayers and singing psalms—not by a long shot."

A few hours later a broad-beamed Jersey cow named Sukey was unloaded at Circle M Ranch, and Nat was displaying his skill as a milker. Next morning after breakfast John delivered two quarts of milk to Lottie and took the rest to Joe Smith's store.

"I wish we had ice to keep it in," he said, when he returned from the trip. "What shall we do with the evening's milk? If I have to make two trips a day to Smith's store, that will eat up all our profits buying gas."

"We can keep the milk in the tin in the water tank, the way we did the meat," suggested Nat. "I'm sure it won't spoil in this cool night air. Then you can bottle it in the morning. I'll get up early and milk Sukey so that you can deliver the morning milk right away."

"Good boy, Nat," said Mr. Merryweather, smiling at him. "What a resourceful fellow you are!"

Later he suggested to his son that he and Nat might share the profits from Sukey's milk just as Jean made pin money from selling eggs. "Or," said his father, "if you have Nat teach you to milk, you can take full charge of the cow and have the profits for yourself."

"Okay," said John, "that will be swell, Dad." The boy had been wanting to earn some money. He remembered that Stetson hat still waiting for him in the shop in Tucson. The small allowance his father was able to give him did not go far for a fellow with John's expensive tastes.

Nat tried hard to teach the impatient boy how to milk. But John tugged away so hard that Sukey got nervous, and began to stamp her feet and toss her head.

"Say, John," Nat called. "That isn't the kitchen pump you've got hold of there. Don't use so much elbow grease

—sort of coax the milk out. You've got to gentle the poor old girl."

But John kept on pulling so clumsily that Sukey revenged herself by kicking over the pail and drenching John with milk. Spluttering, he ran into the house, where Jean met him, convulsed at the spectacle he made.

"You can have that job, Nat, and half the profits, too," John said, after he had changed into dry clothes.

"Oh come now, John," Nat protested. "You will learn how in time if you stick to it."

"No thanks," said John, gruffly. "Believe me, I don't play nursemaid to that old ticklish beast."

Mr. Merryweather looked grave as he listened to this conversation. John's lack of perseverance distressed his father, as it did Jean. It was not his way to scold and nag at his children, so that they felt any reproachful remark of his extra keenly. When, after the milking fiasco he said, "Not much of a cowboy, are you, son?" it stung John to the quick. And he endeavored to make up for it by spending the afternoon trying to rope the snubbing post before the corral. After repeated failures, he once again shrugged his shoulders and decided that trick was not for him, either.

That night Jean was awakened by loud squawks from the chicken yard. She put on her bathrobe and went to the *ramada* to waken the boys. "What do you suppose is bothering the chickens?" she asked.

The boys went to investigate. They found a large horned owl in the yard attacking the chickens. Two of Jean's pullets lay dead on the ground and the owl was getting at a third, when the boys arrived. Seizing poles, they beat the owl off and soon quiet was restored.

Jean was distressed at their report. "Well, thanks to that owl we shall have chicken for dinner tomorrow," she said, "but it is a pretty expensive way to get it."

In the morning Nat declared that the family should have a rifle to shoot at marauding creatures. Mr. Merryweather agreed, and took Nat with him to Tucson to buy a 30-30, light enough for Jean to handle.

"I'll make a pad of rubber for her shoulder so that the gun won't kick too hard for her," Nat said.

Every evening, thereafter, just before sunset, Jean practiced shooting. Her targets were bottles stuck up on posts of the corral. Sometimes one of the boys would throw a tin can into the air for Jean to hit. She found that she had a steady arm and a good eye, and was, as Nat said, a "natural shot."

He suggested that she go gunning for cottontails so he could make them another rabbit stew, but Jean protested.

"I don't believe I could bear to kill a living thing," she declared.

"Not even an owl that was hurting your chickens?" asked Nat.

"Oh, that's different—if one animal were attacking another," she said.

Jean was enjoying the companionship of Nat and her brother, but she longed for a girl friend of her own age to share her experiences in this lonely land. So what happened to John one day in early December was like an answer to prayer.

He had driven to Joe Smith's store with milk. As he came in the door the storekeeper waddled toward him, with a broad smile on his face.

"Here he is, folks, the young fella I was tellin' you about," he called back to a young man and woman standing at the counter.

The man, John saw, looked like a typical cowboy—thin and slouching, faded blue jeans tucked into high-heeled boots, wide brimmed hat and plaid woolen shirt. His eyes were keen under bushy eyebrows. Beside him stood a slender girl, also dressed in blue jeans and boots. Strands of wavy blond hair showed under her Stetson hat. Her eyes were gray-green, her smile warm and friendly.

"Meet Sally and Bert Hazelton, John Merryweather," Joe Smith said, and John shook hands with the two. "The Hazeltons have just got back—they bin tourin' the rodeos all around the country," the storekeeper explained. "Bert, here, is a professional rodeo rider—even Sally rides some, don't you?"

"She sure does," her husband said, proudly. "Sally cleaned up at Cheyenne this summer riding bulls."

John looked at the girl in surprise, for he had never seen anyone who looked less like a rider of bulls than this girl, in spite of her cowboy clothes. Her voice when she spoke to John was gentle and quiet, her manner well-bred and charming.

"Joe tells us you have a sister with you out here," said Sally Hazelton. "I'd like to meet her."

"Why don't you and your sister come to see us sometime," put in Bert. "We'd sure like to have you."

"Yes, do," Sally chimed in. "We live about ten miles from here, off the Nogales highway."

"Well, thanks ever so much," John answered. "We'd love to come."

"How's about coming this afternoon?" asked Bert.

"Okay," said John. "I guess my sister could manage that all right." Bert gave him explicit directions for finding their place and with that the two Hazeltons took themselves off.

"Them two are a swell pair," said Joe Smith, after they had left. "Sally is the daughter of a rich Detroit fella. She came out here a couple of years ago to go to the University. Then she met Bert and fell in love with him, and married him, just like that!"

"What does he do for a living besides ride in rodeos?" asked John.

"Nothing," Joe Smith answered. "He earns a living at that game. He's got more ridin' history tucked under his saddle than you could shake a stick at. And his wife is sure one game kid. Wait 'til you see the house they live in. They built it themselves out of 'dobes and beams from the old railroad that used to run along here. She cooks on the fireplace and they haul all the water they use from my store. You'd think a girl raised like she was would complain about livin' like that—but nary a peep out of her. She's one game kid, all right, all right," Joe repeated.

John lost no time in telling Jean about the friendly pair he had met and after dinner they set out to call upon the Hazeltons, following a very bad road across the desert after leaving the highway. Jean was sure they had taken the wrong road and even John thought he might have mistaken the directions. But at last they saw a tiny adobe house, among the mesquite and palo verde trees. It was so low and so nearly the color of the earth as to be almost invisible at a distance. A sleeping porch at one side of the

single-roomed square house was roofed with ribs of
sahuaro cactus. The little place was separated from the surrounding desert by an interesting fence made of crooked
saplings. Over its gate, for decoration, hung a bleached
cow skull. Inside the enclosure strange varieties of cactus made a desert garden with a border of colored
rocks.

Sally popped out the door and eagerly invited them in.

The tiny place was immaculate. "A place for everything
and everything in its place," thought Jean, as she looked
around. They sat on a low double couch across from the
fireplace where Sally cooked the food, placing the pots on
an iron grill. There was a cupboard against one wall, with
shelves for provisions on top, drawers for clothes in the
middle section, and a place for dishes and pots and pans
at the bottom.

When Jean realized that this girl managed without running water to keep everything so clean, she felt ashamed
of herself for thinking that Circle M Ranch was primitive.
After all, she had running water in her kitchen and a real
stove to cook on.

Far from being embarrassed about their unpretentious
home, the young Hazeltons were very proud of it.

"We built it ourselves," boasted Bert. "We didn't make
the 'dobes. Got a Mexican to make those, but we put 'em
together and plastered the room inside and out and laid the
cement floor. We went around to abandoned 'dobe shacks
and got window frames. The whole house cost us only six
dollars."

"Door and all?" queried John, incredulously.

"Yep," Bert answered. "We found this door on an old

school house that hasn't been used for five years. So no-body minded our taking it—leastwise, nobody said any-thing about it."

"We made enough money out of this season to finish paying for our land," put in Sally.

"John told me that you ride bulls in rodeos, Mrs. Hazel-ton," said Jean. "Is that true?"

Sally grinned and her husband said, "Of course it's true. Why not? Anybody who has a good seat on a horse and ain't skeered can learn to ride bulls."

"Do you mean it?" asked John. "Say, how much can you earn by riding a bull at a rodeo?"

"It's all according to how much money there is up," answered Bert. "For instance, take last season at Houston. There was five go-rounds. I placed first on one go-round and got two hundred dollars. Figure it out for yourself. Of course no one ever won first place on all five go-rounds. Now take here in Tucson—a fella might win four or five hundred dollars—if he placed first two days running, and then got his divvy of the finals money, too. That's made up of a percentage of the entrance fees. Of course at the little shows the total purse can be as low as one hundred dollars to be split up—and then there's everything clear up to Madison Square Garden with a total purse of over five thousand."

"Tell me, please," said Jean, "what is a 'go-round?'"

"That's when all the contestants for any one event have each ridden once."

"The rodeo business seems to have a lingo of its own," commented Jean.

"Gosh!" thought John. "I'd like to earn some of that

money." Aloud he said, "How did you go about learning to ride bulls Mrs. Hazelton?"

"Call me Sally," the girl answered with a wide grin. "You're out West now, John, and you don't have to stand on ceremony."

"Okay, Sally, thanks," said John. "But tell me, how did you learn this stunt?"

"Well," Sally answered with a chuckle, "Bert and I were broke and I saw an ad of a small ranch rodeo. The ad said they would pay any girl five dollars who could stay on a bull's back for eight seconds. That was the first time I ever rode a bull, but of course I'd been riding horses all my life."

"And did you stay on?" asked John.

"Yes, just exactly eight seconds before the bull bucked me off. Anyway I got the five dollars."

"My, you were plucky!" exclaimed Jean. "Then what did you do?"

"Oh, I'd started in then, so I went to all the small rodeos around the neighborhood. Sometimes I got bucked off, but usually I managed to stay on. And sometimes I won. Of course they were only white-faced bulls I rode—not Brahma bulls, like they have in the big shows. Anyway I helped earn the family beans, didn't I, Bert?"

"You bet," answered her husband.

"Have you ever ridden at any of the big rodeos?" Jean wanted to know.

"Yes, I rode at Cheyenne this past summer and at Madison Square Garden this fall—and once I rode here at Tucson."

"Well, you certainly are a good sport," declared Jean.

While they were talking, Sally had set a tin coffee pot on the iron grill over the fire. Soon it was ready and Bert got out four cups.

"Here's some of Sally's coffee, Jean," he said, handing her a cup. "It's strong enough to stand up and speak for itself."

As they drank their coffee and ate some sour dough biscuits which Sally had made in her Dutch oven pot, Jean examined the pictures on the walls of the little house. Bert noticed her looking at a photograph of a very elaborate stone mansion in the midst of beautiful formal gardens.

"That's Sally's old home in Dee-troit," he volunteered.

"Honestly?" asked Jean in surprise.

"Oh sure," said Sally Hazelton, nonchalantly. "That's the old mausoleum. I keep it up there just in case I ever get discontented with Bert and this house—to remind myself what a lot of trouble it used to be living up to that place. Whew! Never again. Not for me!"

"You mean, you really like it out here in this big empty country better than in your old home?" asked Jean incredulously.

"Heavens, yes," said Sally. "Don't you?"

"Gosh no," spoke up John. "Jean is counting the days till we go home."

"Well, you can have the East," said Sally. "I hate it—so many people living crowded together in such a little space. Out here you have room to draw a full breath."

"But don't you miss conveniences?" asked Jean. "And friends and fun and excitement?"

"I have all the fun and excitement I want during rodeo

season—and friends, too," answered Sally. "I'm glad for a little quiet between seasons. And as for conveniences—well, it's my idea that American women spend so much time fussing over gadgets to *save* time that they don't have any time left to enjoy themselves. No sir," Sally went on vehemently, "I think that anybody who doesn't like this kind of life is just a softie."

Soon after, Jean and John took their leave. On the way home, Jean said, "Imagine a girl who was brought up in a home like Sally Hazelton's actually liking that little hut!"

John chuckled. "She sure told you plenty when you asked her about it." He turned and looked thoughtfully at his sister. "I guess it's pretty tough on you out here, isn't it, Jeanie?" he went on, almost tenderly.

"I should say it is," Jean answered vehemently. "But please don't let Dad guess it, will you, John? Nor—nor Nat?"

"Oh well," said John, "Nat never knew anything better than our house here. I bet he'd shy if he ever saw a bathtub or an electric refrigerator, but Sally Hazelton—well, gee, Sis, compared to her father's house, our old house back home is just a dump."

"All the same, I can't wait to get back to our dump, as you call it," said his sister.

They agreed that Sally's point of view was a puzzle to them both, but they liked the young Hazeltons and hoped to see more of them.

The twins could not wait to introduce Nat to these new friends, knowing that he and Bert would take to each other, as they did at once. For the Eastern boy and girl there was a glamour about the Hazeltons, who talked so unassumingly about their dangerous work, riding bareback broncs and bulls, and who were so ingenious at making everything they needed. John never tired of listening to Bert's tales of the big shows and the exploits of fellow riders. Soon he was regaling the family with knowing descriptions of the technique of bronc riding and bull-dogging. He even picked up Bert's salty way of expressing himself, and the family at Circle M became addicted to what Jean called "Bert-isms."

Sometimes in the afternoons Jean mounted her horse and rode across the desert to visit Sally, whom she liked and admired immensely. One day she found Sally putting the finishing touches on a scarlet satin shirt.

"For Bert to wear in next season's shows," the girl explained. "I always make his rodeo shirts, and wine, too. And look," she opened a drawer and took out some handsome Western shirts, beautifully stitched and finished. "I'm going to trade these at the Boot and Saddle Shop in town for a pair of leather chaps for Bert's Christmas present."

"Sally, you are a wonder!" exclaimed Jean. "Is there anything you can't do? But how do you manage this fine stitching?"

"I have a friend in the valley who has an electric sewing machine. I go to her house to do all the machine stitching."

Soon Jean learned of another of Sally's enterprises. One day, when Sally arrived at Circle M Ranch to visit her friend, she found Jean laboring over a tin wash tub, scrubbing the boys' shirts.

"Laundry is so expensive," explained Jean. "I'm trying to help out by doing the washing myself. But how I miss our electric washer."

"It is hard work doing it that way," Sally agreed. "But look here, I'll tell you a trick I learned. There's a place in town where you can rent the use of an electric washer and iron for very little. So now I take all our wash, even our sheets and blue jeans and get it done in no time. Want to go in with me, next time I go?"

"Yes, indeed," Jean answered. After that the two girls made weekly excursions into town with all their heavy laundry.

If Jean was hoping to find in her new friend a confidant to whom she could pour out her homesickness and her dislike of the West and the inconveniences of her life, she was disappointed. Any small complaint that Jean made branded her a "softie" in Sally's eyes. But Jean learned from her many short cuts to her housekeeping problems and inexpensive foods to serve her family.

"Live and learn," Jean said to Sally one day, when they had been shopping together for supplies and she had watched Sally pick out the cheaper cuts of meat and buy some Mexican spices with which to cook them.

"I've learned plenty out here from the Mexicans about how to live without spending much," Sally answered. "I'm crazy about the way they do things. Do they need a house or a fireplace or anything else, they just go ahead and build it simply, using materials that are right at hand. Bert and I could never have had our house if we hadn't watched them build some of theirs. Of course they have to buy machinery for pumps and parts of cars and stuff like that, but they know how to use their brains and their hands. I get a kick out of doing things like that, too. Just like using these herbs and making a stew taste like a swell Waldorf dish.

Give you time, Jean, and you'll be a regular Westerner, too."

Jean smiled at her friend. "Not if I know myself, I won't," she thought. But she didn't say that aloud for fear of incurring Sally's condemnation of "softie."

Chapter VII

CHRISTMAS ON THE DESERT

THE APPROACH OF CHRISTMAS INTENSIFIED JEAN'S HOME-sickness. She longed for crisp snow and evergreens and the gayety of holiday parties. Letters from friends, telling of skating on the lake and the first fall of snow made it all the harder to bear. The "gang" were planning Christmas and New Year festivities, when those who had gone to college would be home for the holidays. "We shall miss you and John just terribly," Dorothy, her best friend wrote.

"And that won't be all the missing that's done, either," John had said, when Jean read him the letter. "How do you suppose you'll know it's Christmas in a place like this? Do you suppose they will hang bells and Christmas tinsel on the sahuaros and put sleigh bells on the cows?"

Jean was thinking much the same thing. What would Christmas be like, anyway, out here in the desert land. But the twins were surprised to see that the streets of Tucson looked much like the streets of any city of its size before Christmas. The shop windows were full of gifts—festoons of greens were hanging from the lamp posts—Salvation Army Santa Clauses tinkled their bells on street corners—and the markets were full of holly wreaths and Christmas trees.

Well, she would go through the motions, of course, and pretend to be happy for her father's sake. Did he ever guess, Jean wondered, how terribly homesick she was? Sometimes she caught him looking at her with an especially tender expression, but she did her best to keep from him the knowledge of how she really felt.

After a family council they decided that instead of buying individual presents they would all chip in and get a small battery radio for all of them to use. Mr. Merryweather said he felt the need of daily news. And they all missed the concert broadcasts and other music which had meant so much to them at home. "We won't be so far away and out of things if we have a radio," Jean said.

Nat did not realize how makeshift their Christmas plans seemed to the twins. For him, a family Christmas was a new and delightful experience which he anticipated eagerly.

A few days before Christmas, Lottie Dawson rode up to the house on her horse and dismounted with a cheery hail.

"Say," she called to Jean who came out to welcome her, "I'm going to have a big Christmas dinner party and I depend on you all to be my star guests. Joe Smith is coming and the Hazeltons. How about it, will you come?"

"Will we?" cried Jean "It will just make Christmas for us, Lottie! We were feeling a bit homesick, you know."

"Sure, we'll do our best to make you forget home."

That same evening Mr. Merryweather came in with another suggestion. He had been spending some time at the mission of San Xavier del Bac on the Reservation, learning its history from the Franciscan father in charge. The dim murals and ancient carved decorations of the interior, naïve and primitive, appealed to the artist in him. The Spanish builders, so he told his family, had designed the decorations, but they had been, for the most part, executed by Indian charges, trained to the work.

Now Mr. Merryweather had learned that every Christmas Eve there was a Midnight Mass at the mission, for the Indians and Mexicans.

"The padre says it is most interesting," he told the family at the supper table. "Shall we go?"

"Do let's," Jean responded. "It will be different from anything we've ever done for Christmas before."

Christmas Eve was a cold crisp night. Moonlight flooded the hushed, mysterious desert as the Merryweathers rattled over the miles to the mission. The large open space in front of the church was crowded with cars and farm wagons of the Papago Indians. A quiet throng of people moved in procession through the arched gateway leading to the church portal. Flickering lights of candles, held in each worshipper's hand, picked out worn faces of old men and women, the dark dignity of Indians, the round eyes of children and of babies in their mothers' arms. Every face was lifted in solemn trust toward the light streaming from the open church door.

Along the top of the high wall before the church, candles set in paper bags contrasted their warm glow with the icy silver of moonlight. The illuminated towers shone white against the night sky. Suddenly, from one of the tower windows, the clear call of trumpets rang out, as two Indian men sent the notes of old Christmas carols showering into the still air. The bells burst into a wild, joyous peal, announcing midnight.

Quietly the Merryweathers found places in the back of the crowded church. Above the heads of the worshippers candle light touched the banners of garish crepe paper streamers draped from arch to arch. The gilded carving behind the high altar shone with a warm glow.

Preceded by Indian altar boys carrying tapers, the priest stepped down from the altar and passed to a side chapel where the scene of the Nativity had been set. He blessed the Christ child figure in its swinging crib, then lifted it in his arms and carried it to the high altar.

The Mass went on, with its solemn chanting, and clouds of fragrant incense. Jean was deeply moved, and bowed her head in sympathy with the adoration she felt in the simple, dark-skinned people about her. For centuries, she thought, their ancestors had been worshipping in this same church and finding comfort there.

"That was a Christmas Eve we shall not forget," said Mr. Merryweather softly, when they reached home after a silent ride through the moonlit night. The boys nodded, and Jean saw that they, too, had been moved by what they had seen.

Lottie's dinner party the next day added the note of
festive gayety to their Christmas. She had set a long table
in her living room and had a tiny Christmas tree in the
center for decoration. The banqueting board groaned
under the weight of good things to eat. At one end Lottie
placed a monstrous turkey, crisp and brown. Next she
returned from the kitchen bearing a roast suckling pig,
complete with an apple in its mouth, which she placed at
the opposite end of the table.

The company cheered. "Never before in my life have
I seen a roast suckling pig," cried Jean, gaily. "This is a
red letter day."

"Now, friend Merryweather, if you will carve up the
turkey, I'll dig into this fellow. Suckling pig is kinda my
specialty," declared Lottie.

She filled their glasses from a gallon jug of sweet cider,
in which they drank a toast to Christmas, to their hostess
and good fortune to them all. She piled their plates with
second helpings until they cried for mercy and then she
produced mince pies, a plum pudding and cups of coffee.

"Well," sighed John, when they were all but reduced to
immobility, "You're just as good at cooking, Lottie, as
you are at herding cattle or riding broncs. In fact, you're
an all around swell guy!"

The young people quickly piled the dishes in the kitchen
and cleared away the table so that they might all sit around
the big fireplace, where blazing mesquite and juniper logs
gave off their aromatic scent.

"Lottie," said Jean, after they were all seated, "I wonder
if you would let us indulge in an old Merryweather cus-
tom. Every Christmas, as long as I can remember, Daddy

has read us Dickens' 'Christmas Carol' on Christmas Day. We brought it along. Do you mind if we read it?"

"Of course not," said Lottie. "Can't say I ever read it myself, although I've heard parts of it on the radio."

"Oh do, please, Mr. Merryweather," put in Sally Hazelton, her eyes starry. "We always used to read it at home on Christmas Eve."

"The first year Sally and I were married," said Bert, "she read it out loud at Christmas—but she bawled so I had to take the book away from her and finish it myself."

"Oh," asked Lottie, "is it sad?"

"In spots," answered John. "But it has a happy ending."

"Okay, then," said Lottie. "Let's go."

For several hours, as Mr. Merryweather read the dearly beloved story, they sat silently listening. Occasionally Lottie's cowboy, Jake, put a fresh juniper log on the fire, but otherwise no one moved.

Jean was close to tears during this reading, not so much at the well-known story, but because hearing her father read it evoked so many memories of home.

At the end Lottie blew her nose loudly and turned shining eyes upon Mr. Merryweather. "God bless us every one," she repeated. "You bet. Now then, Bert, how's about some cowboy songs to finish off with. Wait until I get out the jug to wet your whistle." She poured them each a drink of cider, and then Bert began to sing in the drawling voice of cowboys of the West:

"Walkin' John was an old rope horse
From over Marengo way.
When you stacked your rope on a ragin' steer

> *Old John was there to stay.*
> *As long as your rope was stout and strong*
> *And your terrapin shell stayed on*
> *Dally-welty, or hard and fast*
> *'Twas all the same to John."*

The song went on to tell how they put old Walkin'
John in a livery stable to work, and how he got along all
right with everybody there, until one day a "dude" came
in, dressed up like a cowboy, with chaps and wide som-
brero and so forth, and they saddled Walkin' John for this
drug store cowboy to ride. Poor old Walkin' John couldn't
stand it and bucked the dude off into a cholla cactus bush.
Bert drawled the last stanza slowly and with much expression:

> *"He wasn't dressed for to aviate*
> *But, fellers, he sure did fly.*
> *They picked him out of the cholla bush*
> *And some of his clothes stayed on.*
> *They felt of his spokes*
> *Then wired his folks.*
> *'Twas all the same to John."*

The three young people from Circle M burst out laughing at the end of this song. Jean laughed until the tears
rolled down her cheeks and Nat slapped John on the back
while the two of them howled with mirth.

"What's the special joke?" asked Lottie.

"Oh nothing," answered John. "It just makes us think
of what happened to a dude we used to know." And they

were off again in peals of laughter, remembering John's
"tangle" with the cholla bush.

"More, more, Bert," cried Jean, clapping her hands.

"Say, Nat," said Bert, after bowing to the applause,
"let's have some Texas cowboy songs."

"Okay Bert," Nat answered, "but you'd better help me
sing 'em. I'll begin with 'Git along, Little Dogies.' You
know that one, don't you?"

"Sure," said Bert. And so they sang many songs of the
old West, each matching the other in ditties of humorous
words and lonesome, melancholy tunes.

"Now, Joe," said Lottie after the two boys had sworn
they had "sung themselves plumb out," "tell the folks
about the Christmas when your mother hid you down the
mine hole to save you from Apaches."

"Oh, say, Lottie," protested John, "you're just fixing up
tall tales for tenderfeet."

Joe chuckled. "No, this is really so. My mother was one
of the pioneers out here, you know. This happened about
fifty years ago, when I was seven. My father was working
a mine then, and my mother was the only woman in the
camp. All the men had gone off to celebrate Christmas, so
just our family was there. Well, sir, my mother had cooked
a big Christmas dinner with all the trimmings. She'd even
fixed a little pretend Christmas tree with strings of popcorn
for us children. There was three of us, the littlest only
three years old.

"Well, we'd just sat down to that feast when a fella
from a near-by ranch came up ridin' fast as the wind.
He hollered to my father that the Apaches were comin'.
Father grabbed the baby and my mother took me and my

sister by the hand and we ran to the mine hole and hid down inside it. My father rode off with the rancher for help.

"Pretty soon we heard horses galloping up and some shots."

"Boy, weren't you scared?" asked John.

"Scared? My teeth was chattering, and my mother was trying to hush the other two as best she could. She was afraid the Indians would run off with us children. We heard them go into the house and for awhile it was all quiet. Then we heard them ride away again. After a long while my mother dared to come out of the mine hole with us kids taggin' her, and we crept quietly over to the house. Oh, how me and my sister bawled when we saw the Christmas dinner table. The dishes was licked clean and even the popcorn off the tree was gone.

"Well, sir, my mother went into the kitchen and cooked up some beans and jerky the Indians hadn't found, and she told us the jerky was turkey and the beans was stuffing, and she made it all seem so real that when my father came back with some men we was all jokin' and laughing about our Christmas dinner."

"Good for your mother!" exclaimed Mr. Merryweather.

"Yes," said Lottie, "you should have known Mrs. Smith. She was a real old-timer."

"But Joe," inquired Jean, "would the Indians have stolen you children and killed your mother if they had found you?"

"Oh no," said Joe, with a broad wink. "Those wasn't really Apaches, though the men wasn't takin' any chances when they saw Indians. Those was just hungry Indians lookin' for some food to steal."

After the holidays the winter weeks sped away. Ranch work had fallen into a routine, each one taking care of his share. Jean racked her brains to provide hearty, tasty meals at low cost for her hungry men folks. The *frijoles* which Pedro's niece had taught her to make were a great favorite. Sometimes Pedro provided a treat when he brought a present from his sister, a large pot of savory *tamales*.

There were times when the wind howled in fury for days on end, piling dramatic masses of indigo clouds in the great sky, until at last curtains of rain descended to rush across the land in a fierce tempest. But storms were few and the Merryweathers marveled at the succession of bright sunny days and crisp, clear nights. Lottie, however, shook her head and looked worried.

"We've had several extra dry seasons now," she said, "and these spits of rain we've had this year don't help a mite. It never gets into the ground. The pasturage is poor and the water's getting low. It'll be bad business if we don't get more rain before spring."

But the twins, overjoyed as they noticed their father's increasing strength and alertness, did not join in Lottie's worry. "It's worth all the work and loneliness," Jean told herself, resolutely, "seeing Daddy getting so well."

He was working now on detailed drawings of the San Xaxier mission church, as interested in the history of Spanish influence in the Southwest as in the drawings, themselves. Often he returned from a visit to the University library in town with an armful of books, from which he read his family tales of the old padres and explorers.

Seated snug and cosy beside the blazing fire of fragrant juniper logs, Jean would listen to the desolate sound of the wind as it roared outside, pouncing on the little house as though trying to batter down its sturdy walls. To blot out the sound, she would jump up and turn on the radio, listening to almost anything because it spoke of people—crowds of people—moving and alive. On nights when there was no wind the vast emptiness of the desert terrified the girl. Only the occasional weird hysterical yelping of coyotes— the lonesomest sound in the world, Jean thought—broke the silence. But then, she would look up from her book and see her father absorbed in his reading, with the lines of worry smoothed out on his face, and feel almost reconciled.

One night when Nat was mending a bridle beside the fireplace, he looked up with an amused smile at the "reading circle." Mr. Merryweather was deep in Padre Kino's "Historical Memoirs of Pimeria Alta," Jean was reading a book about the bad old Arizona town of Tombstone, and John was looking through some old copies of the cowboys' own magazine, "Hoofs and Horns" which Bert had lent him.

"Well," said Nat, "you all will sure know a lot about this country when you are through."

Unlike their father, the twins were not interested in history as far back as Spanish days. For them Arizona had a frontier quality, and what interest they had in the land was in the pioneering Americans and Apaches on the warpath. They found it hard to believe that as recently as the 1880's the Apache chief, Geronimo, and his rebellious band, were raiding settlers' ranches and attacking wagon trains—and in the memory of a man they knew, people were still afraid of Indians, even though all they did was steal a Christmas dinner.

So the winter passed away, filled with hard work and varied interests. On an afternoon in February John said, "Let's all ride over and say goodbye to Sally and Bert. They are leaving for the rodeo season tomorrow morning."

"Yes, let's," said Jean, thinking how much she would miss those two good friends.

They found the young Hazeltons busily at work clearing up their small house, and the three young folks from Circle M lent a hand, helping pack away blankets, mop the little house and dispose of rubbish.

"Do write and tell us how you get on," Jean urged, as she kissed Sally goodbye.

"I hate to write letters," Sally answered, "but we'll send you some postcards."

"Goodbye, and I hope you wow 'em!" said John, shaking them both by the hand.

"That's right, Bert," added Nat. "I hope you do some good."

Nat and the Merryweathers took their leave and turned their horses homeward, as the glittering sun slipped down below the Western mountains.

One morning shortly after the Hazelton's departure, Jean was feeling unusually blue and lonely when Pedro came into the kitchen all smiles.

"My niece, Conchita, has come up from her home in

Nogales to celebrate her name day with us," he told Jean. "Yolanda wants all of you to come to Conchita's party tomorrow."

"We would love to, Pedro," Jean answered. "But what is her name day?"

"Her name is Concha Agatha Teresa Gonzales," Pedro replied, "and her saint's day—Saint Agatha—is tomorrow."

"Oh fine," said Jean. "What time shall we come?"

"In the evening," Pedro answered.

"May we bring something?" Jean asked.

"Oh no," said Pedro.

"But isn't it like a birthday?" the girl asked.

"Yes," Pedro smiled.

"All right," Jean thought to herself. "We'll take a name day present to Conchita." Among her things Jean found a pretty scarf that she had never worn, which she wrapped up in some left-over Christmas paper.

The courtyard of the ramshackle Gomez house was filled with people when the Merryweathers arrived. Mexican and American neighbors, children and older people and a few cowboys were there. In the noisy chatter the soft flow of Spanish mingled with English. Under the pepper tree in the center of the court stood a trestle upon which sat a keg of beer, flanked on one side with a washtub filled with ice and piled high with bottles of soft drinks and on the other with pails of *tamales*. From their cages surrounding the courtyard the chickens and rabbits and baby wild cats looked on.

Everyone was doing well by the beer and drinks and *tamales*, Jean though as she listened to the laughter. Lottie Dawson spied them as soon as they stepped out of the sta-

They sang popular Mexican songs

tion wagon and took them under her wing, proudly presenting them to the other guests as though they were her special acquisition.

Conchita was a slender, pretty Mexican girl just about Jean's age with soft curly black hair and large dark eyes. She accepted Jean's gift with a little cry of joy and immediately wound the scarf over her curls with becoming effect.

Later Yolanda and Conchita brought out their guitars and sang popular Mexican songs beginning with "Rancho Grande" and "South of the Border, Down Mexico Way," followed by "La Cucaracha," and many others. The girls had lovely warm voices and they harmoized well and easily as two people do who have sung together for many years. A large acetylene lantern hanging from the tree lit the faces of the two girls and spread a wide arc of light over the courtyard.

At last Conchita handed her guitar to a Mexican dressed in a charro costume and, clapping her hands for silence, she said, "Let's dance!" There were shouts of approval and the Mexican struck up a lilting, lovely tune.

"Oh good," Lottie whispered to Jean, "that's the Varsovianna."

Jean watched fascinated as the couples formed, the men standing behind the girls as they went into the figures of the dance. Dozens of couples swayed gracefully to the music. Then the Mexican struck up "Turkey in the Straw," and the cowboys, one after the other, clogged to the well-known tune on the hard-packed earth of the courtyard. Each performer drew loud applause, but the honors went to a lively, spry old fellow, whose face rivalled in color the red bandana tied around his neck. Soon the courtyard was crowded with dancers as the Mexican played one tune after another—accompanied by the rhythmic clapping of the hands of the onlookers.

When the Merryweathers finally tore themselves away the party was going full blast, getting nosier and gayer with song and dancing.

"That was fun," said Jean on their way home. "Mexicans do know how to have a good time. I must write Dorothy about this party."

"They don't have parties like that in Connecticut," said John.

"No, of course not," Jean answered. She was quiet for a moment.

"Penny for your thoughts, Twin," said John.

Jean shrugged. "Just thinking, John, about our old parties at home. Wouldn't I love to go to one of them again!"

Chapter VIII

SPRING ROUND-UPS

With the coming of spring Jean's thoughts turned more than ever to her New England home. She remembered with an ache in her heart the crocuses, tulips and golden sprays of forsythia in her garden; and the first feel of spring in the air, the sound of peepers in the swamps, and the caroling of robins in the orchards.

She looked out over the rolling land, gray-green with cactus and desert bushes, the clay earth covered with silvery dry grass. "What can spring be like out here?" she questioned. "Just hot sunshine and no flowers, I suppose."

The desert had surprises for her, however. One day,

after a rare shower of rain, Jean found a startling change in the fence of her chicken run. The dry ocotillo branches of which it was made had decked themselves in ruffles of green leaves, from top to bottom, and some were crowned with red tassels of bloom.

"An Arizona wonder—a fence that blooms," she told her family.

Soon the desert was decorated with the graceful, coral-red sprays of the ocotillo. When Jean saw the delicately green palo verde trees burst into showers of golden bloom, she did not miss her forsythia bushes so much. Masses of small yellow poppies and daisies and patches of lavender verbena, tinged the dry earth with color.

Then came the cactus blooms, and Jean almost forgot homesickness for New England in her delight over the fantastic desert flowering. On her walks, she found the small hedgehog cactus lifting brilliant cerise flowers toward the sky. Every variety of prickly pear rimmed its flat leaves with great silky golden or saffron blooms shaped like tulips. Even the sharp, angular cholla bushes dressed themselves in gay rosettes of flowers, which John said looked like Easter bonnets on an old hat rack.

The blooms on the desert inspired Mr. Merryweather to get to work seriously with his water colors. Day after day he set up his easel and after a week or so he had a "one man show" in the living room—nearly a dozen paintings to show his family. Nat and the twins were loud in their praise.

Jean, too, was inspired by all this desert blooming to produce some semblance of a garden in their bare door-yard. Lottie Dawson had given her slips from oleander

bushes, and Mr. Merryweather had brought her a few
rosebushes from town. Yolanda showed her how to plant
petunias in clay pots which hung from the rafters of the
ramada and rewarded her with their delicate flowers. Jean
wore herself out carrying pails of water from the tank to
her garden, but it was discouraging work. Over and over
again she set out small plants, only to have them nibbled
to the ground overnight by rabbits.

"If only I had a thick fence and plenty of water, I'd
have a garden," she declared. "Things ought to grow like
weeds in this hot sunshine."

Affairs at Circle M Ranch were going fairly well. Sukey
was giving a great deal of milk, and Jean, having added
to her flock of chickens, was now sending fresh eggs to Joe
Smith's store along with the milk. Nat reported to Jean
every bit of improvement he could about how her brother
was taking hold—he was riding the range more diligently,
and had become expert at mending broken fences, but still
he was dilatory about practicing roping.

"He really should be learning that if he doesn't want to
look like a boob at the time of spring round-ups," Nat told
Jean. But John, after making a few feeble attempts at trying to rope a steer or young bull on the range every day
or so, would shrug his shoulders and give up.

"He'll be sorry, one of these days," Nat predicted.

"I wish something would happen to make him really
want to learn how," said Jean, little knowing how deeply
that "something" would grieve her when it did happen.

It happened one morning when the cattle were going
into the corral for water, headed by Domingo Third.
Nat was riding the range with Pedro, and Mr. Merry-

weather had gone to Tucson for supplies. John was tinkering around the chicken run. Timmie, seeing the cattle, was barking ecstatically, as usual.

The little dog circled round and round, nearer and nearer to the bull. After that first day, when Timmie had been saved by Nat's skill, Jean tried to keep the dog away from the corral whenever the herd came in. That morning, however, she was too late.

"Here, Timmie, here, Timmie," she called, but the little dog paid no heed to her.

The bull, angered by Timmie's barks, made straight for him, his great head lowered.

"John, John," screamed Jean in alarm.

Her brother ran from the chicken coop he was nailing, and snatched a rope hanging by Pedro's hut. He swung it around his head and let go, but, alas, he failed to catch the wicked horns as Nat had done. The rope fell to the ground. Bellowing with rage, the bull charged at Timmie. Its great horns caught the little dog in the side. There was a sharp yelp of pain, then an ominous silence. Timmie fell lifeless to the ground.

Jean rushed into the corral, ignoring the bull, and gathered her dead pet into her arms. She carried him into the kitchen, vainly bathing his torn side and pouring water on his head. Tears streamed down her face and her shoulders shook with sobs.

"Gee, I'm sorry, Jean," said the crestfallen John. "Now if only Nat had been here! What a boob I've been never to learn how to rope cattle."

His voice was so contrite that Jean momentarily forgot her own sorrow.

"Never mind, John," she said bravely, wiping her eyes. "It was bound to happen some day, I suppose. But I hate that bull—the big brute!"

"Well, by Jove, I'm going to learn to rope cattle now or—or—well, I don't know what—" finished John, vehemently.

He made a small coffin out of some boards and together the twins sorrowfully buried the little Scottie in the grave John dug under a palo verde tree in the yard. Jean knelt beside the grave, patting down the sand with trembling hands.

"I feel as though we'd lost a member of the family, John," she said sadly.

"I know, Sis," her brother answered, huskily. "He was a great little pup." Then, diffidently, he said, "Don't say anything to Nat about how I miffed it with the rope, do you mind, Jean?"

"Of course I won't," she promised.

It wasn't necessary to say anything to Nat, for, when he came back at noon and found that Domingo had killed Timmie, and saw John doggedly trying to rope a fence post, he guessed what had happened.

And how John tried! Every afternoon he could be seen struggling to rope the snubbing post in the corral. He had decided to give up practicing on the calves until he could rope the post, and he had stopped trying to do even that on horseback.

He finally broke down and asked Nat for a lesson. Although the older boy patiently demonstrated again and again how to swing the rope, John seemed unable to get the knack of it. His aim was good, but the loop at the end of the rope rarely caught on the object at which he threw it, and sometimes it even came untied. Although he improved a little, he was never sure that the rope would catch.

"Take it easy, John," Nat advised. "You're trying too hard."

Jean and her father hung over the fence watching him practice and cheering him on, but they soon saw that their presence made him more nervous so they stayed inside the house.

"He's bound to catch on soon, Jean," Nat said reassuringly. "And it sure is swell seeing him try so hard and sticking at it, day after day, isn't it?"

"Yes, but why can't he learn, Nat? You used to say all he needed was wanting to enough—and surely he does now. Just see how he is trying all the time."

"I hope he will catch on in time for the round-ups," Nat replied. "Heaven knows he ought to."

The first of the neighborhood round-ups was to be held on May Day at Lottie's ranch. Mr. Stevens, a nearby rancher, and his two sons, Bob and Roy, were to help as well as the men from Circle M.

Just before dawn Pedro, Nat and John prepared to leave for Lottie's ranch. While Jean served them a hasty breakfast, John said, "Nat, you'll have to show me what to do today."

"Oh, it's just rounding up the cattle on the range and cutting out the young steers to be sold and the cows with calves. Then, when we have the cows in the corral, we rope the calves to bring them to the branding fires."

Jean looked at her brother apprehensively. He was

dreading the day, she knew, afraid that he would appear stupid before these Westerners who had, after all, grown up with cattle. Now the two Stevens boys and their father, as well as Lottie's cowboy, would see what a greenhorn John was.

"How I hope he gets away with it!" his sister thought.

Later, in the hot bright morning, Jean and her father drove to Lottie's ranch.

"I wish I could help herd the cattle," said Mr. Merryweather, as they rode along.

"Oh no, Dad. You mustn't try. You sit in the shade with me and watch the show."

"Yes, I know that is what I must do," he answered with a sigh. "But I wish I were able to do my share on the ranch."

"You will soon," said Jean, consolingly. "You seem ever so much better than you were when you came, and you're so brown you look like a regular Westerner. Besides, look at all the lovely work you have been doing with your water colors. I hope you brought along a sketch book with you today. Did you?"

Her father patted the pocket of his coat and smiled at his daughter. "You are a great comfort, Jean," he said.

In Jean's mind, however, she felt that Circle M could contribute far from their share of the work at the roundup. "Dad can't do anything and John can't rope, so, although it looks as if we had four 'hands,' we've really only two—Nat and Pedro."

As Lottie was to help with the cattle, Jean had offered to serve lunch to the crowd. Lottie and she, the day before, had baked several cakes and prepared supplies for countless sandwiches.

"Good heavens!" Jean had exclaimed. "That looks like enough food for a small army."

"Wait and watch those fellows eat," Lottie had replied with a chuckle. "You'll see it isn't any more than enough."

Jean found Mrs. Stevens at work in Lottie's kitchen making sandwiches and she joined in with a will. Lottie had left with the men at dawn. She had told Mrs. Stevens that the lunch was to be spread under the mesquite trees near the corral and that at noon Jean was to give the "come and git it" signal by banging on the old wagon tire hanging by the kitchen door.

Mrs. Stevens was a voluble, sociable woman. While she and Jean worked she told the girl her life's history. They had come from Indiana, which, to Jean's amusement, she called "the East." Mr. Stevens had been very ill with tuberculosis when they had arrived in Arizona.

"The doctor didn't give him six months to live," said Mrs. Stevens. "That was seventeen years ago and look at him now!"

Jean was deeply interested. If a man in such a condition had made so fine a recovery, she had high hopes for her father. It was seldom that he complained as he had that morning about his inability to take an active part in the work. She knew, of course, how eager he was to be able to do his share. Many a time she had had to urge him to rest, when he was bent on doing some labor beyond his present strength.

"What did your husband do to get so well, Mrs. Stevens?" she asked.

"At first he just lay in the sun in the daytime, and slept on a porch at night," was the answer. "Then, little by little, he commenced to do some work. I raised chickens and he started in to feed them. Later he began to ride horseback, and now he is as well and strong as you could want. We run over four hundred head of cattle, and you know that takes some work."

Jean and Mrs. Stevens went out to watch the cattle come in. As they sat on a slope under the mesquite trees they saw a group of riders gently easing the cattle along over the rolling land toward the corral. Lottie and the men were spread out around and behind the shaggy red cattle with white faces. Occasionally a rider slapped his reins or coiled rope against his leather chaps, making a sharp sound to bring stragglers into line. When an enterprising steer started to run away a cowboy galloped after it with a high-pitched "Yip-pee!" turning it back to the group. The mournful, throaty bawling of uneasy cattle filled the clear air.

As they neared the corral the cowboys rode among the herd, some driving part of the animals out into a large fenced field, while others urged the cows and calves into the corral.

"Those steers they are cutting out are the ones they mean to sell," Mrs. Stevens commented. "I guess we'd better start bringing out lunch," she went on.

Jean looked at her wrist watch and was surprised to see that it was nearly noon. Mr. Merryweather helped them carry the food and coffee to the shade of the mesquites, where they set out sandwiches and cakes, paper plates and a great dish of baked beans, on table cloths spread on the

ground. When all was ready Jean banged on the wagon
tire with a hammer in accordance with Lottie's instructions.

Soon she and the men flocked to the inviting lunch. As
the pile of sandwiches quickly diminished Lottie caught
Jean's eye and gave a great wink, as much as to say, "What
did I tell you?"

The men discussed when they would go to the Stevens
ranch and to Circle M for their round-ups. "Let's go to
Circle M day after tomorrow, Friday," said Mr. Stevens,
"then come to our place the following Monday. Okay?"

They all agreed to the plan, and Jean thought to herself
that she must spend the next day baking cakes and getting
together the wherewithal for a mountain of sandwiches.
She decided to have Pedro butcher a calf as soon as they
got home that night, so that she would have meat for sandwiches for their round-up on Friday.

After lunch the men rolled cigarettes with nonchalant
deftness and, while they smoked, went to start the fires to
heat the branding irons in the corral. Lottie's brand was
a rocking rafter.

Now came the ordeal which John had so dreaded, the
roping of the calves which were to be branded. In Lottie's
large corral, three fires were going in the far corners. Mr.
Stevens, Pedro and Roy each took charge of a fire, while
Lottie and the men remained on horseback.

Lottie rode among the cows and gently dropped the
loop of her rope over the head of a calf. She and the horse
pulled the struggling little creature by the rope to Pedro's
fire. Then the cowpony stood still, holding the rope taut,
until Pedro had the calf thrown and had tied its legs to-

gether. The poor distracted cow mother of the calf lowed
pitifully and the calf bellowed, as Pedro burned the brand
mark on its side.

From their vantage point on the slope above the corral,
Jean and her father watched the proceedings with intense
interest. Mr. Merryweather's nimble fingers were busy
with pencil and sketch pad, putting fleeting impressions
of the scene on paper.

Mrs. Stevens explained to the two Easterners what was
going on. "They have to cut a notch in the calf's ear as
well as branding the hide. That's so that when the men
are looking over the cattle on the range and it's hard to
see the brand mark, they can tell whose critter it is by the
shape of the cut in its ear. Then they have to castrate the
bull calves and give them a shot of vaccine for black leg.
And they smear the wounds with grease and a creosote
mixture to keep out flies and screw worms."

"Good gracious!" exclaimed Jean. "It's a regular operation."

The men worked quietly and swiftly, bringing the
calves to the branders.

Jean watched her brother go after a calf, but, alas, his
loop slipped off the animal's head. He had missed. Nat rode
right behind him, caught the calf and brought it to Roy
Stevens' fire. Jean looked on in tense anxiety, as again
and again John swung his rope with nervous energy, but
missed every time. She saw with what quiet ease Lottie and
the men dropped their loops over the heads of the calves,
and thought, unhappily, "John works too hard at it. He is
scared of it. Oh I wish he could do it, just once."

She noticed that her father had slipped his sketching pad

back into his pocket, and was watching the scene with a perplexed look on his face.

The corral became a swirling mass of cattle and horsemen, milling back and forth in clouds of dust, while the bawling of the frightened animals grew louder and louder. One after another the calves were caught, tied and branded. Jean marvelled at the skill of the cowponies, who seemed to know their job as well as the men and worked right along with them.

Never once, in that endless afternoon, was young John Merryweather successful in roping a calf. At each miss of his, the other young men grinned at each other. John grew more and more awkward as his failures mounted. Jean's cheeks were burning with shame for her brother. Sorry as she was for him, she could not but remember his attitude toward this job before Timmie's death. If only he had really worked at it all winter. This past week of working so hard wasn't enough, she thought.

Finally she saw her brother ride over to Lottie. He was asking her if there were not some other way he could make himself useful.

"Sure," she boomed. "You help Pedro with the grease and stuff. He's trying to do the whole thing himself."

So, chagrined beyond words, John dismounted from his horse and took his small part in the branding operation.

By evening all the calves were branded and turned loose to be comforted by their mothers. The neighboring ranchers prepared to leave. As John remounted his horse he overheard Roy Stevens say to Lottie's cowboy, "So long, Jake. See you Friday at the gunsul's ranch."

Jake laughed. "Yep," he answered, then in a high falsetto voice, "Good night, fella."

"Gunsul," repeated John to himself. "I wonder what that means."

Lottie came up to him and said in a low voice, "Come on down here tomorrow morning, John. I think I can show you a trick or two."

"I'm afraid it's no use, Lottie," John answered bitterly. "I guess I'm too dumb to learn to rope."

"Come on, don't get discouraged," Lottie urged. "Really, I mean it. I couldn't get the hang of it myself at first, but then an old cowpuncher took me in hand and taught me the right twist to give. Come, be a sport. I'm sure I can teach you."

"All right, Lottie, thanks," said John, huskily.

That evening back at the ranch, the household tried hard to be nonchalant about John's failure, but he felt their unspoken criticism of him. At the supper table he said to Nat, "Say, what's a gunsul?"

"That's cowboy talk for greenhorn. Why?" asked Nat.

"Oh nothing." John's voice was bitter and Jean flinched at the pain in his eyes.

Next morning, while his sister was baking cakes for the morrow, John was also preparing for the day. He arrived at Lottie's ranch soon after breakfast. Apparently Lottie had sent Jake away, for she was alone.

"Now then, son," she said in a kindly tone, "let's get going. Watch me." She took the rope in her hand, swung it around her head, gave a deft twist of her wrist, and the loop fell neatly over the post in front of the house.

"I noticed yesterday, John, that you swung too low and

too wide, and also your loop was too big for calves. That would be all right for range roping, but catching a calf is a little different. You want a smaller loop and an easy swing. Now put your hand on my wrist," she ordered, "and feel what I do just before I let go."

John did so. "I think I see," he said. "Let me try now."

Lottie handed him the rope. He swung it close to his head as she had done, took careful aim, giving his wrist the all-important twist, and let go. The loop caught the post neatly.

"There you are!" exclaimed Lottie happily. "I told you that you could do it. Nobody ever showed you that twisting trick, did they?"

John was elated at his success and tried again and again, each time catching the post.

"Now let's go practice on some calves from horseback," suggested Lottie. "Just pretend that the calves are moving posts, that's the only difference. I noticed yesterday that your aim was okay. It was just that your loop slipped. Now come on, let's go."

The first and second times John missed his calf. "Take it easy, son," Lottie shouted. "You swing too hard."

For the rest of the morning he kept at it, trying to be calm and careful, and presently he was succeeding every time. Now he felt at home with the rope and sure of his technique. As he started to leave, he tried to thank Lottie for her help, but she would have none of it.

"You can thank me by giving a good account of yourself tomorrow—and, son," she added, "don't let these cowboys around here get your goat—just remember they've been roping and branding calves practically all their lives.

Now looky here, this afternoon I'm going up to your place to help your sister get ready for tomorrow, but let's you and me keep it a secret what we've been doing this morning. Maybe your folks will be in for a big surprise tomorrow, eh?"

John went home with a lighter heart than he had carried for some time past. His reception at home was cold indeed. All morning Nat and Pedro had been hard at work gathering wood for the branding fires, mixing the creosote and getting everything ready for the morrow. As for Jean, she had been in a veritable whirl of roasting meat, baking cakes in preparation for the big eaters who were to be her guests. She had tried to find John to send him to Joe Smith's store to buy extra bread and butter and jam for sandwiches.

"Well, there you are at last!" she exclaimed, when he made his belated appearance at the dinner table. "What in the world have you been doing all morning?"

"That's some more of my business, Bossy," John answered.

"See here, son," said his father, "I won't have you talk to your sister like that. As a matter of fact, you chose a strange time to go away. You were needed here."

It was seldom that his father spoke so severely and John longed to justify himself by explaining what he had been doing, but his desire to surprise them in the morning won out, and he said, merely, "Sorry, Sis, I'll make up for it this afternoon." He was as good as his word, helping in every way, both with the work in the corral and lending a hand to Jean and Lottie in the kitchen.

It was a very weary Jean who tumbled into bed after supper that night. She must be up betimes, she knew, to give the men breakfast before dawn and to get everything ready for the noon meal.

At breakfast Friday morning Nat tried to suggest tactfully that it would be a good thing if John helped at the branding fires as he had done at Lottie's.

"Oh no," John said. "I'm going to rope calves myself today."

Nat started to say something, but thought better of it. As for Jean, she stared at her brother in amazement, his confident tone was so different from his former hang-dog air.

"Don't look at me like that, Jean," he said with a chuckle. "Maybe I'm not a gunsul any more."

And indeed he was not! To Jean's great surprise and delight, at the branding that afternoon, the first calf was caught by the skillful roping of young John Merryweather. After he had roped it, he could not resist turning to Roy Stevens, who was riding near him, to say, "Not so bad for a gunsul, eh, Roy!"

The Stevens boy flushed under his tan, but did not answer. As for the other cowboys, they were as surprised as Jean, and although they said nothing, John was conscious of belonging at last. And so for the rest of the afternoon, he did his share of the roping, never once missing.

Jean was surprised to see how large their herd had grown. Unlike Nat and her brother, she and her father never rode the range, so neither had realized how many calves had been born.

"You've got a fine bunch of young calves here, Mr. Merryweather," said Lottie as she got ready to leave. "You'll be able to make a good profit if you sell 'em this time of year. But if you want my advice, if I was you, I'd keep most of those calves and all your heifers, and only sell your yearlings now. Then you can really go to town next time you want to sell."

"That's good advice, Lottie," answered Mr. Merry-weather, "and I think I'll take it."

Lottie turned to John, and said in her great voice, "Well, cowboy, you did fine today."

"Just look who was my teacher," answered John, sweeping off his hat and making her a low bow.

"So that's what you were up to yesterday morning when I was so mad at you for being away from the ranch," said Jean. "I see it all now."

"Not mad, any more, Jeanie?" asked John with a broad grin.

"Mighty proud of you, Twin," answered his sister, to which Nat added, "You bet, fella."

Chapter IX

A DESERT THIEF

"I FEEL LIKE GOING ON AN ALL-OUT BUST," ANNOUNCED John, on the Saturday morning after the Stevens' round-up. "Our big spring job is done and, after all, every cow-hand has Saturday night off to play."

John did not express the thought in his mind, his need to celebrate because he had conquered the difficult business of roping and had shown himself as good a cowpuncher as any of them, but it was evident in his self-confident swagger. Jean understood her brother's feeling. As for herself, the very thought of a party was a delightful prospect.

"I'm with you, boys," she cried. "What shall we do?"

"How about Nat and me asking you to one of the night spots in town—not an expensive one, of course. I know a little place where I went once—" he stopped and blushed and all three remembered that first dreadful Saturday night when their hearts had been so heavy.

"How John has changed," Jean thought with pride.

"And the Stevens boys were talking about a joint they go to," John went on, "where they have a good dance floor and some Mexican musicians."

"Marvelous!" said Jean. "I only hope I haven't forgotten how to dance."

That evening, by the dim light of the oil lamp, Jean prepared for the party with as much care as though she were going to a big dance at home. She slipped into the pretty frock which had hung unworn in the closet all winter, and studied her reflection in the mirror. The pale green silk of the dress with its long full skirt and tight bodice, enhanced the deep golden tan of her skin, and her shiny, honey-colored hair. Her gray eyes were alight with anticipation. As a finishing touch she put on her diamond earrings. They were her most precious ornament.

"Well, do your stuff, girl," she said to her reflection. She did not admit to herself that she wanted to look especially nice to impress Nat.

Jean stepped into the living room and dropped a little curtsey to the two boys.

"Will I do?" she asked, demurely.

John whistled. "Now you look like the gal who used to knock 'em cold back home," he said. "It's swell to see you in something besides pants. How about it, Nat, will she do?"

Jean saw the warm light of admiration which leaped into Nat's dark eyes, so that his laconic drawl, "She sure is an eyeful!" satisfied her.

It was fun to forget their months of hard work in a whirl of dances to the gay lilt of the Mexican band. John was an excellent dancer and Nat's lean grace proved as effective on the dance floor as on a horse. Once he tightened his arm about her and smiled down into her eyes.

"You dance like a dream girl," he said, softly.

"I didn't know you could make pretty speeches," she teased.

Late in the evening the Stevens boys appeared with girls, and, although they were a little afraid of Jean at first, the ice was soon broken. Jean enjoyed the triumph of having four partners competing for her dances.

Dawn was lighting the sky when the three reached home, sleepy and happy, to fall into bed. Everyone overslept, so that, although Sunday morning was a time of leisure, Jean scrambled into her clothes and hurried out to get breakfast without noticing the disorder in which she had left her things the night before.

Later, when she was tidying up her room, she saw that the box in which she kept her few bits of jewelry stood open on the dresser. She looked into it, to pick up the lovely earrings which had made part of her success at the dance. They were gone! Frantically she searched through the box, for the earrings were not only her favorites but a dear memento of her mother. They were certainly not in the box, and strangely enough, John's gold cuff links were gone, too.

"That's queer," thought Jean. "I'm sure I remember taking the earrings off last night. Maybe I was so sleepy that I put them somewhere else."

She searched her room and then the living room, brought the broom and swept them both diligently, but the jewelry was nowhere to be found. At dinner her father noticed her worried face.

"What's the matter, Jean?" he asked.

"Oh, dear, I'm so worried. I can't find Mother's earrings. I wore them last night, you know, and I've searched every inch of the rooms but they just aren't there. The strange thing is that John's cuff links are gone, too, and he didn't wear them last night."

"Are you sure you didn't lose the earrings on the way home?" asked John. "You know you've lost several others by having them slip off."

Jean was certain she had taken them off after they had returned, but the boys hurried out to search the station wagon and the ground around the house. Pedro, when questioned, said he had not seen them. Jean grew more and more unhappy.

"They're not just earrings to me," she said, "beautiful as they are. But they belonged to Mother and I can't bear to lose them."

"Cheer up, Sis," comforted John. "They are sure to be found sooner or later, and as for my cuff links, don't worry about them. The things can't have been stolen because there is no one within miles but Pedro and us, and I'm sure Pedro is as honest as daylight."

"No, there's no one but us," said Nat in a strange tone. They all gazed at him, startled. The old hunted, black look was in his eyes once more.

"Why Nat seems frightened," thought Jean. "Oh no, it couldn't be Nat—that's impossible!"

Suddenly they all remembered what had been forgotten for months: Nat's story of having been unjustly accused of stealing. But they knew him now. They knew how fine and straightforward he was. Surely, surely they couldn't have been mistaken in him.

"Well, that's that," said John, stoutly. "There is no one here but us, therefore the things were not stolen. They'll turn up, sooner or later."

"Yes, of course," said Jean forlornly. "I guess I'll get supper now."

They all tried valiantly to maintain their usual gay talk, but it was no use. A question hung in the air between them. Jean dared not say anything reassuring for that would be an admission that there was doubt in their minds. Nat looked from face to face and bitter lines tightened about his mouth. His shoulders took the old aggressive hunch, as though to ward off a hostile world.

"They don't say anything," he thought, savagely, "but they don't trust me. I might have known. Once branded, you're done for."

Jean tossed and turned that night, thinking of Nat as they had known him all winter, as he had danced with her and smiled into her eyes at their party. "No," she thought, struggling with tears, "there's nothing wrong with Nat. This thing has got to be cleared up. Something must be done about it."

But both twins remembered that day when John had bought his Stetson hat—how they had talked about the great value of those earrings—before Nat.

When the family assembled for breakfast in the morning the atmosphere was worse than ever. Nat ate in black silence, and the efforts of the twins to act as usual were forced. Mr. Merryweather tried in vain to draw Nat from his gloom by light friendly talk.

Finally Jean said, timidly, "Nat, please don't be like that. Surely you don't suppose for a moment that we think—"

Nat jumped up so suddenly that his chair fell over with a crash. Hot-headed and supersensitive, like a true son of Texas, rage surged up in him. "I can't stand this," he cried. "You're just like everybody else—you don't trust me. I thought that old trouble could be forgotten, that I could stand up and be self-respecting like any man, but I might have known better. Now you think I lied to you when I told you I didn't steal my boss' watch. You're wondering who else could have taken your things. Oh no, you don't *say* anything, but I feel you doubting me. I can't stay here and be suspected. I'm through!"

He slammed the door and started down the road at a run.

"Nat, Nat, come back!" screamed Jean, rushing to the door. "It's not true what you said. Oh Dad, John, go after him!"

Mr. Merryweather ran out, jumped into the station wagon and hurried after Nat. The boy was striding along at full speed, shoulders hunched and head bent. Mr. Merryweather drew up beside him.

"Stop, Nat," he said quietly. "Jump in here, I want to talk to you."

"No thanks, sir," Nat answered sullenly. "I can walk until I get a hitch!"

"Come, Nat, it's not fair to rush off without giving us a hearing."

Reluctantly Nat climbed in and Mr. Merryweather drove slowly along the road.

"Listen," he said to the angry boy. "I understand how the old wound smarts and it seems like the same old pattern of suspicion directed against you. In your sensitive pride you are feeling that we have questioned your honesty. But I assure you, and please try to believe me, that no one of us doubts you. We couldn't live with you all this time without knowing the kind of man you are. I ask you to come back. This painful incident will never be mentioned again."

"No," said Nat. "It's all spoiled now. I've been very happy and you've all been wonderful to me. But Jean and John showed that they suspect me—in spite of themselves, I reckon. I guess it's too much to expect that I could really live down a jail sentence, even though it was a frame-up. I'll be on my way."

"If you must go, Nat, here is the balance of what I owe you. This will redeem the last three I O U's. Luckily the rent check for our home in the East arrived a few days ago."

"I don't want the money," the boy replied angrily.

"Come, come, Nat, don't be ridiculous. It is money you've earned and you'll need it to stake you while you look for a job, if you persist in leaving us. I know you are angry and hurt, but when you've cooled down I hope you will see that you are making a great mistake. Then come back to us, Nat. Your home is always waiting for you." Mr. Merryweather held out a roll of bills to the boy, who stuffed them into his pocket.

"I had meant to add to this sum after we sold off the cattle, Nat," he said kindly. "You deserve a bonus for your good work."

Nat blinked tears from his eyes, but rage still held him. "Thank you, sir," he said stiffly. "But please let me out. I'll get a hitch to town."

Sadly Mr. Merryweather watched Nat disappear into the distance, plunging along with an air of desperation. "Poor boy!" he thought. "And what am I going to say to those two at home?"

It was difficult indeed. Jean clung to him in tears. John was more upset than he had been since their mother's death. Nat's going off like that made him seem almost guilty in their eyes, yet they couldn't believe he had done this thing. John clumsily expressed this feeling.

"Listen, my dears," said their father. "You must be patient and try to understand poor Nat. When anyone has met with injustice, especially one so young, so proud and sensitive as Nat, it leaves a scar. He was accused of stealing, unjustly, I am sure. But when a similar situation arises, he is thrown back into the fear and antagonism of the past disaster and sees suspicion where none exists. Then anger against the world blinds him to reason. I only hope and pray that when he has time to think it over, he will see that he was mistaken and come back to us."

"Oh Daddy," sobbed Jean. "It just breaks my heart!

The poor boy—we were his only friends and we failed him. I'll never forgive myself for this."

"Nor I," growled John, pacing the floor. "I could kick myself. Why didn't I do something to show him we believed in him? But that's just the trouble. He must have felt that there was a little doubt in our minds."

Heavy-hearted, the various members of the family went about their work. "Now I will have to learn to milk the old cow," John said. "Why didn't I let Nat teach me when he tried to?"

"You learned to rope cattle, John, when you really put your mind to it," his father reminded him. "I imagine you can learn to milk Sukey, too."

"I'll try, sir," John answered in a new, grown-up tone.

John managed to bring in about half a pail of milk his first time. "Cheer up, Sis," he said, grinning at her. "I'll do better tomorrow. At least the old girl didn't kick the pail and give me a milk bath the way she did the last time I tried."

The boy was as good as his word. He was managing to "gentle" Sukey as Nat had done. "He is learning to take responsibility," Jean thought to herself, "but what a price we have to pay for it—losing Nat!"

The twins missed Nat at every turn, his companionship, his wide appealing grin, the quiet skill with which he put through the ranch jobs. They had not fully realized how much he did to make things run smoothly. John tried hard to take his place—even to starting the fire in the kitchen stove in the mornings.

As for Jean, she concentrated on thinking of extra tasks to keep her busy so that she would not have so much time to grieve over Nat. With this end in view, she decided, a few days after the disaster, to make a batch of candied orange peel, of which both John and her father were very fond. She collected a bowl of orange peelings and left it on the kitchen table overnight, ready for use the next morning. But when she looked into the bowl after breakfast it was entirely empty—every peeling was gone.

"That's funny," she thought. "I'm sure I put the peelings in that bowl—I know I did. Maybe Dad or John emptied them into the garbage pail, thinking I wanted them thrown away."

But the two, when questioned, said they had not touched the peelings. Maybe Pedro had thrown them out, though that was unlikely, for he seldom came into the kitchen. Nevertheless, she went to his hut to consult him about the puzzle. Pedro's brown face wrinkled into an amused smile when he heard her tale.

"Might be pack rats," he suggested. "They like orange peelings and they are sure big stealers. There's a big pack rat nest right in the woodpile outside the kitchen door. Mebbe we look there."

Often, since Timmie was no longer there to keep them away, Jean had heard at night the scurrying feet of those little desert rodents. "Surely one pack rat couldn't have taken all those peelings during one night!" she exclaimed.

"Si, Miss," Pedro answered. "Very smart animal, is pack rat."

With that he began tearing down the woodpile. At the bottom of it they came to a nest. It was a strange looking affair, guaranteed to keep away intruders, for it was piled all over with cholla cactus joints. There were sticks and stones and bits of cotton, and under them, neatly tucked away in heaps, were the orange peelings.

"Well, for heaven's sake!" exclaimed Jean.

Pedro worked busily, destroying the nest. "This Mr. Pack Rat have to go somewhere else to live," he chuckled. As he picked it apart with his fingers something bright shone in the sunlight. There, lying in a tiny hollow lined with fluff from some plant gone to seed, lay John's gold cuff links. Jean pounced on them and dug eagerly into the hollow with her fingers. Yes, there they were—her mother's earrings!

"Oh Pedro, look, look!" she cried. "The jewelry we lost!"

"*Ay, que lastima*, that I did not think of pack rats before Nat run away," sighed the Mexican, shaking his head.

Followed by Pedro, Jean rushed into the house to her father and brother.

"See," she cried, holding out the jewelry to them. "The thief is found! A pack rat had them in his nest. Oh, our poor Nat!"

"Cripes!" exclaimed John. "What do you know about that?"

"But they can't eat those things," said Mr. Merryweather. "Why do they take them? They are regular little animal magpies, I guess. Probably that fellow ran up the side of your dresser, Jean, and the bright things in the open box attracted him."

Oh, if Pedro had only thought about pack rats before, said Jean to herself. But then, the old Mexican wasn't used to seeing jewelry around, and Nat, of course, had been too hurt and angry to think of pack rats or anything else.

"If only we could find Nat," said Jean. "Surely he would come back if he knew the things were found."

"I say we go into town and try to locate him," John suggested. "If he got a job anywhere nearby, the post office might have his address. We might ask at the garages, too."

"Suppose we consult our good friend Mr. Farmington about how to find him," suggested Mr. Merryweather.

"And hurry!" cried Jean.

She rushed into her room to change into her town clothes. Soon the three Merryweathers were urging Joshua as fast as possible over the winding miles to town. Mr. Farmington suggested that they broadcast for Nat over the missing-persons hour, sending a description of the boy over the ether, and asking that anyone who had seen him write to that station. Then the lawyer took them to consult the sheriff, but they received little satisfaction from him. They, themselves, put an ad in the local paper, which read: "Nat Barton. The jewelry has been found. Please come home. The three Merryweathers."

It proved a fruitless search, however. The post office had never heard of Nat nor was he employed at any garage in town. Day by day went by with no response from any of their appeals, not even from the broadcasting. Nat had, apparently, walked out of their lives forever.

Chapter X

IMPROVEMENTS

SHORTLY AFTER NAT'S DISAPPEARANCE, LOTTIE'S COWBOY, Jake, arrived one morning at the Merryweather ranch. He said the man from the Tucson packing house was at her ranch making a bid for her cattle, and would stop at Circle M if Mr. Merryweather wanted him to.

"Miz Dawson says not to take what he first offers you," Jake reported. "She says he is a bargainer. You must ask him more than you are willing to take and he will offer you less than he is willing to give. She says you ought to get thirty-five dollars each for your yearling steers and about forty dollars for your heifers."

"Well, thank Mrs. Dawson for her advice," said Mr.

Merrymaker, "and ask the fellow to come up here after he is through at your ranch."

After Jake left for the Lottie D Rancho, Pedro and John went out to round up the cattle for the speculator's inspection, and just after their noonday meal, he arrived. When he saw Domingo Third he said, "Your brother paid a thousand dollars for that animal. You'll have a fine lot of calves when you get the ones he has sired."

"Yes," Mr. Merryweather answered. "We are expecting big things of that bull."

The speculator went to stand beside the corral and look over the cattle.

"You've got about thirty yearling steers and twenty-five heifers, I see," he said. "I'll pay you twenty dollars each for your steers and twenty-five dollars for each heifer."

"No," answered Mr. Merryweather, "that's not enough. Anyway I don't want to sell any heifers, for I want to increase our herd. But I'll take forty-five dollars each for these thirty young steers."

"Not from me, you won't," the man replied with a shrug. "Well, I'll give you twenty-five dollars each for the steers."

"Make it forty," said Mr. Merrymaker.

"Look here," said the speculator, "what kind of business were you in before you took up cattle raising? Okay, I'll pay you thirty-five dollars each for the steers—you to pay the cost of trucking them into town—and that's my last word!"

"Sold!" said Mr. Merrymaker with a grin. "Send out the truck for them tomorrow and the boys and I will have them ready."

"Now how about some calves?" asked the speculator. "I'll take fifty if you can spare that many."

"No, I'll sell only the steers now, I think," said Mr. Merryweather. "As I told you I want to have a much larger herd next year, so I'll want to keep these little fellows. I understand it's easier to sell a ranch if you have a large number of good stock on it. I want to improve the herd before I offer the ranch for sale."

"Very well," the other answered. "Suit yourself. But the truck will cost you seventeen dollars for thirty head and there would be room in the truck and trailer for seventy-five head. It seems a pity to waste the room, but I guess you know your business best. The inspector will come out tomorrow to look at the brands. We have to be sure these cattle all really belong to you, you know. He charges ten cents a head for inspecting them."

"All right," said Mr. Merryweather, "and goodbye to you."

"Gee, Dad, you sounded like a regular pawn-broker!" exclaimed John admiringly when the man had left.

"Something else we owe Lottie Dawson," answered his father. "If it hadn't been for her message I'd have taken his first offer of twenty dollars a head. Bless the woman, what a neighbor she is!"

Next morning, bright and early, John and Pedro rounded up the thirty yearling steers and had them waiting in the corral for the truck from the packing company. It was a big day for the Merryweathers, for this was the first real money earned on the ranch since they had come.

Soon the transaction was completed, the cattle inspected

for the brand marks, and Merryweather Incorporated the richer by nearly a thousand dollars.

"Now, you two," said their father, "I'm going to pay each of you one hundred dollars toward the work you've done this year."

"Gee, Dad," said John, overwhelmed at this unexpected windfall, "I don't think I deserve it."

"You gave a very good account of yourself after Lottie taught you how to rope—and you've taken on Nat's work excellently. You may not have deserved it in the past, but perhaps you'll keep up the good work now," said his father.

"You bet I will, sir," answered John, eagerly. "Now," he thought to himself, "I can go and redeem that Stetson hat. I hope the storekeeper has kept it all this time."

"Let's take some of our earnings from the sale of the cattle to improve the house," suggested Mr. Merryweather the next day. "It will help our chances of getting a good price for it when we sell, and also make the rest of our stay more comfortable."

"A bathroom, Dad?" asked Jean.

"Yes, dear, a shower, not a tub, of course. And two new bedrooms. We'll get Pedro's nephew, Roberto, to do the building. I'll draw the plans right away, and Pedro can teach John how to make adobe bricks."

"Good enough," said John. "But let's go see Roberto and make arrangements for him to do the building. Shall we?"

"Yes, and we'll take Pedro along to help make the price," answered his father.

They set off in the station wagon to Roberto's home. Pedro took his nephew aside and talked to him very fast in Spanish while the Merryweathers looked on. Finally

Pedro turned to Mr. Merryweather and said, "All right, Boss."

Roberto stepped up and added, "I'll work for you for eight dollars a day for myself and helper. I'll start next week after Tio Pedro and young Mister have the adobes ready. The earth on your place is good for making 'dobes. It will take me two-three weeks to build two rooms with roof and windows and doors and cement floors. Bring me the plans and I will go to Tucson to order windows and doors."

"That's fine," said Mr. Merryweather, rising and offering his hand to Roberto. "I'll get the plans ready and send them to you tomorrow."

That afternoon Jean watched her father busy with pencil and T-square.

"Look here," he said, pointing to the sketch, "I've an idea to build a small wing on each end of our house, a bedroom in each. The bathroom can be built off the kitchen. Then I will carry the ramada along those wings like the Spanish farmhouses which open on a patio. The roof of one wing can be a sun deck, with outside steps leading up to it. A wonderful place to take sun baths, don't you think?"

"Yes indeed," answered Jean. She watched her father sketching for a few minutes, then she contributed an idea. She remembered that, according to Mrs. Stephens, her husband had slept outdoors while recovering from tuberculosis. "Let's build a sleeping porch while we're at it," she suggested. "It won't add too much to the expense, will it?"

"That's a fine idea, Jean," responded her father. "It can go across the back of the present house, and then my design won't be spoiled. Go ask Pedro to come here a minute, please, dear."

When the Mexican had come into the room Mr. Merryweather said, "Pedro, I want to add a sleeping porch on the back of the house. So you and John must make more adobes than Roberto reckoned he would need. It will probably take him a week longer to build that, also, won't it?"

"No, señor," said Pedro. "Only half a wall for sleeping porch. It not take so long as whole room."

"It may take a little longer, Pedro, because it will be a longer wall than either bedroom. Anyway, you tell Roberto that I want to add a sleeping porch."

"While we're at it," suggested Jean, "how about a low wall to enclose the wings of the old house like a regular patio? That will keep out rabbits that eat my flowers. Would that cost too much?"

"No," her father answered. "While Pedro and John are making adobes they might as well make enough more for your wall. And perhaps they can build the patio wall themselves—so we can save on Roberto's wages."

"Good!" said Jean. "Now I'm going out to watch them make adobes." She tied a kerchief on her head and went out into the hot, blazing sunlight. Each day, now, seemed hotter and drier than the one before. The Merryweathers had never imagined such intense light and heat as showered down from the metallic blue sky.

"Hi, Jean," called her brother. "Want to help make mud pies? I feel like a kid—messing around with this mud."

Jean saw that they had dug a deep hollow in the ground and that John was mixing the loose clay earth with water which they had hauled from the tank. He had taken off his boots and socks and was tramping the mud with his bare feet. Soon Pedro joined him. John was whistling a dance tune while he tramped the mud up and down, up and down.

"That looks like fun," said Jean.

"Come on in, the water's fine," her brother invited, with a grin. So Jean took off her sandals and began to dance in the mud, keeping time to her brother's whistling. But she stopped suddenly when she saw Pedro looking at her, his face one great wrinkle of disapproval.

"This no lady's work," he spoke solemnly. "Better you work in kitchen."

"Nonsense, Pedro," Jean answered tartly. "Why can't I have fun making mud pies, too?"

But the Mexican stopped working and kept looking at her, his arms folded across his chest.

"I guess you'd better quit, Sis," said her brother. "Old Pedro is staging a stand-up strike."

"Oh dear!" said Jean, but she remembered her father's admonition that "when you're in Rome, do as the Romans do," and she realized that she was up against a Mexican prejudice that she could not gainsay. So she obligingly washed off her bare feet and put her sandals on again. She sat down beside the pit, enviously watching her brother dancing in the wet earth.

"That's more better," said Pedro, smiling at her.

After a while Pedro told John that the earth was mixed well enough to be put into molds to dry. They wheeled loads of the clay to a wooden frame laid out in squares which was on the ground nearby. While John wheeled the barrow full of clay, Pedro filled the spaces within the frame, patting down the wet earth, after he had emptied the barrow, with his hoe.

Soon the whole frame was filled with the brown earth. Then Pedro carefully lifted it from the ground, leaving the large squares of mud to harden.

"It looks like a giant's platter of fudge," Jean commented to her brother.

All the rest of that week John and Pedro worked at making adobes. After three days the mud was hardened in the hot sunshine so that the great square chunks could be moved. John helped the Mexican lift the bricks and stack them up near the house where they were to be used. This was back-breaking work, as each brick weighed fifty pounds or thereabouts.

Jean was delighted to see that her brother, unlike his old self, worked steadily at this job, never complaining about the hard work. Although he scarcely realized what was happening to him, John was finding a great deal of satisfaction in what he was doing.

One evening after supper, Jean noticed that her brother had a strange, almost eager look on his face. "Penny for your thoughts, Twin," she said.

John blushed. "I was thinking of something Nat once said to me," he answered almost shyly. "He said, 'Honest, fella, I get more fun out of doing a job right than anything else in the world.' I thought he was nuts," John amended.

His father looked at him quizzically. "What do you think about that now, son?" he asked.

Embarrassed, John laughed. "I guess maybe I understand what he meant, sir," the boy answered.

"Good boy!" exclaimed his father.

Jean smiled at her brother tenderly. She, too, was thinking of something Nat had said: "Maybe the West will make a man of him."

I really believe it has, his sister thought. How I wish Nat could see him now.

"By Jove, I like it here," John was thinking to himself. "If somebody gave me the choice tomorrow of going back East or staying here, I really believe I'd vote to stay." But he did not confess this to his sister, who was, he knew, still counting the days until their return.

By the first of the next week, when Roberto and his helper came to start the building, there was a goodly pile of adobe bricks waiting for them.

The twins and their father watched Roberto's skillful work. The adobe bricks were placed one on top of another with plaster made from sifted earth and water between them. Pedro worked right along beside Roberto and his helper, handing his nephew the heavy bricks which Roberto set in the plaster.

While the walls were going up, Jean and her father searched their land for dead sahuaro cactus plants, the ribs of which would make a proper ceiling for a desert adobe house. Then John and Pedro took the station wagon and brought home piles of the bleached dry stalks.

Building progressed rapidly, and soon the house was high enough for the roof to be put on. The Merryweathers were fascinated by that process. The walls were built two bricks higher than the ceiling beams, over which sahuaro ribs made a solid layer. This was covered with thick wet mud, for insulation, Roberto explained. Then there was an air space of about six inches, over which the two-by-fours were laid. At last the roof of wood about an inch thick was nailed on, to be covered by layers of tar paper.

John had worked with the men, learning by watching, so that soon he felt he could almost build an adobe house himself. At any rate, he did a very workmanlike job on Jean's patio wall, and made her a little wooden gate for it.

"Now," said Jean, "no rabbit will ever be able to get in and ruin my flowers again. Oh folks, isn't it getting to be swell—our ranch home?"

"Yes," thought John, "too swell to give up," but aloud he only said, "You bet, Sis."

"I know another expenditure I think we ought to make, family," said Mr. Merryweather. "I find I can get a gasoline engine for seventy-five dollars and a pump jack for twenty-five more. Then we won't have to depend on the windmill to keep our water tank filled. We'll be needing more water now with the shower bath, and Jean has often spoken of how low the pressure gets in the kitchen after a week of no rain. How about it, do we make it unanimous?"

The twins agreed eagerly, remembering the time when the tank had been completely empty and they had had to haul all their water.

As the rooms approached completion the family began to plan a house-warming.

"We must invite Lottie and Jake, of course, and Joe Smith and the Stevens family," began Jean. "And let's have Roberto and Yolanda, too."

"How about Mr. and Mrs. Farmington from Tucson?" asked John.

"Good idea," agreed Mr. Merryweather. "They have a son and daughter who go to the University, Mr. Farmington told me. This might be a good chance for you to meet them."

"I wish Bert and Sally were here," John said.

"And Nat," added his sister. A shadow came over her face as it always did when she thought of Nat.

And so, one night some days later, the Merryweathers gave their first party. All day Jean had been hard at work, making the house attractive, baking chocolate cakes, preparing sandwiches and squeezing lemons for lemonade.

"How I wish I could import an air cooler from Tucson!" she said, as perspiration streamed down her face.

Each morning Jean carefully followed Pedro's advice for keeping the adobe house cool. She shut the windows and lowered the canvas shades early, to keep out the sun and preserve the fresh night air within. Then she sprinkled the brick floor of the living room from a watering can. Although it could not be said that the house was cool, the difference between its atmosphere and the heat outside was tremendous.

As the guests arrived John and Jean took them in to see the new rooms and the sleeping porch which were greatly admired. But after they had exclaimed over the improvements each group of guests sat down quietly in the living room, saying nothing. The three Mexicans were especially shy. Pedro acted as though he had no business to be there, in the boss' house, and Roberto and his wife sat in a corner without a word to say for themselves. Even the voluble Lottie seemed silent.

The twins were dismayed and at their wits' end to know what to do about their party, especially as the young Farmingtons looked so nice and jolly. They wanted to show them a good time, so that they would come again. Esther Farmington, just the twins' age, had flaming red hair, an impudent face with a freckled snub nose and merry blue eyes. Her brother, Howard, two years older, had dark brown hair and eyes and a snub nose like his sister's. These two sat by their mother and father on the couch, solemnly eyeing the assembled guests as though they were a lot of strange animals.

"What can we do to make this party go?" Jean asked her brother in despair, when they went into the kitchen to put ice in the lemonade. Joe Smith had brought the ice from his store along with a case of ginger ale.

"Gosh, I don't know," said John. "Let's ask Lottie." Whenever he needed a solution to a problem, John instinctively turned to Lottie Dawson. They made an excuse to get their good neighbor into the kitchen and put it up to her.

"They just need some little thing to break the ice," she assured them. "I tell you, go look in the Stevens' car and see if Roy's guitar is there. He makes a hit singing cowboy songs, and I'll bet he brought it. We'll start him singing, that will help."

Sure enough, Roy had prepared for a possible call to entertain. Jean brought the guitar and started him off by asking for some of the songs Bert and Nat had sung at Lottie's Christmas party. Roy strummed his guitar gaily and sang song after song in the slow, drawling manner of cowboys the West over.

Finally he said, "Have you heard the one about tying knots in the devil's tail?"

"Oh, let's have that one," begged Jean.

He sang a long involved ballad of many verses, ending with:

> "If you're ever out in the Sierry peaks
> And you hear an awful wail
> You'll know it's only the Devil himself
> Raisin' heck 'bout the knots in his tail."

When the laughter had subsided, Roy proposed, "Now let's have some Mexican songs. Come on, Yolanda."

Yolanda got up shyly, and, standing behind her chair, sang several lively Mexican ballads to the accompaniment of Roy's guitar, as she had at Conchita's name day party. Then Roy struck up some old American favorites—"Old Black Joe," "Way Down Upon the Suwannee River," and many others, and all of them joined in.

"Now I think we need to wet our whistles," said John. "Come on, Jean."

Jean brought in a huge pitcher of ice-cold lemonade, followed by John with Joe Smith's ginger ale. Then John passed sandwiches and cake, and soon they were all chatting happily like old friends.

Then Lottie whispered into Roy's ear. He cried, "Git your partners, now, for the Varsovianna." He struck a chord and broke into the lilting strains of that popular Mexican dance which the Southwest has adopted as its own. The Merryweathers had heard it only once before—

the night of Conchita's name-day party, but to the rest of the guests it was as familiar as it was well-loved. The family was delighted to see Joe waddle up to Lottie and lead her out to the sleeping porch. "Let's go, Miz Dawson," he exclaimed. While the others watched he stood behind her and, taking her hands, led her through the steps of the dance.

"Isn't that what they were dancing at the party at the Gomez' house?" Jean's father asked her. "It's like an old-fashioned schottische, only more graceful."

"Oh come on, now, the rest of you folks," cried Lottie. "Joe and I ain't exhibition dancers."

Jean was wishing she had learned it that night at Conchita's party, when Howard Farmington came up to her with a little bow, and said, "May I have the pleasure?"

"I'll try," she said, smiling up at him, "but I don't know how to dance it."

"Oh, it's easy," Howard assured her. "Look, Sis," he called to Esther, "get John to try it with you."

"Thanks, fella," said John. "I didn't quite have the nerve to ask her, as I never did this dance before."

The twins were soon imitating the steps being done so skillfully by Lottie and Joe Smith, and enjoying it immensely. Several other couples followed suit, until the sleeping porch was full of dancers and others spilled over to the open ground outside.

"Now then," said Lottie, jovially, "how about a Virginia reel? You call the figures, Joe."

"Good," said Mr. Merryweather, and went up to the shy, smiling Yolanda, and, taking her by the arm, led her to the head of the line. With that Mr. Farmington led out

Mrs. Stevens and Roberto went up to Lottie. Then Mr. Stevens bowed to Mrs. Farmington and they joined in. Bob Stevens and Howard Farmington both made a dive for Jean and Bob won out. John and Esther were dancing together and Howard said, "Well, come on," to Jake. "One of us will have to be the lady for this dance."

"Not me," said Jake. "But maybe you'd be my girl."

"Sure," answered Howard. "There never are enough girls to go around at a Western dance." He bowed and smiled and danced with mincing steps across from Jake.

After this grand finale the guests began to leave. The young Farmingtons asked Jean and John to come to see them soon. When the last car had departed the family went up the outside steps to enjoy their new sun deck. The vast star-studded sky stretched above them and moonlight flooded the land with silver.

"Moonlight on the desert," murmured Jean. "It's all they say about it—and more." You never see the moon like this in Connecticut, she thought, but quickly put that idea away as disloyal.

"How clear the mountains are against the sky!" her father was saying.

"Yes, and each cactus plant has its own sharp shadow," the girl answered. "Oh beautiful world!"

"Getting to like it, after all, eh, Jean?" said John, teasingly. Then, "Gosh, I miss Nat, tonight. Do you remember how he and Bert sang cowboy songs at Lottie's Christmas party?"

"Indeed I do. Oh John, do you suppose we shall ever see Nat again?"

"Heaven knows I hope so, Jean, but who can tell?"

Their father rose, taking one last look at the silvery landscape.

"Well, my hearties, let's go to bed, for tomorrow is another day," he said. "Our first night on the new sleeping porch, John."

"Yes, and the first night we can have real shower baths, don't forget," added Jean happily.

Chapter XI

DISASTERS

Day after day the sun showered its relentless heat over the land. Coming from the shelter of the house, the outer air felt like the hot, dry breath from a furnace. Sometimes furious winds roared across the desert, filling the sky with black masses of clouds. The dry soil was caught up in whirlwinds of dust which rushed by with a sharp spatter against the windows, to disappear in the distance, but no rain fell.

The twins were up at sunrise each day to utilize the freshness of the early hours, for work was difficult in the blazing midday. Jean tried to do all her cooking right after breakfast in order not to have the stove going during the hot hours. How they longed for ice! Even the desert cooler served only to keep the food from spoiling. Butter did not

stay hard. She wished that she could serve her family re-
freshing chilled food, but that was out of the question.
The clay olla, however, swinging in the shade of the
ramada, continued to provide deliciously cool water.

After midday they all took refuge in the shadowy
interior of the house, to endure, as best they might, the
long hot hours until the brazen sun disappeared behind the
mountains. Evenings they spent lying on the new roof
deck, gazing at the stars, like jewels in the huge velvety
dome of sky, while they drank in the reviving coolness of
the night air.

Each night Jean marked off with a red cross one more
day on her calendar and counted up the days that must be
endured before their return home. Would the time ever
pass? she thought. Once she caught her father's eyes upon
her, after she had struggled with the problem of finding
something for her family to eat for supper, and she smiled
at him, wanly.

"I'm afraid the heat is too much for you, darling," he
said, tenderly. "Perhaps we'd best give up and go home.
Shall we, dear?"

How she longed to say yes, to pour out all her despair
of this place into her father's ear, but she sensed his desire
to stay, so she answered, brightly, "Oh, no, Daddy. It
really won't be long now. October fifteenth will come
sometime, won't it?"

He chuckled. "That's one thing we can count on, even
in the desert," he answered. "Time will pass—it always
does."

The scanty pasturage was withering to nothing in the
dry heat. Water was getting low. The Merryweathers

shared the worry of other ranchers over the diminishing water holes and hungry cattle. They scarcely dared use the precious water for the new shower, which was their only relief from the heat. Jean's flowers, over which she had worked so hard, were dying for lack of water.

One Friday afternoon Jean heard a car drive up to the door. She went outside and to her delight there were Esther and Howard Farmington.

"We've come to take you and John and your Dad home with us for the week-end," Esther called to her. "Hurry up and pack a bag and let's go. Dad has installed a swimming pool at our place and we want you to help us christen it!"

What a wonderful idea! Jean hurriedly got out of her sun suit and into a cool dress, and packed a bag for herself and one for her father and John. She almost wept for joy at the prospect of a whole week-end away from the dreadful heat of the ranch.

But, to her surprise, John demurred at going, although she could see that he was as eager for the trip as herself.

"Maybe you and Dad had better go without me," he said. "I shouldn't leave Pedro to do all the work by himself."

What a different John he was, thought Jean proudly. Pedro, when consulted, assured the boy that he could manage, and to Mr. Merryweather he said, "Young Mister's getting to be a good hand, all right." So John's scruples were laid to rest, and he climbed into the Farmington's car, as excited as Jean over the prospect of a vacation.

And what a week-end it was! Jean luxuriated in the swimming pool and the air-conditioned home of the

Farmington's set in the midst of a grove of eucalyptus trees on the outskirts of Tucson. The lawn of fresh green grass rested her eyes after the glare of desert sun. She lay for long delicious minutes in a bath tub with cool water exquisitely scented with pine bath salts. In the evenings the four young people went dancing in the air-conditioned ballroom of one of the large hotels.

Jean wished the week-end would last forever, but Monday morning came inexorably and they went back reluctantly to the hot desert ranch.

"We must have Howard and Esther out here for a week-end sometime, Jean," said her brother, after they had returned.

"Not while it's so hot," said Jean.

"No, of course not," John answered. "I meant after the rains come, of course."

"And when will that be?" queried Jean.

"Goodness only knows," said John, with a deep sigh, "but let's hope it will be soon!"

As a matter of fact, John was almost worn out with the work on the range. The thirsty animals, in their desperate search for water, often tore their hides against the barbed-wire fences, which left open sores into which screw worms lodged. These were maggoty creatures which ate away the good flesh, so that, in addition to their regular work, John and Pedro had to inspect the cattle every day for screw worms and treat them with creosote.

One day in early August John told his father and sister that Domingo Third had a sore on his shoulder that had to be treated. Pedro was going to bring the bull into the corral for the treatment, he said.

"Well, do be careful, John," said his sister. She could never forget what that terrible bull had done to her beloved little dog.

"Oh, Pedro can manage Domingo all right." John spoke confidently.

After breakfast Mr. Merryweather left the ranch on horseback to see Lottie Dawson. Jean, who was washing the breakfast dishes, heard Pedro calling, "Get on there, you Domingo, you." And she saw the Mexican proudly riding on his pinto with the bull fastened to the saddle by a rope. Apparently Domingo was not going to give them any trouble this time, Jean thought, as she stood at the window watching Pedro's skillful handling of the bull.

John went out to the corral with a pan of creosote mixture. It was not safe to get close enough to the bull to apply the mixture to its wound by hand, so Pedro had fastened a wad of cotton to a long stick. With this dipped into the creosote mixture he was going to paint the bull's wound.

Jean watched him pick up the stick and dip the cotton-covered end into the pan. Very slowly he rode his horse near the bull. He was just about to apply it to the wounded shoulder of the animal, when the great creature snorted and began to paw the ground angrily.

"He doesn't like the smell of that stuff," thought Jean. But Pedro was not intimidated by the bull's behavior and he edged his horse closer to the animal. Before they had gone many paces, however, Jean saw Domingo lower his head and come tearing across the corral right at Pedro's horse. The pinto screamed as the bull's sharp horns tore into his breast. He bucked, throwing Pedro to the ground. The bull charged the horse again, and the pinto lost his balance and went down, pinning the Mexican under him.

John rushed to Pedro's aid, trying to pull him from under the horse, but he could not move him. The bull, further enraged by the smell of blood, came on again with head lowered, straight for Pedro's prostrate figure. Jean saw her brother wildly waving his arms to distract the bull, but it was useless.

"Save Pedro," was the only thought in Jean's mind, as she snatched her rifle from the wall and rushed to the corral.

"Stand back, John," she cried, and, raising the rifle to her shoulder, she aimed at the bloodshot eyes of Domingo. She pulled the trigger, sobbing a prayer that she would not hit the helpless Mexican. With a great bellow the bull rolled over dead!

"Oh, señorita," gasped Pedro, still pinned under the horse, "you killed the champion bull!"

"He would have killed *you*, Pedro," cried Jean. "Quick, we must get him free from the horse," she shouted to her brother.

He jumped to help her, and with frantic struggles they managed to get the Mexican out from under the wounded horse.

"He must go to the hospital right away," said John. "But what about the poor horse?"

"The horse will have to wait," Jean said firmly. Between them they carried the Mexican to the station wagon where Jean made a bed of blankets on the floor. With Pedro's head in her lap, they started for Tucson, John driving as fast as he could without jarring the wounded man.

He glanced back at his sister, admiration in his eyes. "That was quick work, Sis. You saved Pedro's life."

"I never stopped to think," Jean replied in a shaky voice. "I don't know how I did it." She found that she was trembling violently now that the crisis was over.

"My pinto, my pinto!" Pedro moaned.

"Don't worry about your horse, Pedro," John called over his shoulder. "We'll take a vet back with us to see him."

The twins waited at the hospital until they had a report on Pedro's injury. His hip was badly crushed and his leg was broken in two places. Then they hunted up a veterinary surgeon for the wounded horse and drove rapidly home.

"We ought to change the name of this place to 'Hard Luck Rancho,'" said John, bitterly, as they turned into their driveway.

"Cheer up, John," Jean responded briskly. "Think how much worse we would feel if that great brute had killed Pedro."

"That was sure a wonderful shot of yours, Sis," her brother said.

"It was luck, mostly," Jean declared. "To tell you the truth I was scared to death the bullet would hit you or Pedro instead of the bull."

When they reached the corral they saw that their father was already there ahead of them trying to help the injured horse. The veterinary surgeon, whose car had followed the twins, took charge of it.

They quickly told their father what had happened. "I'm sick that I had to kill the bull, Daddy," said Jean, "but he was about to gore Pedro. There wasn't anything else to do, was there, John?"

"No," her brother spoke up. "And gee, Dad, you sure would have been proud of Sis, the quick way she acted. I didn't know what a sure-fire shot she was!" Jean flushed with pleasure at his words.

"Poor Pedro thought I should have let him be killed in order to save that thousand dollar bull," she said. "All the way in to the hospital, when he wasn't worrying about his pinto, he was bewailing the fact that I had killed Domingo. He was sure you would be angry."

"Of course Pedro knew that I was expecting great things of the herd because of that bull," her father answered. "But you couldn't have done otherwise, darling, and I'm proud of you. What did the doctor have to say about Pedro?"

Jean reported to her father what she had learned about the Mexican's condition at the hospital. "As for internal injuries, the doctor didn't know yet. Anyway, Pedro will be laid up for several months, of course, and perhaps he will never be able to work as a cowhand again."

"Well, I will drive in to the hospital tomorrow and see how he is and arrange for his care there," said their father. "And what about the horse?" he asked, turning to the veterinary surgeon.

"I think he can be saved," was the answer, "but I'm afraid he won't be much use as a cowpony from now on. What shall I do with him—save him or shoot him?"

"Oh by all means save him," cried Jean. "Pedro loves that horse above everything in the world. If he can't be a good cowpony he can at least be ridden, can't he?"

"After a few weeks' rest, he can," said the man. "But his days of real usefulness are over."

"Just like his master's, I'm afraid," said Jean. "Well, they can grow old together—the Mexican and his horse."

The Merryweathers went into the house for a light supper. Afterwards, while sitting on the roof deck, his father said, "John, do you think you and I can manage alone? Or shall I try to find a cheap cowhand? I wish I could be more help!"

Jean felt a thrill of pride when John spoke up, "Sure we can manage alone." But he sounded more confident than he felt. There was a lot more work to running the cattle this time of year, what with flies and screw worms for which the cattle had to be doctored. And his father mustn't overdo.

"If only we had Nat!" Jean thought.

"I'll take over the complete charge of Sukey," said Mr. Merryweather. "Can you teach me how to milk her, son?"

"What will we do with the carcass of Domingo?" asked Jean. "We can't leave it in the corral."

"Dad can arrange for the meat packing man to come and get it tomorrow, can't you, Dad?" John answered.

Next day the twins watched the men from the packing company load the huge bull into a truck to be carted off to town.

"Well, there he goes to the bologna factory, Jean," said John, "the cause of so much of our troubles. I know he was valuable to the herd, but I can't help but be glad to see the last of him."

"I feel that way, too, John," answered his sister, "but I know how terribly disappointed Daddy is, so I feel guilty about being relieved that we won't have old Domingo Third around here any more."

Indeed, Mr. Merryweather's troubles were mounting. At the hospital he found that Pedro must remain there for several months. To his dismay he learned that the hospital expenses and the doctor's fees would more than eat up what remained of the money he had obtained from the sale of the cattle in May.

And the weather remained unbearably hot. "Oh if it would only rain!" Each day some member of the family made that outcry. But the sun kept up its blazing heat and the cloudless blue sky looked down relentlessly. One morning when John rode the range, he found several little calves dead beside the empty water hole. The other cattle were so thin and shrunken-looking that sometimes John could stand it no longer and drove into town for a load of alfalfa hay for them. All they could afford to buy was, as he said, a mere drop in the bucket. "The cattle are starving and there's nothing I can do," John thought bitterly.

"Say, family," said Jean one morning at breakfast, when she looked at the calendar, "if we are going to sell this ranch in order to go home in three months, I think we should be putting it in the hands of a real estate company."

"Nobody would buy this ranch now, Jean," her brother answered. "Come out and look at the cattle—and you'll see that nobody would give us five cents a head for them. We will have to wait until after it rains before we will have anything saleable to offer."

Their father agreed. He had been making unsuccessful attempts to dispose of some of their cattle in order to have some ready cash. He often wished he had not taken Lottie Dawson's advice about keeping those heifers and calves when he had had the chance to sell them after the spring round-up.

"All right," said Jean, reluctantly. "I suppose you're right, but I wish it would hurry up and rain."

John secretly congratulated himself that he had put off the evil day when they must offer the ranch for sale. Even those long hard days of drought had not served to change John's enthusiasm for his new-found pride in work. He had lost all desire to return to the East.

One day John went to see Lottie Dawson to ask her advice about food for the cattle. Neither Lottie nor Jake was near the house, so John rode over Lottie's ranch looking for them. At last he found them. Jake was burning the leaves of a prickly pear bush with a blow torch.

"What's he doing that for, Lottie?" John asked, when he rode up to her.

"He's burning off the spines of the prickly pears so we can feed the leaves to the cattle," Lottie answered. "There's juice in them leaves, so they get a drink as well as feed by eating them."

"Good," said John. "I'd just come over to ask you what in the dickens I can give our poor cattle to eat."

"Well, drive down here tomorrow and pick up this blow torch, so you can fix some feed for your cattle, too, until it rains."

"Thanks," said John. "Say, Lottie, can't you act like the Indians and do a dance to make it rain?"

"I wish I could, boy," Lottie answered, with a chuckle.

"I haven't known the rains to be so late as this for years. And we've not had a drought like this since I was knee high to a grasshopper. I remember when I was a kid and my old man's ranch went completely dry. We didn't have a drop of water to wash our faces let alone anything for the cattle to drink. I didn't mind not being able to wash, but it sure griped me when my favorite little pony died of starvation and thirst. Then, just as Ma and Pa had decided to quit and give up the ranch for good—boy, a storm broke that was the great-grandaddy of any storm you ever saw! The washes ran so that they overflowed for a quarter of a mile around almost. Who knows, maybe the weatherman is fixing up a surprise for us like that."

Lottie's eyes strayed from John's face and swept over the barren earth. "Hi, Jake," she called. "Come and help me lift that heifer." She pointed to a heifer lying down in its tracks. "These Herefords give up every once in a while," she explained to John, "and if you let 'em lie, they die sure."

Jake put down his blow torch and went up to the back of the fallen animal. He wrapped its tail around his neck, and Lottie put her arms under its head, and together they lifted it to its feet. Then Lottie smacked its rump and it feebly walked away. John made a mental note of how Lottie and her cowboy had handled the heifer. "I guess Dad is strong enough to help me lift our cows when they give up like that," he thought.

Lottie's weather predictions brought no relief that week, however. And one morning John had even more cause to call their place "Hard Luck Rancho." It was just after sunrise, and he was circling the fence near the southern boundary of their ranch when he made a dreadful discovery. The strands of wire fence were down and there were marks of many hooves in the sandy earth nearby.

"It looks as if some of our herd had taken French leave," said John to himself. He dismounted and made a swift but secure job of mending the fence. Then he went over the range in search of the herd. "I wonder how they got away," he mused. Memories of stories of the early days of cattle rustlers came to him. But surely no one would steal such sorry-looking beasts as their herd was now.

"No," he thought, "they must have just broken through in their desperate thirst and hunger, looking for better pastures."

After riding half the morning, he came upon the remnant of the herd. He looked them over carefully. Every bull was gone and many of the heifers which his father had refused to sell to the speculator.

"Those were the strongest of our herd," John said to himself, "of course they would have to be the ones to go. Oh, drat it all, why didn't I ride the whole range every day?" But he well knew that, since Pedro's accident, he had not had time, what with his other jobs, to cover the whole range oftener than twice a week. Nevertheless he upbraided himself for carelessness, and suddenly the memory of Nat Barton's words the time he had carelessly neglected to fasten the Texas gate swept over him.

"What a pain in the neck I used to be," thought John. Had he been "careless and shiftless" again?

This was a terrible loss! What could he do about it? As usual, when in trouble about the ranch, he rode hastily to Lottie's house to ask her advice.

"Oh John," she cried, when the boy had poured out his tale of woe, "what a dirty shame!"

"What can I do to find them, Lottie?" he asked.

"It's no use trying, John," the woman answered. "You don't even know when they got away, since you say you haven't ridden that part of the range for several days. Oh, I don't blame you," she said, seeing the look in his eyes. "I don't see how you manage to do all the work you do on your place, single handed. But if they did get out a few days ago, I'll bet some of those roughnecks down by the border have already butchered them for beef."

"Mighty stringy beef, they'll be," John replied. "Poor things—they are nothing but skin and bones. But I think I ought to look for them anyway."

"Well, you probably won't be satisfied until you do," said Lottie. "So hop into my car and we'll go down the road and have a look-see."

Although they searched diligently, turning down every road along the way, they found no sign of the lost cattle.

"I can hardly bear to go home and tell the folks about this," said the heart-broken boy. "You know Dad felt awfully badly about the loss of Domingo Third—not that he thought Jean could have done anything but what she did, of course. All the same, that bull was worth a lot of money—and now to have lost these, too—oh why didn't I ride over that part of the range yesterday?"

"Well, fella," said Lottie, in her friendly, hearty voice, "it's just one of those things that happens. Nobody's to blame, you least of all. Twenty-four hours wouldn't have made any difference, in case the herd did break out a few days ago, instead of yesterday. We wouldn't have been able to find 'em anyway."

"Maybe you're right, Lottie," said John, sadly, "but you can bet your bottom dollar I'll ride along every fence on the whole blame ranch every day from now on."

"Don't be a goof, John," said Lottie. "You can't possibly do that with all your other chores—not in screw worm season, anyhow."

They had returned to Lottie's ranch by this time and she invited him to come in.

"No, thanks, Lottie," he answered. "I must go and break the news to the folks about our latest disaster. First it was Nat we lost, then Pedro and Domingo, and now the best of our herd. I can hardly bear to tell 'em. How on earth can we build up our herd without any bulls?"

"As far as bulls are concerned," she answered cordially, "I'll lend you a couple of bulls after it rains. And don't worry about your folks. Your father and sister will be good sports about it, I'm sure."

Lottie Dawson was right. They were good sports. And neither Jean nor her father would let John blame himself for the loss. Jean said he worked like a trooper every day and his father agreed.

"See here, John," said Mr. Merryweather, "I've been riding horseback since a few weeks after I got here. Why not let me take on some of the work of inspecting fences? I'm sure I could stand a couple of hours every morning. Would that help any?"

"Yes, sir," said his son. "If you did it very early in the morning before the sun gets too hot. You shouldn't be out in this heat, you know. But that would interfere with your taking the milk to Joe Smith."

"I'll take on that job, folks," said Jean. And then, when her father started to protest, she went on, "Oh I know I have a lot to do, but I can manage to add that morning trip. And now, let's go to bed. I'm sleepy."

"Me, too," said John. "Good night, folks. Gee, I'm sorry about the herd."

"Don't worry, son," said his father. "We'll get along somehow."

Long after the twins had gone to bed and to sleep that night, however, Mr. Merryweather lay awake, trying to figure out ways and means to keep going with the scanty funds at his disposal, for the last report from the hospital was that Pedro must stay there for at least another month.

Chapter XII

JOHN FINDS A WAY

"THOSE CLOUDS HAVE JUST GOT TO BRING RAIN TODAY," said John desperately, one blazing afternoon in August. He was looking at the stormy sky over the eastern mountains. For days their hopes had been disappointed, as each afternoon towering clouds gathered over the mountains and thunder muttered, without bringing rain.

Another storm was brewing in the west and the twins watched eagerly as the cloud armies rushed toward each other across the great sky, blotting out the sun. Thunder reverberated and livid chains of lightning quivered against the black clouds. They watched the storm advance across the great plain below them, obliterating mile after mile under purple curtains of rain.

Then the wind struck with the force of a hurricane and with it came a solid sheet of water, hissing over the dry land. Rain! Rain! The twins rushed out into the storm, jumping up and down, shouting with joy as the torrents poured over them. Jean lifted her arms toward the sky, letting the water stream over her parched skin, surprised to find tears running down her cheeks.

The two storms clashed overhead in a mighty symphony of wind, thunder and roaring water. Soon the twins were driven indoors by pelting hailstones, drumming on the roof, whitening the earth in the patio. Gradually the rage of wind and water diminished and in the lull which followed the rain fell gently.

Jean and John went outside again, drinking in the fresh moist air in ecstasy.

"What's that?" asked Jean, listening to a rushing sound of water.

"I do believe it's the big wash running," declared John. "You know Nat once said that in cloudburst summer storms the water rushed down from the mountains through the gulleys. I used to think that was only a 'tall tale.' "

They ran across the land to the big wash which had always been a wide crooked "river of sand," lined with palo verde trees and desert willows. They could scarcely believe their eyes when they saw a muddy, rippling stream tearing along between the banks.

"Cripes!" exclaimed John. "This is the weirdest country!"

More wonders followed, for, as the clouds lifted above the western mountains, rays of sunlight reached across the land, and above the vast valley an immense, perfect rainbow arc sprang out against the inky clouds. Even as they watched its burning beauty a second bow appeared above it. The double arc spanned the heavens in unearthly brilliance.

"Oh John," whispered Jean, breathlessly, "it's like a miracle."

Thunderstorms of almost equal violence burst over the land in the next few days, ending in thrilling rainbow shows. The air had a crystalline purity, and men, animals and thirsty earth revived and took heart.

One afternoon Jean, preparing to get supper, realized that in their preoccupation with heat and storm they had neglected to go to town for supplies. The larder was very low.

"John," she called, "I'll have to go down to Joe Smith's store to get some canned goods and some bread or we won't eat tonight." They had not been making their daily trips to Joe's store because Sukey was dry.

Jumping into the station wagon, they jounced over the road worn into worse gullies than usual by the torrential rains. When they reached the river in the valley just before Joe's store, John stopped the car with a jerk.

"Will you look at that!" he cried.

Like the desert wash which had given them such a surprise, the wide bed of dry sand and rocks was now a whirling brown stream. John got out and tested the depth of the water with a stick. He shook his head.

"It's too deep to cross," he shouted. Then he pointed to the sign at which he had so often laughed. "Floods. Cross at your own risk."

"Now I know what the Stevens boys meant when they

said you had to go around by another road to the valley when the river was running. I never thought to see it."

They took this roundabout road to reach Joe's store, where their friend chuckled when they expressed their astonishment over the running river.

"This country has a lot of surprises for you," he said. "But you don't have to worry about your cattle any more. Now the rains have begun, everything will be all right."

So it proved as the September days went on. New grass sprang up on the range, the water holes began to fill, and the bony frames of the cattle took on a little flesh. Although the well was still low, the family dared to have the luxury of shower baths once more.

The desert landscape became flushed with green as every dry bush put out fresh leaves. Jean laughed at the giant sahuaro cacti, which had become swollen with new moisture so that each gaunt limb looked rotund, its "accordion pleats," as Jean called them, distended.

The girl sowed new petunias in her hanging pots on the ramada and began setting plants in the border along her patio wall. In the sparse grass yellow flowers like daisies sprang up, and close to the ground, Jean found tiny rosettes of plants with delicate, miniature flowers. She began to believe that she might have a garden after all.

"Say, Jean," said her brother. "Things look so much better around here now, let's ask the Farmington kids out for the week-end."

Jean agreed and the four young people had a jolly time. John took Howard riding the range with him, proudly showing off some of the duties of cowboy life to his admiring city friend. Esther was equally impressed with Jean's ability as a cook and housekeeper.

On Saturday they went on an all-day horseback ride, taking a picnic lunch with them. In spite of the long day in the saddle, they were ready to attend a dance that evening in a roadhouse down on the Nogales highway, where they danced gaily with neighboring cowboys and some "dudes" from near-by guest ranches.

Sunday they all went to Lottie Dawson's ranch to a barbecue to which came the Stevens family and Joe Smith as well as the Merryweathers and their guests.

"Gee, we had fun," said Howard Farmington, as they were preparing to leave on Monday morning.

"Be sure to come again," said Jean.

"Could we come for the fall round-up?" asked Howard.

"There isn't going to be any fall round-up this year," John answered sadly. "The long drought saw to that. But next May we'll have a pip. Be sure to come to that one."

"What makes you think we are going to be here next May, John?" his twin asked. "Aren't we going home the middle of October? Of course we are, silly."

"Oh sure, I suppose so," said John without enthusiasm.

During the past months of drought and disaster it had taken all the courage and determination of the Merryweathers to keep things going on the ranch. John and his father had been too preoccupied to think beyond the problems of each day. But Jean still ticked off the days on her calendar—and counted the few remaining weeks happily.

One morning in late September Mr. Merryweather returned from the mail box with an open letter in his hand, and called Jean and John into the living room.

"I want a family council of Merryweather, Incorporated," he announced. "This letter is from our tenant asking me to rent him the house for another year. Of course we have always planned to offer the ranch for sale and go back some time this fall. But I want your opinion. What answer shall I make to this letter?"

Jean's heart constricted at his words. Oh surely, surely they would go home this fall—nothing would stand in the way of that—would it? She felt her father's eyes upon her, and quickly got out her handkerchief and wiped imaginary perspiration off her face so he could not read the look that must surely be there. Then she turned to her brother and was puzzled and worried by the strange expression on his face.

"What do you say, Dad?" John asked finally.

"No, son. I want the opinion of the junior members of the firm."

"Ladies first, Jeanie," said John.

"Not this time," replied the girl, slowly. She sensed in her brother's manner a great excitement.

"Okay, Sis," he answered. "You asked for it. Well, here goes. The way I feel, Dad, is that I don't want to quit when things are bad. We've lost some of our stock and the rest are still in poor shape, in spite of the rain. Nobody would give us a decent price for the place now. And anyway, I want to build up the herd and make more improvements. Then, if you still feel that you want to sell, next year, we'll have something to offer. But I'm so much interested in cattle raising and Western life that I want to stay. I've never felt like this about anything I've ever tried to do, before. I guess you—you—might call it—ambition," he finished.

Jean listened to John with mixed emotions, her own disappointment over the possible delay in returning home momentarily lost in pride in her brother. Nat's prophecy had come true. The West *was* making a man of John.

"I mustn't, just mustn't stand in his way," she thought resolutely. But another long year stretched endlessly before her, and she almost faltered. Then she turned to look at her father. The light of pride in his eyes as he gazed at his son decided Jean to make the most unselfish speech of her life. "For both their sakes we must stay another year," she told herself firmly.

Now her father turned to her. "Your turn, Jean," he said, softly.

Jean hesitated. She *must* find words that would convince them, and they would be the most difficult words she had ever had to speak. Noticing her hesitation, her father said, "See here, John, you and I are asking too much of our Jean. We mustn't be selfish, son."

"Then he *does* want to stay, too," Jean thought.

"No, you're not being selfish, Daddy Merryweather," she spoke with a rush. "Of course I've always thought before that I'd jump at the chance to go home, but now—I don't know—I'm not so sure. As John says, we're making something here. Why I've been so proud of everything we've achieved! Even this terrible summer has been a challenge to us and I'm proud that we've stuck it out and conquered it." She stopped. "Well, that's no fib," she thought to herself. "I *am* proud of us for *that!*"

They were waiting, so she went on carefully. "I'm getting to—to love this country," she said at last.

"I mustn't overdo it," she was thinking, as John turned incredulous eyes upon her. "And I'm grateful to it, Daddy, for making you well," she went on, aloud. "Of course, we *will* go home after next year, won't we?"

"Oh of course," answered her father, with a happy smile. "But I agree with John that we shouldn't quit now when things are bad. To tell you the truth, I'm glad you've both put forth such good reasons for staying on another year."

"Then he really believes I meant it," Jean thought, wryly.

"I have found renewed health here, to be sure," her father was saying, "but I don't feel able yet to cope with full-time business. As for occupation, I am strong enough now to carry a larger share of the ranch work this winter, and besides I want to go on with painting this landscape. I even dream of trying to get enough paintings together for a one man show some day, either here in Tucson, or perhaps in New York."

"That makes it unanimous," shouted John, joyfully. "We're broke, and we've got to work our heads off, but we'll get on all right. I'll find a way."

"There's just one thing that worries me," said their father, "and that is the fact that you are both having to put off college for still another year—although even if we did go home now there would be no chance for college for you, as I'm still without funds."

"Well," said Jean, "now that we are going to be here, I, for one, am going to study Spanish seriously this winter.

When Esther Farmington was here for the week-end, she was telling me about correspondence courses at the University. I could take a Spanish course by correspondence, I know. Then I could go to town once a week and spend the night with her and for two days running go to a teacher she knows, who'll give me practice on pronunciation. Do you two men think you would be able to bach it one night a week, without your star cook and dishwasher?"

"Of course we could, dear," answered her father. "I am glad you will be staying in the city one night a week. I've felt that you two needed more companionship of people your own age out here. Except for the Stevens boys, you have no contemporary friends at all."

"Don't forget Bert and Sally," said Jean. "By the way, I got a postcard from Sally saying they will be back early in October."

"Good!" said John.

Thought of the Hazeltons gave John his inspiration. Now he knew what he would do to earn money. He remembered that first time he and Jean had visited them, when Sally had told them how she had learned to ride bulls and, as she said, "helped earn the family beans." Bert had declared that anyone who could ride a horse and had plenty of nerve, could learn to ride bulls. "Why not me?" John asked himself. When Sally and Bert were back, he determined, he would consult them.

Soon after the Hazeltons returned, the young Merryweathers went over to welcome them home. It was good to see them again. They had much to talk about—the loss of Nat, and Pedro's accident, and their hard luck about the cattle and the long months of drought.

"You sure had a run of tough luck," said Bert. "But cheer up, maybe you're due for a couple of good breaks now."

"We're awfully glad that you decided to stay another year, in spite of your troubles," said Sally.

While Sally and Jean were talking John made an excuse to get Bert outside and out of his sister's hearing. Then he said, "Look here, Bert, I want to try to learn to ride bulls so that I can enter the Tucson rodeo. Any chance, do you think, that I could learn to ride well enough by that time? Let's see, the Tucson rodeo is toward the end of February and this is early October—that's about four months and a half. What do you think?"

"Well, I dunno," Bert answered. "It might be done. See here, Lottie Dawson's got a chute and some mean bulls. Let's meet at her ranch tomorrow at about two o'clock and you can try out and see if you can ride 'em. It's a trick, but you're a real hand with a horse, and you've got plenty nerve, so there's no reason on earth why you shouldn't. I'm sure Lottie will be glad to let you practice on her bulls, and I'll train you."

"Gee, that's swell of you, Bert. But don't say anything about it in front of my sister, will you? What the folks don't know won't hurt 'em. I've got to earn some money so that I can replenish our stock. That's why I want to learn to ride. See?"

"Okay, pal," Bert answered. "We'll try you out to-morrow afternoon. I'll be able to tell then whether or not you can learn enough to stick your neck out at the Tucson rodeo."

Next day John met Bert at Lottie Dawson's ranch and the two boys told her their scheme.

"Sure you can use my chute," said Lottie jovially. "And I've a couple of mean bulls you can practice on, too. But say, John, does your family know about this?"

"No, Lottie, and please don't tell them," John begged. "If I win at the Tucson rodeo they'll be there to see me— but in the meantime I don't want them to know about it. They might try to stop me."

"All right, boy," said Lottie, grinning at him. "I'll be mum as a tomb. Now I'll saddle up my mare and round up a couple of bulls for you to practice on. You'd better show him how, first, Bert," she suggested. "Let's see, you have your spurs on, haven't you, John?"

"That's right, John," said Bert. "You've got to spur 'em, you know—you mustn't tight leg 'em. But first, Lottie, I think he'd better just try to stick on for the eight seconds without trying to use spurs, don't you?"

"You're the doctor, Bert," she answered.

Soon she came riding in behind a pair of white-faced bulls. One of them she drove into the chute, and the other she put in the corral. Bert was perched on the gate of the chute, while Lottie and Jake put a rope under the bull's belly. Then Bert squatted above the bull, taking one end of the rope in his hand. Jake handed him the other end and he pulled the two together tightly. Then he shouted, "Let's go, girls," and while the gate of the chute was thrown open, he slid down onto the back of the bull. The animal, surprised at the sudden weight, began to buck and prance on the ground in front of the chute. Bert raised his legs and dug his spurs into the creature at which the bull leaped, and whipped his rear end around and around.

Lottie blew a whistle and Bert slid off the bull's back. The animal ran away as fast as it could go, but Lottie followed, using her rope to bring him back to the chute again.

"Do you want to try it now, John?" Bert asked.

John's heart sank into his boots, but this was no time to show his fear.

"Sure thing," he answered bravely. He climbed onto the gate of the chute as he had seen Bert do. "Okay," said Bert, "now grab a-holt of him."

John adjusted the rope and cried, "All right!" Then the gate was opened and he slid down onto the back of the bull.

The next thing John Merryweather knew he was lying on the ground in front of the chute. The world was going around and around. He was dizzy and felt sick. Lottie was holding a glass of cold water to his lips, and, judging by his wet hair, they had doused his head with water.

"Hello," said John, groggily.

"Hi," answered Bert. He turned to Lottie and shook his head, solemnly. "A salty tenderfoot runnin' wild can sure head himself into a passel of grief," he commented with a chuckle.

"Had enough, boy?" asked Lottie.

"No, sir!" John declared vehemently. "Bring him back and this time I'll stick on him or—or bust!"

"That's the spirit!" said Lottie.

So, although shaken and sore from his spill, once again John got himself on the bull's back. "I must have been on this thing more than eight seconds," he thought, as the creature under him stamped and twisted and bucked his big head. At last came the welcome sound of the whistle, and he slid to the ground.

Bert rushed up to him. "That was swell!" he exclaimed. "You stayed on fine."

"Now let's try the other bull and use your spurs on him," suggested Lottie.

"No, Lottie, no spurring today," said Bert. "John better tight leg 'em today. He's got to learn to stay on first before he gets fancy, you know."

So once again John Merryweather mounted, but this time the bull was a spinner. As soon as the gate of the chute was opened, the animal began to spin around. "Lean into the spin!" shouted Bert, as the bull was spinning to the left. But John did not hear the warning. Once more he was thrown off, landing in the soft earth. Dazed but not hurt this time, he picked himself up.

"Get him a drink of water, Bert," ordered Lottie. "Isn't that enough for today, John?" she asked in a kindly voice.

"Oh no," said John. "I've got to learn to stay on that fellow, too, before I quit."

"All right, if you're not too sore," Lottie agreed.

"Look, John," said Bert. "You must lean the same way the bull spins. Now this bull whirls to the left, so you should lean that-a-way. And by the way, when you get to spurring bulls, remember never to spur one that's spinning. Are you ready to tangle with this fellow again?"

"Yes," answered John, and limped over to the gate of the chute. This time he managed to stay on for the whole eight seconds, but when he slipped off, the bull butted him with its horns.

"Ouch!" said John, as he sprawled in the sand. "I sure am a goof!"

"You've done fine, just fine!" said Lottie heartily. "Now that's enough for today. Come on in the house and I'll wash your scratched-up face and put some sticking plaster on your cuts. What will you tell 'em at home when they ask how you got hurt?"

"I'll kind of imply that my horse threw me," John said with a grin. "They'll think I lit on some cholla cactus, like the dude that Walkin' John bucked off. It wouldn't be the first time that happened to me, either."

"Good enough," answered Lottie. "That will account for everything."

"How about it, Bert?" John asked his friend. "Do you think I'll ever be a bull rider?"

"You bet I do!" Bert's voice was enthusiastic. "You've picked it up like you was born on a bull's back. But you got to keep at it—practice as often as possible. A lot of good fellows compete at the Tucson rodeo, you know. There's good money, there."

So for many weeks, whenever John could get away from the ranch, he met Bert at Lottie Dawson's to practice. Each time the younger boy grew more confident, although he was often thrown from the bull before his eight seconds were up. When he had been at it a week, he dared to use his spurs. The first time he was immediately thrown, but that was because he lost his balance.

"It's just like flying, after you've had a smash-up," John said to Lottie and Bert when they suggested that he stop for the day. "You have to make yourself go up in the air right away again before you have a chance to get scared."

"Attaboy!" cried Lottie, giving John an admiring glance. She liked this clean-limbed, courageous young Easterner. "And if there's any justice under heaven," she told herself, "he will win some prize money at the Tucson rodeo."

John was having a difficult time at home, hiding his secret. Some days, after a particularly hard jouncing on one of Lottie's bulls, he was so sore and tired that he could scarcely sit at the supper table. And he noticed that both Jean and his father observed his discomfort, although they said no word to him about it.

Whenever, during his practice at Lottie's, a car came down her driveway, he always ran into the house, lest it should be Jean or his father coming to call. But his luck held and neither of them came to Lottie D Rancho.

They were more concerned about him than he knew, however. Indeed one day Jean asked her father what he thought was the matter with John.

"He never seems to have any time at home in the afternoons any more," she said. "Surely he can't be working on the range all day, now that you are riding some of it, too. Besides he isn't so busy now that what he calls 'screw worm season' is over. Sometimes he starts off in the morning without waiting for breakfast. And at night he goes to bed right away after supper—dead tired. And he is so quiet—not a bit like himself."

"I'm afraid the work is too much for him, dear," her father answered. "I, too, have noticed how tired he seems every night. I'm afraid he doesn't let me ride enough of the range to be much help."

"If only Pedro hadn't been hurt," sighed Jean. "Does

the doctor hold out any hope that he will be able to work when he leaves the hospital?"

"Not much, I am afraid," her father answered. "And by the way, Jean, Pedro will be able to leave the hospital day after tomorrow, his family told me this morning. Let's drive in and bring him home to Roberto's house—maybe we could arrange a small celebration for the old fellow."

So Jean and her father drove in to the hospital and fetched the old Mexican home. He was so happy to be back with his own people, and so pathetically grateful to his "Boss and the little Missy," that tears came into Jean's eyes as she watched him. With a deep happy sigh, he ate a huge plateful of *frijoles*, the first he had tasted for months. "Nurses very kind," he said, "but cook's no good at hospital."

Pedro insisted to Mr. Merryweather that he would be able to come back to work in "two-three weeks," but Roberto shook his head, and took Jean and her father to one side as they were leaving. "I'm afraid that Tio Pedro won't be able to work at all any more," he said. "Poor old man!"

That night Mr. Merryweather reported this conversation to John, and asked his son if he shouldn't perhaps try to find someone else to help on the ranch. "You seem much too tired out at the end of the day."

"Oh no, Dad," John answered quickly. "You and I can manage alone." He thought to himself secretly, "I must watch my step or they'll begin to suspect something." That night he took down a book and sat with the others in the living room, valiantly trying to stay awake. But Jean and her father both noticed that the book soon fell from his hand, as, weary beyond words, he dropped off to sleep in his chair.

The next time Jean went over to call upon the Hazeltons, she confided to Sally her concern over her brother. Poor Sally! It was all she could do not to relieve Jean's anxiety, but she had promised John to keep his secret.

"He and Bert are off together a lot, I know," said Sally. "But I don't worry about it. I never pay any attention to Bert when he's up to some funny business that he doesn't tell me about."

"Funny business," Jean repeated to herself. "Oh dear, is John hanging around with loafers somewhere?" But quickly she thrust that thought away. Surely not—not the hardworking, self-reliant chap her brother had become!

Sally's words, however, and especially her manner, served only to increase Jean's worry.

One day Bert met John at Lottie's with news. "There's to be a small ranch rodeo on Sunday at Bud Fletcher's ranch, John," he said. "Entrance fees are only five dollars. Come on, let's you and me enter. What say?"

"Do you think I'm ready yet?" asked John.

"There's got to be a first time some day," Bert replied. "Why not now?"

And so, on the following Sunday, Bert and Sally and Lottie and John drove to Bud Fletcher's ranch beyond Tucson. John had had to steel himself against the appeal in Jean's eyes when he had said he was going out with Sally and Bert. Jean was hurt and bewildered when she realized that she was not invited on this excursion.

"Why don't you take Jean with you, son?" his father

asked, as the boy saddled his horse to ride to the Hazelton house.

"Why—uh—uh," stammered John. "There isn't room. We are picking up some people in Tucson. The Hazelton's car will be full." John knew that his explanation sounded very lame. His father looked at him quizzically, but made no reply.

John hated to deceive his father and sister—but what else could he do? If his scheme worked out and he was able to compete successfully at the big rodeo, he could then confess what he had been doing all this time. But if he didn't win? Shucks, he *had* to win!

The rodeo at Bud Fletcher's ranch was a small affair, not very well attended. At the small ring, surrounded with grand stand seats, Sally and Lottie said goodbye and good luck to the two contestants as they went to get their numbers and pay their entrance fees.

"Say, John, you've drawn a muss-hog—that means a very tough bull," Bert explained. "His name is Dynamite, and he's a terror. Don't worry if you can't stick on him. But, boy, you'd better jump if he starts to throw you!"

John's heart was in his mouth when he heard his name called. He had registered as "Jack Merry." Bert was in the chute holding the rope around a great gray creature with a huge lump on his back. John had seen many pictures of Brahma bulls but this was the first one he had ever encountered in the flesh. What a powerful beast he was! John adjusted the rope as Bert had taught him. Then, saying faintly, "Okay," he slid down onto the bull's back and the gate of the chute swung open. He had no more than lunged into the arena when he felt himself lifted high over the horns of Dynamite and thrown on the sand. It was all he could do to pick himself up—so great was his pain and disappointment. But he managed to get to his feet and stagger to the stand where Lottie and Sally were sitting.

"Tough luck, boy," said Lottie, sympathetically. "Cheer up. Better luck next time! That Dynamite's famous for bucking boys off."

"That's right, John," said Sally. "I bet there isn't a wolf in the business that can stay on him." Then, seeing John's puzzled expression, she explained, " 'Wolf' means rodeo performer."

Their words were poor comfort to the boy who wanted so much to win. However he was soon applauding Bert, who had won first prize in both bull riding and the bare-back bronc contest.

On the way home Bert wanted to celebrate with his prize money, but Sally prudently reminded him that they had a long time ahead of them with nothing coming in. John was glad when Bert acquiesced, because he was eager to get home early. He remembered with a pang Jean's wistful expression as he had ridden away.

"Don't be discouraged, John," said Sally that evening as John left their house. "Sometimes it takes a year or more for a fellow to get where you've gotten already. Bert says you're a natural born bull rider and, believe me, he knows."

So next afternoon saw young John Merryweather again riding bulls at Lottie Dawson's ranch. Lottie sat on the fence keeping time, her wrinkled face glowing with pride under her big Stetson hat, and wisps of her curly blond hair blowing in the wind.

Chapter XIII

FIESTA DE LOS VAQUEROS

FOR JOHN MERRYWEATHER, FEBRUARY SPED AWAY ALL TOO
fast, bringing ever closer the date of the Tucson rodeo.
Now that it was so nearly here, he looked forward to that
crucial time with mingled excitement and dread. All unconscious of her brother's part in it, Jean was learning from
Bert and Sally about the big annual Western festival—the
Fiesta de los Vaqueros. For an entire week, then, Tucson
lets loose and plays "Western." The festival begins with
the live stock and horse show, followed by two days of

Indian celebrations, when groups of dancers from various tribes come to give performances. The rodeo, on the last three days, is the climax of the week. This year Bert was entering the rodeo, in both the bronc and Brahma bull riding contests.

Jean, who had never seen a rodeo, was keenly interested in Bert's descriptions and eager to see the show. She supposed, of course, that her brother was equally ignorant, and attributed his knowing attitude to his companionship with Bert. John told his family that he was going to help Bert in the chutes, and that was all he said about his own participation.

On a Friday morning late in February, the Merryweathers were up early getting ready to go into town, to watch the colorful parade that opens the rodeo.

"Be sure you wear Western clothes, or else the Vigilantes will get you," John warned his family.

He, himself, clad in a bright gold sateen shirt and his Stetson hat, looked very dashing.

"That's a beautiful shirt you're wearing, if I may say so," commented Jean. "Where did you get it?"

"It's one of Bert's," John answered. "As a matter of fact, Sally made it for him. She's a pretty clever girl, don't you think?"

"Indeed I do. Shall we see Bert ride this afternoon?"

"I think so," said John. "By the way, he and Sally are coming here to pick me up. I want to go around to the chutes with Bert before the parade—to—to—learn just what I have to do to help him," he finished lamely. "But we can all meet and watch the parade together and have lunch before Bert and I have to leave for the show."

They arranged a place to meet from which they could watch the parade. Then, "Just what will you be doing in the chute when you 'help' Bert?" Jean wanted to know.

"Well," said her brother, "somebody has to hand him the rope that goes around the bull, and help him get seated on the bull's back."

"Oh," said Jean. "Well, be careful of yourself, Twin. I hear those Brahma bulls are very mean creatures."

"You don't know the half of it," thought John to himself.

The streets of Tucson were gay with flags and pennants. Many shop windows bore the scrawled warning, "Go Western or Else!" The population, young and old, native and winter visitor alike, had obeyed the admonition joyously. People swaggered along the streets, playing "Western" in every variety of outfit: big hats, shirts and pants, from the most gorgeous of fringed suede jackets and suits to simple ranch shirts and neckerchiefs. It was a field day for children, who, even to the tiniest, played they were cowboys in gay attire.

While Jean and her father took their places on the street where they had arranged to meet John, they saw what happened to a citizen who did not obey the command "Go Western!"

A huge cage was standing on the top of a truck. Beside it stood a policeman, pistol in hand. He shot off his gun and called to two men who were near the truck, "Get him!" The men went up to a soberly dressed citizen, who had not one redeeming bit of Western clothing upon him. He was hustled into the cage, and the truck drove away after more victims. The man who had been "arrested" took it in good humor, and of course the crowd laughed merrily.

"There is something pretty swell about this part of the country," Jean was thinking, "something outgoing and friendly." Suddenly she realized that she would miss this heartiness when she got back home—then she quickly wondered at herself for letting such a silly idea that she'd miss *anything* when she got back home, come into her head.

No sooner had Mr. Merryweather and Jean taken their places in the crowd lining the curbstone than they heard a hail, and Bert and Sally and John appeared. Bert looked very picturesque in a large curly-brimmed hat and blue plaid shirt, and Sally wore a cowgirl outfit although she herself was not riding in the show.

The spirited music of a band drew every eye to the street vista and on came the parade, bright with costumes, exciting with its group of horsemen, its amusing floats and ancient, horse-drawn vehicles. Leading the procession were the officers of the city on splendid horses, a Mexican official from across the border in stunning charro costume of brown leather trimmed with gold, and two queens of the Fiesta, American and Mexican. The American girl, dressed in a white suit, bowed and smiled from her prancing horse, while the pretty Mexican señorita, riding side saddle in her native attire of embroidered blouse and full skirt glittering with spangles, drew equal applause.

Cavalcades of riders passed by: show groups mounted on magnificent horses, the riders' chaps and saddles and bridles of their mounts heavily studded with silver; long lines of cowboys and cowgirls on their good clever ranch horses; "dudes" from guest ranches and boys from the fashionable desert schools proudly taking their part in the show.

The crowd cheered rapturously the loved reminders of frontier days and history of the Old Pueblo, Tucson, in the procession of ancient vehicles. Old ore and freight wagons filled with laughing groups, lumbered by drawn by teams of mules or oxen. Along came one of the original stage coaches which, long ago, had transported passengers across desert roads, filled with men and women dressed in the fashion of that period. An ancient Spanish ox-cart with solid wheels, creaked along, drawing cheers for its oc- cupants, girls in Spanish costumes and Mexican musicians strummings their guitars. From old fashioned buggies and landaus elegant ladies of the '80's bowed to the spectators. A float went by representing a saloon of the "Wild West" with its mustachioed bartender and gay girls, swaying and lifting their gaudy skirts. Another showed pioneer women in sunbonnets working at an old fashioned spin- ning wheel and cooking on a primitive stove. Not a single "gasoline buggy" was allowed to appear in this show of the "old West."

Groups of feathered and painted Indian dancers spoke of the original population, and the Chinese quarter was represented by a colorful wagon in which a New Year's dragon swayed his ornamental head.

In between the floats and riders came high school bands, swinging along to their tootling and drumming, preceded by beautiful girl drum majors, tossing their batons high in the air and doing acrobatics in time to the music.

As the procession streamed by, picturing times old and new, representing the varied peoples which had made this

Arizona land, Jean found herself waving and cheering. John, too, was shouting with enthusiasm at the groups of horsemen and their mounts.

"The horses are the best of all, aren't they, John?" exclaimed his sister.

"Yes sir, out here horses make the show," John agreed. Although this was an old story to the young Hazeltons, they were amused and pleased by the Easterners' enthusiasm.

When the last band and float had gone by, the three Merryweathers took the two Hazeltons to lunch.

"Shall we see you ride this afternoon, Bert?" Jean asked as they seated themselves around the luncheon table.

"Yep," Bert responded gaily. "If you look fast enough you'll see me mounted on a big gray bull named, unluckily, 'Number Thirteen.' Boy, I hope that will be a lucky number for me. They say that's quite a bull. But I didn't draw a horse for today, so I guess you'll have to wait until tomorrow to see me ride a bronc."

Bert and Sally were full of talk, but John had fallen suddenly silent. He seemed nervous and scarcely touched his food. "What is the matter with him?" Jean speculated. "Surely there is no reason for him to be nervous when Bert isn't." For the hundredth time she wondered what had come over her brother these days.

"Well, fella, time to get goin'," said Bert when they had finished lunch. Sally went with the boys, leaving Jean and her father to drive by themselves to the Fairgrounds.

"We'll be rooting for you, Bert," Jean called as they departed.

Under the great turquoise dome of the sky the arena and

grandstand were a bright spectacle. Flags snapped at their staffs, and the red-coated band played lively music. In the background groups of horsemen trotted to and fro.

Then from the official booth above the chutes came the announcer's voice, magnified by loud-speakers:

"Good afternoon, rodeo fans. We welcome you to our annual Fiesta de los Vaqueros. This is not a Wild West show, or a circus; it is a contest. Many of these boys have come from a great distance to compete. We have all the top hands here, some of them world champions. They've all paid their entrance money, but they're taking a chance. If you like their performances, give them a great big hand, but if some of them have a little tough luck, let's give them, too, a big hand, folks, just the same."

The band burst into a swinging march and a procession rode down the arena, turned and lined up before the grandstand: queens and officials, show horses in their silver trappings, rangy cowboy performers on their pet horses, last, but by no means least, two clowns wearing overalls and false beards, mounted on their trick mules. Their part in the show was to amuse the audience between events and to help the contestants get away from angry bulls and steers.

The announcer proclaimed the first event, calf roping, explaining that the calf was given a sixty-foot start, that the cowboy must rope it, throw it and tie any three of its feet together. At one end of the arena Jean saw a half-grown calf come galloping, followed by a cowboy, riding full tilt, whirling his rope around his head. The rope swung out, the loop fell neatly on the calf's neck, jerking him backward. The horse stopped short, holding the rope taut as Jean had seen them do at the spring round-ups. Like a flash the rider was off his horse and struggling with the kicking, bawling calf.

"Watch that wrap-up, folks," intoned the announcer. "He's got a kicker there!"

With unbelievable speed, three of the calf's feet were tied together by the rider, who carried the rope for that purpose in his teeth. Then he lifted his arms and let them fall, signalling that the job was done. The mounted judge lowered his flag, and in a few moments the announcer said, "Toots Bacon's time on that was nineteen seconds flat. How did you like that, folks?" The audience answered with loud clapping.

As one after another of the contestants pursued and tied their calves Jean and her father marvelled at their speed and skill. Some few missed catching the calf with both the two loops they were allowed, whereupon the announcer said, "No time on that one. But let's give him a big hand, folks, for that's all he'll get." The audience always responded generously.

Remembering John's humiliating struggles with roping, Jean felt especially sorry for each who missed. She studied her program to see when the Brahma bull riding would take place, eager to see Bert in action. Several contests came before that, however, so she gave her attention wholeheartedly to the exciting happenings in the arena.

Next came the bucking horse contest. The announcer made much of the wildness of the horses and danger to the riders. "But remember the old saying, folks, 'There never was a hoss that couldn't be rode and never a cowboy that couldn't be throwed.' These hosses are real outlaws and they hate to be ridden."

He explained that the riders must keep one hand free, holding the reins in the other hand, "so you can see six inches of daylight between his hand and the saddle." He continued, "Some of these boys are going to stay on and some are going to get bucked off. Coming out of chute number one is Bud Henley of Casa Grande, mounted on Reckless Red."

The gate of the chute was opened and out sprang a bucking whirlwind of a red horse. He plunged and kicked and twisted, while his rider jerked back and forth, staying on only by skillful balancing. The horn sounded and the mounted helper rode alongside the bucking animal, allowing the rider to scramble on behind him. Each bucking bronc seemed faster and more vicious than the last, and when one of the riders was thrown, Jean held her breath in terror. But the man picked himself up and limped away to the applause of the audience.

The team-tying contest followed. In this two riders pursued a steer which had a sixty-foot start. One cowboy was to rope the head while the other caught the hind feet in his loop. They had to deal with rugged range cattle.

"Heeling steers is one of the most difficult of all roping catches, because the steer is fighting on the end of another rope which is around his neck," the announcer informed the audience.

As he spoke the steer came thundering down the arena pursued by the riders, who swung their loops on head and hind feet with speedy precision. The head roper jumped from his horse, threw the struggling steer and tied its hind feet in record time.

"Isn't it marvelous, Dad?" exclaimed Jean. "Did you ever see anything so fast and skillful? I hope John is watching this wonderful roping!"

The two Merryweathers sat forward, tense with excitement, as sixteen pairs of team-tyers competed. It was to them the most interesting event so far.

But Jean was terrified at the ferocity of the next thing on the program—the bull-dogging. The first contestant was a heavy-set fellow.

"Here's the steer and here's the dogger," called the announcer, jovially. "Lots of steer and lots of cowboy, folks. He's handling a lot of beef."

It did look dangerous, seeing the cowboy leap off his galloping horse to seize the sharp horns of the steer, going at full speed. With his feet braced and his arms wrapped around its neck, the cowboy struggled to throw the animal by twisting its head. When the steer was lying on its side with its feet straight out, the job was accomplished successfully.

"What a way to make a living!" commented Mr. Merryweather.

"Yes," agreed Jean. "It's so dangerous and so chancy. If they don't win, they have paid their entrance fees for nothing." She was really glad when the bulldogging was over, so sure was she that one of the men would be gored while struggling with the furious animal.

Now came the event they were most eager to see—the riding of the Brahma bulls.

"Next will be one of the most dangerous contests of the rodeo," came the announcer's voice. "Brahma bulls are the sacred beasts of India, and they're mighty ferocious,

Plunging out of chute number seven

came a huge gray bull

believe me. Watch the chutes, folks. They'll try to hook those boys down there."

The audience sat forward, staring in breathless anticipation. The clowns wandered out on foot and stood near the chutes.

"Don't think those clowns are down there just to be funny," called the announcer. "Their job is to distract the attention of the bulls while the riders dismount. An important job, that is, for those bulls are only too willing to take care of the boys with their horns and hooves. Let's show these boys we're with them, folks, by giving them a great big hand, even if they don't stick on the bull for the full eight seconds they're supposed to. Now then, each contestant will be marked fifty per cent on the bull and fifty per cent on how he rides him. He must spur the bull once in the first three lunges out of the chute. After the horn sounds the rider will dismount as best he can. Okay down there? All right! Coming out of chute number one is Kid Meridith of Tulsa, Oklahoma, riding Sky-High. There's the bull and there's the rider!"

An enormous creature dashed out of the open gate of the chute, bucking and jumping, kicking and snorting, trying to throw the man on his back. A cowbell fastened around his belly did not help his disposition. It was the most frightening thing Jean had ever seen. She was glad when the horn blew and the rider dismounted safely. The clown ran toward the head of the bull while the performer picked up the rope by which he had held on and walked back to the chutes. The applause was tremendous.

Jean was looking for John's gold shirt behind the gates of the chutes but she did not see him.

"It is strange that Bert would let John help him with the rope," Jean said. "John is an amateur."

Her remark was not answered because at that moment the band blared forth another gay tune. Over the music came the words of the announcer: "Coming out of chute number two is Bert Hazelton of Tucson, riding Number Thirteen."

Jean forgot herself and shouted, "Go to it, Bert," as she watched his slight figure balancing precariously on the back of the bucking, spinning creature. Then the horn blew and Bert's dangerous ride was over. He slipped neatly from the back of the plunging bull, rescued his rope, and strolled nonchalantly to the group of cowboys beside the chutes.

"How did you like that ride, folks?" demanded the announcer. "Bert is a bantam and he drew a spinner!" The crowd showed how they liked it with much applause.

So it went on as four other contestants tried their luck. One bull, named Poison Ivy, threw his rider after the first lunge out of the chute and the clown cleverly distracted the furious animal until the rider could pick himself up and get to safety.

Jean heard a man behind her remark, "I've seen Poison Ivy in rodeos for the last three years and no one ever stayed on him for eight seconds yet."

"I'm so glad Bert didn't draw that bull," said Jean, and Mr. Merryweather agreed fervently. He had watched the bull riding with an excited interest almost equal to Jean's.

"Out of chute number seven," they heard the announcer's voice, "comes Jack Merry of Tucson. It's his first big time rodeo. Folks, here's a plucky boy. Let's give him a big hand. He's riding Joe Lewis. That bull ought to pack a wallop."

Plunging out of chute number seven came a huge gray bull, kicking and twisting. Jean gasped, for, on his back, was a rider in a gold shirt.

"Dad!" she cried, clutching her father's arm. "It's John, it's John!"

Breathlessly they watched while John swung and balanced on the back of the bucking animal, holding on to the braided rope for dear life. The horn sounded and John slipped off, landing lightly on his feet instead of tumbling off as some of the riders had done.

Jean relaxed with a great sigh. "Thank heaven he's safe!" said John's father, mopping his perspiring forehead.

"*That's* what John has been doing all this time, Dad," cried Jean, with swift realization, "learning to ride bulls. Oh, why didn't he tell us?"

"I guess he wanted to surprise us," sighed her father, "and he certainly succeeded!"

"Aren't you proud of him, Daddy?"

"Yes," he answered with a quizzical smile. "Very proud. But I hope he doesn't intend to follow in young Hazelton's footsteps and make this his profession."

Jean was much too excited to pay attention to the rest of the show. Now she understood what John had been up to. Of course—he was trying to earn money to replenish the herd. How she hoped he would win a prize! But what a hard and dangerous way he had chosen to earn that money!

Exciting performances continued in the arena, but the Merryweathers saw them in a daze. They waited impatiently for the end of the show so that they might find John and tell him what they thought of him.

They had agreed to meet in the parking lot and as Jean and her father hurried toward their car, they saw John approaching with Bert and Sally. He waved at them with a broad grin. Jean had an impulse to run up and throw her arms around her brother but she knew that would never do.

"Hello, Jack Merry," she called gaily. John ran up to his family. "We're so proud of you we could bust!" declared Jean with more fervor than elegance.

"Good work, son," said Mr. Merryweather, patting the boy on the back. "Let's go and celebrate this revelation of the evil deeds of Jack Merry, alias John Merryweather, with a cold drink."

"Right, Dad," answered John. He was about to climb into the car when the loud voice of Lottie Dawson stopped him. "Hey there, Jack Merry," she shouted, "don't go off without giving your old pal a tumble."

"Indeed I won't, Lottie," said John, fervently. "A pal is right, if there ever was one! Dad and Jean," he went on, "Bert taught me to ride at Lottie's ranch and I used Lottie's bulls. Furthermore, Lottie put up the money for my entrance fee. Wasn't that taking a chance, though?"

"Nonsense," answered Lottie, wiping her eyes. "I've got a hunch you won something today. That was a beautiful ride. What do you think, teacher?" she asked, turning to Bert.

"You bet," Bert assured her. "I'm sure John placed high on today's score. Of course, we won't know for sure until after the first go-around is over tomorrow. There's thirty contestants on the Brahma bulls at this show, so we can't get our scores until all thirty have ridden."

"I can hardly wait until we know for sure that you've won something, John," said his sister. "You too, of course, Bert," she added belatedly.

"Now come on, folks," said Lottie. "I feel this calls for a celebration. You're all to come and eat dinner with me —my party," she continued, eyeing them severely. "Bert and Sally, too."

So the three Merryweathers and the two Hazeltons had a fine dinner as Lottie Dawson's guests that evening, and there was much laughter as John recounted his many mishaps while learning to ride bulls. He told them he had attended all the small ranch rodeos that had been held in the neighborhood during the past two months, and that he had managed to stay on every bull he had ridden except that first time at Bud Fletcher's ranch.

"He's a natural born bull rider," Bert proclaimed. "I never saw anybody pick it up so fast—and imagine what a performance he gave today, with nearly every wolf in the business competing—he got the biggest hand of all. And I'll bet he placed, too."

"Well, just look what a good teacher I had," answered John. Bert grinned and gave John a salute.

"So that's where you've been all these Sunday afternoons when you hade to go out for a while, folks," Jean mimicked John's voice. "Dad and I have worried ourselves sick about you—thinking the work was too much for you, and wondering what you were up to. Haven't we, Daddy?"

"Well, please forgive me, family." John's voice was

contrite. "But you both know why I wanted to earn some money—to help replenish our herd. And if either of you had gotten wind of what I was up to, you would have made me stop, now wouldn't you?"

"You're right, John," answered his father. "And we both forgive you for the worry you've caused us, don't we, Jean?"

"Of course we do, John, whether you win or not, I think you're swell to have tried," answered his twin.

"Do you remember that day when you asked me what I thought was the matter with John?" Sally asked Jean. "It was all I could do not to break down and confess it all to you."

"Good girl for keeping my secret, Sally," said John, smiling gratefully at her.

"He's one game kid," Lottie whispered into his father's ear. "He don't know the word quit—it just ain't in his book. You ought to be mighty proud of him!"

"I am, Lottie," replied Mr. Merryweather, "and very grateful to you. What a trump you have been!"

"Well, young Brahma bullers," Lottie said, "I think we'd better get on home so you all can crawl into your beddies, because, as the sayin' is, you've got to go to town again tomorrow."

Chapter XIV

THE RETURN

ON THE SECOND DAY OF THE RODEO JEAN AND HER FATHER took their places once more in the grand stand. They were eagerly looking forward to the Brahma bull event, hoping to see both John and Bert ride and win. John had warned them, however, that they might not draw bulls that day.

Neither of the boys' names was called by the announcer on the first section of Brahma bull riding
. "I hope they will each draw a good bull when they do ride," said Jean, "and not either that old Double Trouble or Poison Ivy. According to Bert neither of those two has ever been ridden for eight seconds at any rodeo."

The first section of bronc riding was on when Jean got

her second great shock at the Fiesta de los Vaqueros. In a daze she heard the announcer say, "The next rider is Nat Barton of Tucson, coming out of chute number four, riding Whirligig."

"Daddy!" cried Jean. "Did you hear what he said? It's Nat. How wonderful!" Jean's heart sang with happiness. "Maybe John has already spoken to him. Do you suppose so?"

She jumped up in her excitement, straining to watch the young man on a huge black horse, which sprang out of the chute.

"That horse is a terror," said the man who was sitting behind her to his companion. "He almost killed the fellow that rode him last year."

The man's words terrified Jean. "Oh nothing must happen to Nat," she thought.

But the horse bucked and kicked, leaped into the air and came down with a jarring thud. Nat held tightly to the reins and hugged the animal's sides with his knees, but the horse gave a final mighty plunge and threw the boy flat upon the ground. A gasp went up from the audience and Jean wrung her hands in distress. How still Nat lay! She had never seen anything so quiet as Nat's body, lying there in the arena.

"Daddy," she sobbed, "is he dead?"

"I don't know, darling," her father answered. Horrified, they listened to the announcer call for the automobile ambulance and watched it driven into the arena and saw Nat lifted onto a stretcher and put inside.

"Let's go see what we can do for him, Jean," said Mr. Merryweather. Hastily they left the grand stand and went

around behind the chutes. There they found Bert who told
them that John had gone to the hospital in the ambulance
with Nat. Jean and her father inquired which hospital he
had been taken to and decided to follow.

"Did Nat know him, Bert?" asked Jean, tremulously.

"No," Bert answered, "Nat didn't know anything. He
was plumb knocked out when they took him away. But
John told the doctor he was a friend of Nat's and so he
persuaded the doc to take him along. Gee, I hope you
find he's not bad hurt. I can't come with you, because I've
drawn a bronc to ride in the second section this afternoon.
Neither John nor I drew bulls today."

"Do be careful on that bronc, Bert," begged Jean.

Bert grinned at her. "Never been hurt yet," he answered.
"Knock wood!"

As they left the rodeo grounds they heard the voice of
the announcer telling the audience not to be worried about
the accident.

"Please don't be distressed or let it interfere with your
enjoyment of the rest of the show," the announcer said.
"That's the last thing Nat Barton would want to have
happen. When we get the report from the hospital, we
will announce it."

But such reassurance was not for Jean. She and her
father hurried to their car and went quickly to the hospital. Outside the door of the emergency ward they came
upon John, walking back and forth, his face creased with
worry.

"How is he, John?" cried Jean.

"He's still unconscious, Sis," answered her brother.
"The doctor promised to let me know as soon as he comes

to. They have already taken some X-rays to see if his skull is fractured. Poor guy! He'll have one heck of a headache when he does wake up. Did you see how he landed? Right on the back of his head."

Jean joined her brother, pacing back and forth outside the closed door, while their father sat on a bench in the hall. Once the door was opened and Jean stopped to look inside. She saw Nat lying in one of the beds. His eyes were closed, but he was breathing! A doctor in a white coat was standing beside him, taking his pulse.

He turned his head and saw the girl standing in the doorway.

"See here," he said, in a low, stern voice. "You shouldn't be here. What are they thinking of downstairs at the desk, letting you come bursting in like this?"

"Please let us stay, doctor," begged Jean, her lips trembling and her eyes filled with tears. "This young man who came in the ambulance with him is my brother. And my father is waiting out in the hall. We are Nat's friends."

"Very well, but you must wait out there on the bench with your father. I'll tell young Barton you are here, when he regains consciousness. What is your name?"

"Tell him it's Jean and John and Dad, please, doctor," Jean replied.

"The last name is Merryweather," put in John.

"Very well," answered the doctor. "Wait outside and I will tell him."

They sat silently apprehensive waiting for Nat's return to consciousness. Each one was living over in his mind that painful last day of Nat's at the ranch—wondering what they might have done to give the frightened boy the reassurance he had so sorely needed. Each one blamed himself for the haunting doubt of theirs which Nat must have felt, and which had hurt him so badly.

"We will make it up to him, now," said John.

"Yes," replied Mr. Merryweather. "Surely we can say something to make him willing to go back to the ranch."

"I hope he isn't still angry at us," added Jean.

At last the door opened. The doctor stood looking at them.

"He is conscious now," he reported, "and, for your information, I don't believe he is badly hurt, but I will have to wait to see the X-rays before I can be sure. One of you may come in to speak to him. I've told him you are here, and I think he tried to ask for you, Miss."

Jean rushed into the room and threw herself on her knees beside Nat's bed.

"Oh Nat, Nat," she sobbed. "Will you please forgive us?"

A hand clumsily stroked her bent head. Nat's voice was a faint whisper. "There's nothing to forgive you for, Jean," he said, making a great effort to speak naturally. "It was all my fault—my darn temper."

"Will you come home with us, Nat?" the girl asked. "Daddy and John and I want you so much, so much!"

"You bet I will, Jean," the boy answered brokenly. "As soon as they'll let me out of this place."

"You'd better not talk to him any more now, young lady," said the doctor. "Let's let him rest. How do you feel?" he asked Nat.

"As if I'd been kicked in the head by a mule," Nat managed to say.

"When may we take him home, doctor?" asked Jean, when they returned to the others in the hall.

"You had best let him stay here for another hour. I've just looked at the X-rays. There is no sign of a fracture, but he'd be wise to take it easy for a few days. Keep him in bed if possible. And no horseback riding until he is entirely well. Here are some pills to help stop the pain. Give him one every hour until he goes to sleep."

"Will it be all right for him to ride in our station wagon, doctor?" asked Mr. Merryweather.

"Yes, but try not to jounce him any more than you can help," the doctor answered. "I'll give him a sedative before he leaves."

After an hour had slowly passed, they walked out of the hospital, Nat supported on either side by John and Mr. Merryweather. Jean got into the back seat of the station wagon and the two men lifted Nat in beside her. She patted her shoulder and said, shyly, "Put your head here, Nat. You will ride more comfortably."

Nat smilingly obeyed, and with John driving at a crawl, they rode toward the outskirts of town. As they passed a drug store Nat came to enough to murmur, "Say, look here. I've got a sort of job driving for a lady from the East—name of Clarissa Hodges—she's stopping at the Pioneer Hotel. Will you phone her about my accident, please?"

"Of course I will," said Jean. "By the way, Nat, is she nice? Do you like her, I mean?"

"You bet," Nat answered. "She's swell—very rich, but you'd never know it—she's so kind and sort of—of simple."

"Then I'll invite her to come out to the ranch to see you," declared Jean impulsively.

Over the telephone she arranged with Miss Hodges, who had a very nice voice, that Mr. Merryweather would bring her to the ranch on Monday.

"She was awfully distressed about you, Nat," Jean reported. "Says you're not to worry about your job with her, or anything else."

There was so much to tell Nat on the drive out from town—about Pedro's accident the lost cattle, the new rooms, and, of course, their great surprise about John and his riding Brahma bulls. Jean talked on and on, holding Nat's head against her shoulder, while he muttered faint replies.

"Did you ever find the earrings and stuff, Jean?" the boy asked.

"Of course we did," said Jean, going on to describe their discovery of the pack rat thief. "At first I thought I'd never forgive Pedro for not thinking about pack rats—two old timers like you and Pedro and neither of you thought of them and their thieving tricks. Of course now," Jean went on soberly, "I'd forgive Pedro for anything. Poor old fellow. Oh Nat, he is so crippled and so brave and good-natured, it breaks your heart to see him."

"As far as I'm concerned," Nat answered, "I've never lived in a house before where there was any jewelry lying around for pack rats to steal—and I guess it was about the same for Pedro."

Then Nat heaved a great sigh. "Gee, I'm glad you found the stuff," he said, happily. Then he went on: "You don't know how I've wanted to come back. When I cooled down

I knew how wrong I'd been. You never really doubted my honesty; it was just what your father called 'the old pattern of suspicion' that made me get so hot and bullheaded."

"Why didn't you come back, Nat?" Jean asked.

"I reckon I just didn't have the nerve, but, gee, what a fool I've been!"

At last they were home and the two men helped Nat to a bed on the sleeping porch. In spite of his pain he noticed the improvements on the house. As he settled into his bed he sighed deeply, "Gosh, it's good to be home!" And Jean's heart warmed at the words.

She made him some hot tea and toast and a poached egg and carried the food to his bed. After he had eaten, Nat's head cleared somewhat, and looking up at Jean with his old appealing grin, he began haltingly to tell his story.

"I hung around Tucson for a long while after I left here, doing odd jobs, just in hopes I'd meet one or the other of you on the street and we could make it up."

Jean broke in, "We were trying so hard to find you, Nat. Didn't you see our ad in the paper? Or hear our broadcast on the lost-persons hour on the radio?"

"No," said Nat. "I didn't. Of course I wasn't listening to the radio, and I must have missed it in the paper." He went on, "Once I hitched a ride out to a ranch near here and then I walked up the road of Circle M and stood for about an hour lookin' at the lights in your windows. It was my home, all right."

"Oh Nat, how awful!" exclaimed Jean. "To think of you standing out there in the dark. Why didn't you come in?"

"I wanted to, Jean," he said softly, "but I was too stiff-

necked, I reckon. So I moseyed on back to town—feelin'
sort of empty—like I'd lost my last friend."

"Poor boy," said Jean and laid her hand over his. Nat
clasped his lean fingers around hers.

"Say," he said suddenly, sitting up, "how come you
folks are still here? I thought you were all set to go home
in the middle of last October. That's all you and John
talked about before I—I lit out," he finished lamely.

"John wanted to stay and build up the herd after all
our disasters," Jean explained.

"*John* did?" repeated Nat, incredulously.

"Yes," John's sister answered proudly. "Oh Nat, you
wouldn't know John, he's changed so. Do you remember
how you once said, 'maybe the West will make a man of
him'? Well, you were right, Nat. It has. He's just stood
up to one disaster after another—the worse things have
been, the better he's gotten."

"Good enough," said the boy. Jean seemed more contented than he remembered ever having seen her, Nat was
thinking. She was ever so much more sure of herself. "I'll
bet she likes it here now, too," Nat thought to himself,
"and doesn't know it."

"How about you, Jean?" he dared ask. "Did you want
to stay, too?"

"Oh I still want to go back home—the sooner the
better," Jean answered blithely, but the thought passed
through her mind that maybe she wasn't so eager to go
back, after all, especially now that Nat had come home.

"Go on and finish telling me about you," Jean told him
then.

"Where was I? Oh yes. Well, I didn't have much luck with jobs around Tucson, so when I saw an ad in the paper from a ranch near Safford, wanting an experienced cowhand, I applied and got the job. I've been working there since early fall. They had a rodeo at Safford last month and I took a notion to enter the bronc riding contest. I won a hundred bucks at that show, so I took the money to come back to Tucson still hoping to run into you folks, in case you hadn't gone back East. You see, I never could bear to be far away from here. Right after I got back I saw Miss Hodges' ad, wanting someone to drive her around the country, and I've been doing that ever since."

"How did you happen to enter this rodeo then?" Jean asked him.

"Well, I just got the itch to try my luck again, having won at Safford. Miss Hodges paid my entry fee—you know the way people do. They gamble on a rider, then, if he wins, the sponsor gets a third. Not that the money meant anything to her, of course, but she's awfully kind, and she saw how much I wanted to do it."

"But then, why didn't you see John yesterday?"

"I didn't draw a horse yesterday, so I didn't stay to watch the show. But I saw him today and I was gettin' up my nerve to go and speak to him after today's show, but instead old Whirligig fixed it so that you found me."

Jean and Nat had been so absorbed that they had not heard a car drive up. Now came Bert's jovial hail, "Hi, fella, where are you?" He and Sally came out to the sleeping porch, each seizing one of Nat's limp hands, to shake it heartily.

"We stopped at the hospital after the show," said Sally, "and they told us the good news that you'd left with the Merryweathers."

"Gee, it's good to have you back, Nat," added Bert. "Why, I didn't see you with the other wolves around the chutes, I don't savvy."

He looked quizzically at Nat's drawn face. "That was a tough spill you took, fella. That Whirligig is twelve hundred pounds of the meanest, orneriest hoss flesh I've ever seen wrapped up in one hide. Yep, I bet he was raised on wild grass and jumpin' beans, and never got over his rearin' either."

John joined the group around Nat's bed, saying, "Here's to the Fiesta de los Vaqueros! Thanks to it, we've got Nat back."

"How did you make out on the bronc you rode today, Bert?" asked Jean.

"I didn't," Bert answered with a wry smile. "But maybe tomorrow I'll get a break with a better one—and maybe both John and I will do some good with our bulls. And say," Bert went on, fishing in his pockets, "shut your eyes and hold out your hand, Jack Merry!" John did as he was told and felt some crisp new money put into his hand. "Congratulations! You placed second yesterday"

"Really?" cried Jean. "How wonderful! How much is that, Bert?"

"One hundred and twenty smackers!" Bert replied, grinning broadly.

"Gee!" said the proud and beaming John. Then, "How about you, fella. Did you win?"

"Yes, he did," Sally answered for her husband. "But

the pupil beat the teacher. Bert placed fourth. Forty dollars."

"How do they divide the money?" asked Mr. Merry-weather, after he had shaken hands with both boys and added his congratulations.

"Well, you see," explained Bert, "the purse for the Brahma bulls is eight hundred dollars, and there are two go-rounds. That's four hundred dollars a go-round. The money is split first prize forty per cent, second, thirty per cent, third twenty per cent and fourth, yours truly, ten per cent."

"Tell them about the finals, Bert," suggested Sally.

"Oh sure," said Bert. "Top man for the two go-rounds gets forty per cent of the entrance fees. There are thirty contestants at ten dollars each—that's three hundred dollars. The same division as the day money applies to the finals."

"In other words," said Jean, "if John wins again to-morrow, he will get some of the entrance money, as well as his part of the day money?"

"Right," said Bert. "And who knows? Maybe he will!"

"I've got a hunch," said Nat. "And see here, Jean, you and your father ought to be in town tomorrow to watch John ride. Nobody has to be out here with me."

"Will you promise to stay in bed quietly while we are gone?" Jean asked him.

"Cross my heart," Nat answered, making a sign on his chest.

"All right then, we will," the girl said, smiling affec-tionately at him, "but we'll spank you if you dare get up."

And so, on the following day, the three Merryweathers

said goodbye to Nat and rode into town for the final performance of the rodeo.

Jean was beside herself with impatience for the Brahma bull event to take place. Would her brother win again? He must, he simply must, she told herself. She had overheard his talk with their father about what he was planning to do with the prize money. He was going to buy some heifers from the Stevens to replenish the Circle M herd. How proud she was of him, and how grateful to Bert and Lottie for their help and encouragement!

At last the announcer was stating that the Brahma bull event was on. Jean squeezed her father's hand in excitement as she waited to hear him call for "Jack Merry."

"Oh please let him draw a good bull!" she prayed. She had learned from John and Bert that it was almost as disastrous for the rider to draw a slow-moving bull as one of the "muss-hogs," since they were marked partly on the kind of bull they rode.

"Coming out of chute number five," she heard the announcer saying, "is Jack Merry of Tucson, riding Banana Horns."

Jean watched breathlessly as the gray bull lurched and kicked and swung around, with her brother holding on to the rope. She soon saw why this bull was called "Banana Horns," for, at every lurch, one of his horns dangled down before his eyes, looking for all the world like a banana. What a bucking brute that fellow was! John looked so small and slender on the great beast. But he sat there with unconcerned composure, balancing himself, apparently, with the greatest of ease.

At last came the welcome sound of the horn and John

slid to the ground. He dodged around behind the bull, which was making a lunge at the clown, picked up the rope, while the audience applauded, and the announcer shouted, "How did you like that ride, folks? Wasn't that a pip?"

"You bet," said a lean-faced man who was sitting beside Jean. "That was a beautiful job. If I was the judge I'd give him first prize on that ride. Did you take note how he spurred the bull?"

"I thought I did," Jean answered. "But why do they have to spur them? Isn't it dangerous enough just riding the bulls?"

"Wal," drawled her companion, "it's the rule, you know. Got to spur the bull at least once on the first three lunges."

"I wish you were the judge," Jean confided. "That rider is my brother."

"Wal, how you tell me," said the man. "Wal, miss, I hope he wins. I've bin attending rodeos all my life and that was one of the purtiest jobs of Brahma bull ridin' ever I saw."

"Oh will this show never end?" Jean asked her father again and again during the rest of the afternoon.

She had watched Bert ride his bull successfully. He had done well, too, so it appeared, on a bucking bronc. However, she was so eager to hear the outcome of her brother's ride that she could scarcely pay any attention to the performance in the arena.

At last the show was over, and Jean and her father waited in the car for John and Bert to come from the office where they had gone to learn their fate. One look at the smiling face of her brother told Jean the good news. Apparently the judges had agreed with the opinion of the stranger in the grand stand, for John had won first prize for that go-round, which meant that he was second man in the finals, for Dan Irving of Salinas, California, who had won the first go-round, had kept up his good work the second day, so he was ahead.

And now, not only had John won one hundred and sixty dollars for the first prize of that day, he had also won thirty per cent of the finals.

"Let's see," said Jean. "One hundred and twenty dollars for Friday, one hundred and sixty for today and thirty per cent of the entrance fees is ninety dollars more. That's —good gracious—you bloated millionaire—that's three hundred and seventy dollars! 'Ray for Jack Merry!"

"Did you win, Bert?" asked Mr. Merryweather. "You certainly did a beautiful job on your bull today."

"Yep," Bert answered. "I placed second—right after your loving son."

Back at the ranch Nat greeted them and was loud in his praise of John and his success.

"And to think you used to be a gunsul," he said with a chuckle.

Chapter XV

NEW JOBS FOR THE TWINS

Mr. Merryweather drove into Tucson the next afternoon to bring Clarissa Hodges to see Nat at the ranch. He had heard very little about her from the young man, nothing, indeed, but that she was well-to-do and from New York City. So he was quite unprepared for the person she turned out to be.

Clarissa Hodges, tall and well-built, was smartly dressed and well-groomed in the New York manner. Her expression was humorous and intelligent, and her large brown eyes held a twinkle in their depths.

As they drove out to the ranch Mr. Merryweather responded with pleasure to the talk of this charming woman.

Her voice was low and well-modulated, and what she said had point and flavor. Ever and again through her conversation ran the theme of her love for this country, which, until a month before, she had never seen.

When Mr. Merryweather helped her from the station wagon before the house, Miss Hodges turned to look back over the way they had come. She caught her breath in delight over the view of the valley, indigo blue in the late afternoon light with great crouching mountains surrounding it.

"It looks like the Bay of Naples!" she exclaimed. Then, "See the waves breaking on the beach," she said, indicating a streak of sandy soil in the distance.

She met the twins with eager friendliness, and Jean at once took her out to the sleeping porch where Nat was lying in bed.

"Hello, Nathaniel," she said. "Well, you've certainly got the prize spot in all Christendom to recuperate in, haven't you?"

"I'm awfully sorry I'm laid up, though, Miss Hodges," Nat answered. "I don't like to disappoint you, and I know you were counting on seeing a lot of the country hereabouts before you go back East. Have you found anyone to drive in my place, while I'm laid up?"

"No," answered Miss Hodges. "But I have another plan in the back of my mind."

She did not say at the moment what her plan was, but asked Jean to let her see the rest of the ranch house. Jean proudly displayed the two new rooms which her father had designed and Roberto had built. And proudly she took their guest in to see the bathroom.

"You haven't any idea how you appreciate a thing like this until you have to live without one," Jean commented. Then she told how she had longed for a bathroom when she had first come to the ranch and that, after her father had sold their cattle in the spring, he had put one in.

"I can imagine how you must have missed the comforts of your old home in the East when you first came out here," Miss Hodges said.

"Yes, I did at first," Jean replied, "but after we got the bathroom in I got accustomed to everything else. And it is so beautiful out here—it is a good place to live—this Arizona desert—" Jean stopped suddenly, surprised at her own words. "What am I saying?" the girl asked herself.

"You should see how two of our friends around here live," she went on hurriedly, and told Clarissa Hodges about the little shack of Bert and Sally Hazelton's.

"I'd like to see that place," said Miss Hodges with interest. "They sound like a fine young pair!"

"Oh they are!" Jean replied enthusiastically, going on to tell about Bert's training her brother to ride bulls, and how he had won so much money at the rodeo that they would be able to buy some cattle to add to their reduced herd.

"How many head of cattle will John's earnings buy you?" Miss Hodges asked.

"He hopes to buy eight heifers. Of course we ought to get a bull, too, but we can't afford that yet. Did Dad tell you that we lost our good bull?"

"Indeed he did," answered Miss Hodges. "He told me what a crack shot you are and how your promptness saved the Mexican's life."

"Well, that bull was worth a thousand dollars. It was a big loss."

They had left the house and Jean was showing Miss Hodges her chickens and garden when her father came upon them.

"Let's ask Miss Hodges to stay to supper, Jean" he said.

"Please do, Miss Hodges," said Jean eagerly. She liked this straight-forward woman very much and wanted to keep her there as long as possible.

"Why, I'd love to stay. Thank you both so much," Clarissa Hodges replied with a friendly smile.

It was at the supper table that she asked if she could come and stay with them as a paying guest.

"I'm in love with this stretch of the desert," she said, "and I want to come out here and stay as long as I can. I like simple food so you won't have to go to any extra trouble for me. If this delicious fried chicken and biscuits is a sample of your cooking ability, Jean, I'm afraid I'll put on weight. I realize, of course, that you and your father and brother will want to talk over my plan and decide whether or not I would be more trouble than my board and room rent would be worth. Let me hear from you by mail when you have decided—and I hope you will let me come."

Jean looked at her father across the table. He was looking very pleased at the idea, and so was her brother.

"I don't think we need to have a family conference, Miss Hodges," Jean said promptly. "I vote 'yes!' How about it, Dad and John?"

"Yes, indeed," said her father, meeting his daughter's gray eyes with a smile.

"That goes double for me!" exclaimed John, emphatically.

"That's wonderful!" said Miss Hodges. "Now you must be sure to charge me enough so that you will make a profit out of having me here."

"I should think twenty dollars a week would be fair," said Jean.

"No, my dear," answered Miss Hodges, "that isn't enough. Let's make it thirty-five—five dollars a day. And extra for a riding horse. I have already seen that you have some beauties. When Nat is well, he can keep on driving me around the country-side when he isn't busy working on the ranch."

"Five dollars a day is too much," said Jean. "Why not compromise on twenty-five dollars a week, since you insist?" And so it was settled.

"By the way, Jean," Miss Hodges added, "you mustn't give up your Spanish lessons your father was telling me about, just because I will be here. Let me take on the supper for the one night a week that you will be in town. I'd love it."

"You are a dear, Miss Hodges," said Jean, happily. "You think of everything."

Later that night John and Jean drove Miss Hodges to her hotel in Tucson and arranged to return for her in three days' time. On the way back to the ranch John said, "Look here, Sis, won't you need to buy some extra things for the house now that we are to have a lady like that living with us?"

"Well, I *do* wish we could put in a tank gas ice box and stove in the kitchen. That's what we need if we are to have a paying guest. But how on earth would we be able to afford it?"

"You can take my winnings to buy those things, Jean," her brother said. "Then, later, we can buy the cattle with the money we make by having her here."

"Would you really let me take your money for that?" asked Jean, eagerly.

"Sure. A guest in the hand is worth two dozen cows in the bush," he said, misquoting the proverb to suit his convenience. "And besides, I'll never forget what you did for *me*, Jeanie, when you agreed to stay out here another year." He stopped, embarrassed, then went on, "I know it was a heck of a sacrifice you made. I've wanted to say something about it for a long time."

"Oh that's all right, Twin," answered his twin, huskily. "Maybe as it's turned out, it wasn't so much of a sacrifice, after all."

"Jean," John then said, in a low, confidential tone, "I've a plan I want to talk over with you and Dad. Now that Nat is back, he can look after our herd, just as I've been doing since Pedro got hurt. You see, I want to go on the road to the rodeos with Bert, and earn more money. There is a special reason why I want to have a nest egg by next fall. Do you think Dad will agree to my going?"

"I don't know, John," answered his sister, slowly. "Perhaps he will. But tell me, why you want a nest egg by next fall, especially?"

"I want to learn to be a real cattleman," John's voice was serious, "not just go on being an amateur as I am now. So, I want to go to the University and take the agricultural course, specializing in animal husbandry. If I ride in the rodeos with Bert and Sally, I can share the expenses of their car with them, and we three can live very cheaply in their tent. Then I could save my winnings, and have money enough for my college expenses—tuition and living in town and so forth."

"Why John!" Jean's voice was enthusiastic. "I think that's a wonderful idea! I'm sure Dad will agree when he knows that's why you want to go—not just for the excitement of riding in rodeos.

"But see here," she went on, as a disturbing thought struck her, "if you are thinking about going to the University here, that means you won't be coming home with us in October as we were planning. Had you thought of that, John?"

"Of course I have, Sis," John answered. "That's the only thing about all this I don't like—the fact that the family will be separated. But, Jean, I want to stay here. This is where I belong—it's the sort of work I love and I want to be tops in it. Of course I won't stand in your and Dad's way—if you still want to sell the ranch and go back East, next October. But it's Arizona for me for the rest of my natural life. It's got me, this country. I want to stay here forever."

Jean sat silent awhile, brooding over what her brother had said. It was the first time she had ever thought that they might not eventually return to their old home. All her plans had been made in that direction—all the improvements they had made on the ranch had been to the end that they would be able to get a better price when they sold it. And now John wanted to stay here, forever.

And her father? Would he want to stay, too, Jean wondered. His health had improved so much out here. Perhaps it was the best place for him to live and now that he was painting he had work that kept him contented.

"Well, Jean Merryweather," she said to herself, "what about you?"

"Of course," she heard her brother saying, "whether or not I can go on the rodeo circuit with Bert and Sally depends on Nat. If he is willing to stay and run our cattle, I can go. Otherwise, of course, I can't. But I bet he will."

"If he is still awake when we get back tonight, let's ask him," said Jean. "And John," she went on timidly, "I think your plans are wonderful even though I hate to think of the Merryweathers being separated."

Both Nat and their father were awake when the twins returned, and they all sat up late listening to John's scheme. Nat needed no persuasion at all to agree to stay. Mr. Merryweather was very pleased to learn that one of his children wished to go to college, and gave his wholehearted endorsement to John's plan.

"But, Daddy," said Jean, "this will mean that the Merryweather family will be broken up. Because when John is through college, he plans to stay in Arizona and be a cattleman."

"Of course, dear," her father answered. "To tell you the truth, Jean, I would like to stay here, too. I love this land." His eyes turned to the great window through which the bright moonlight was streaming.

"Really, Dad?" asked John, eagerly. "Well, say, when I learn to be a good cattleman we can run enough cattle on the ranch to support the whole family. After all, Uncle George made a living off it."

"Yes," answered Jean, "but there was only one of Uncle George—and there are three of us—four, counting Nat."

"Nat and Pedro cancel each other," John reminded her.

"Well, anyway," Jean went on, slowly, "we don't have to settle our whole future life tonight, do we? The immediate problem is whether or not you are to go on the rodeo circuit—and since Nat agrees to stay in your place, that's all settled."

Nat had been listening to this family discussion, turning eagerly from one to the other. It began to sound as if the Merryweathers might settle in Arizona for good, he thought. How he hoped that would really happen!

"Gosh, Nat," said John. "You'll never know how glad I was when you came back here. Bert and I had this plan all cooked up, but we didn't see how I could leave the ranch without hiring a strange cowhand. Then, providentially, you turn up. Honest, fella, I hate to say it, but I'm glad Whirligig bucked you off."

They all laughed. "To tell you the truth, John," Nat answered, "so am I!"

They went on, then, to discuss ways and means of buying some heifers as well as putting in the tank gas.

"Let's have a gas ring put under the hot water tank, while we're having the other things done," Jean suggested. "Don't you remember how hot it was in the house last summer whenever we made a fire for hot water? Our guest won't like that. How about it?"

"Good enough, answered her father. "And we will have them install an overhead gas light in the kitchen for you to cook by, Jeanie."

"Hurray!" said Jean. "With all these new gadgets I'll have a lovely time keeping house. And it will take away a lot of Nat's work, too, for with the gas, he won't have to gather stove wood—and don't forget the fine cold place we'll have in which to keep the milk."

"Here's my contribution to our business plans," said Nat. "Why not get a bull on credit from Lottie Dawson? I'm sure she'll be willing to sell one to you on time."

"No, Nat," replied Mr. Merryweather. "We mustn't go into debt. For the present, we can go on using Lottie's bull. It's heifers we need. I think that with Miss Hodges' board and John's earnings we can manage to buy a few."

"I don't know about the rest of you," said Jean, stifling a yawn, "but I must get some sleep. 'Night, folks."

It was some time before sleep came to the girl, however. With eyes open in the dark, she lay quietly in bed, having what she called to herself a "soul-searching." What about this plan of John's to stay out here? If he really wanted to be a cattleman, they shouldn't sell the ranch. They should keep it so that he could have it after he graduated from the University. But what would happen in the meantime? Would Nat stay here alone, after she and her father returned East, with John spending weekends and holidays helping him? How could those two manage without a woman to do for them?

Jean tossed and turned in her narrow bed. Her mind went back to her Connecticut home—she thought of her friends running in at all hours, of the phone ringing, of dances and parties and everything else thad had made up her life. "The West has captured John and Dad—and almost—almost me!" she whispered to herself. She remembered what she had said to Miss Hodges, and how startled she had been to hear herself saying those words, "It *is* a good place to live—this Arizona desert."

"That was me—Jean Merryweather—saying that," she told herself. "That may be what I really think. Maybe it's just habit—thinking that I want to go back East—back home, I mean."

Suddenly, before her mind's eye, came the picture of her father when he had first come to Arizona over a year ago—how white and frail and drawn he had been. Then, as he looked now, brown and well with a sparkle in his eye, with energy and an alert mind, painting away day after day on his beautiful water colors.

Still puzzled and unsure, she went to sleep, at last.

Busy days followed getting John ready for his great adventure. As soon as the gas installation was completed, Mr. Merryweather and John drove into town to fetch Miss Hodges. To Jean's delight, she, herself, suggested that she pay a month's board in advance.

One day, shortly after, Bert and Sally drove up to the ranch to pick up John. They had a small wagon trailer hitched on to the car, loaded with camping paraphernalia. Jean hated to see her brother go, but she smiled at him and watched the car as long as she could see it. They were headed east for Houston, Texas, for their first show.

"Write often, John," Jean had said, when her brother kissed her goodbye, "and tell us really how you are getting along—don't make up fairy tales to keep us happy."

For the first few weeks the people at the ranch received only picture postal cards from John. One morning, however, Jean came into the house waving an envelope. "Here's a real letter from John, folks," she said to her father and Nat and Clarissa Hodges who were all in the living room. "Do you want me to read it aloud?"

"Yes, do," they answered.

"Dear Folks at Circle M," Jean read, "Herewith is some news of your wandering boy. Don't ever let anybody tell you that riding in rodeos is any bed of roses. For the first five shows neither Bert nor I made a cent, and, of course, our expenses went right on—win, lose or draw.

"One day, after we'd paid our entrance fees at the Fort Worth show, we had exactly six cents among the three of us—and nothing to eat. But that's where Sally showed her stuff. What does she do but take her rifle and go out and bring back nine quail for dinner. Then she went to a bakery and persuaded the proprietor to sell her two cents worth of lard and she went to the market and got the owner to sell her four cents worth of potatoes—and honestly, folks, I never tasted a better meal than that one.

"And next day both Bert and I won riding bulls—he won ninety-five dollars and I won sixty-five, so we were sitting pretty again. It's a life of ups and downs, all right, but luckily we've been up for some time now. I'm expecting to be able to send a money order soon, for you to bank for me to help pay my expenses at the U.

"Gee, how I miss all of you! Of course this is lots of fun and very exciting, but I'd love to be back at Circle M Ranch right now, sitting down to one of Jean's messes of fried chicken. Not that Sally isn't a first rate cook—she is, sure enough!

"Your letters are very welcome. I've heard from Jean at every town where we've stopped.

"How are the cattle coming along? I don't suppose you've had money enough yet to buy a good bull—I wish I could make enough to buy a real champion to take the place of the not-so-lamented Domingo Third. And speaking of Domingo that makes me think of rifles, and Sally is as crack a shot as Jean. Last night we had stewed rabbit for supper which Sally had shot—almost as good as the rabbit stews Nat used to make.

"Do you know what happened to me today? I rode my first bronc in a show. Here's another 'Bert-ism' for Jean. When I asked him if he thought I could try to ride bucking broncs, Bert said, 'Sure, all you need is iron in your muscle, salt in your gizzard and plenty of hoss savvy—and boy, you've got all three!' Well, that set me up no end, so I entered and didn't get bucked off either. Of course I didn't win, but then I never thought I would the first time. Poor Bert got bucked off the first lunge, but then he had drawn 'Holy Terror' a bad horse that lives up to his name. My horse was pretty tame, I'm glad to say. His name was 'Mussolini.'

"Now, with two strings to my bow, I should be able to make some real money at this game. I certainly hope so, for, unlike Sally and Bert, I must say the excitement of this business isn't enough to keep me at it. Sally said the other day that even if Bert never won she would try to figure out a way to attend all these rodeos. She never gets tired of it, but as for me, except for the differences in geography, I think when you've seen one rodeo you've seen them all.

"No, it's the possibility that next time I may win that keeps me at it—not any foolishness about what an exciting life it is. As a matter of fact yesterday I saw a poor chap who used to be a champion bronc rider. He was thrown off his horse at Madison Square Garden a few years ago and got such a wallop that he's never been right since. He hit his head something the way Nat did—only, unlike Nat, he never came to. He is really crazy now, but he attends almost all the rodeos and tries to compete. Of course the authorities won't let him, but the poor chap begs from the other wolves and gets a handout of food or cigarettes from some one or other every day or so—that's all he has to live on.

"I tell you when you see a fellow like that it makes you think. Gee, I hope nothing like that ever happens to Bert.

"Did I tell you that I have met Sally's father and mother? They were out West on a trip and stopped off at Dallas for the rodeo. They are both awfully nice and devoted to Sally. Her father has an important job in one of the auto factories in Detroit. Of course while they were around we lived high. They took us to all the best hotels in Dallas for meals, so Sally got a rest from cooking for us.

"I told them about our ranch and how Jean is taking a paying guest and they said they would love to stay at our place next winter when they come out to visit Sally and Bert. They will be here—near Tucson, I mean, for about six weeks. So I told them I was sure my sister would be glad to have them. I hope I didn't talk out of turn, Jean. Did I?"

"Well," said Jean, with a toss of her head, "it sounds as if he thinks Dad and I are still going to be here next winter."

"I wish he were right," said Nat with a sigh.

"Go on and finish the letter, Jean," said her father.

"Well," Jean continued, "as I said, I hope to be sending you a money order in the near future. Bert and I have been getting good breaks lately and we've both 'done some good.' As a matter of fact I have won third place in the last three shows.

"Goodbye, family, and much love,

"From John."

Jean put the letter down after she had finished reading it. "He says he hopes nothing like that ever happens to Bert," she said. "How about himself? I wish he hadn't started riding bucking broncos."

"That isn't any more dangerous than riding bulls, Jean," said Nat. "And honestly there are very few accidents in rodeos. Just think how many boys competed here in Tucson, and of them all, I was the only person hurt and not badly either. Please don't worry about John. I'm sure he will be all right!" Nat gave her his most comforting smile.

"That is very reassuring, Nat," said Mr. Merryweather. "But I must say I share Jean's apprehension about bronco riding. We'll never forget seeing you thrown," he said, smiling affectionately at Nat. "You gave us a bad scare!"

"But look how well my accident turned out, sir," Nat answered. "It meant that we all got together again—and John was able to go away to earn money for college, and Jean started her guest ranch—and you all and Miss Hodges got together!"

"Hear, hear!" said Clarissa Hodges, gaily.

Chapter XVI

WESTWARD THE LAND IS BRIGHT

MANY GOOD THINGS CAME OUT OF THE FRIENDSHIP OF
Clarissa Hodges and the Merryweather family. She
watched with keen interest Mr. Merryweather painting in
the patio and suggested, one night shortly after she moved
in, that he put on a "one man show" in the living room.
She was enthusiastic about the pictures and got him to
put a price on two especially beautiful paintings of cactus
bushes in bloom. These she sent to two friends back East,
who immediately ordered more. From one of these gifts
of Clarissa's resulted what Jean thereafter always called
"Dad's Miracle." The picture, sent to a wealthy New York
woman, was hung in her living room where it was

seen by a prominent art dealer who operated a famous gallery.

It was a very surprised and pleased Mr. Merryweather who, shortly thereafter, received a letter from the art dealer, suggesting that he arrange a one man show in New York City in November. After much consultation it was decided that Jean and her father should go East to the opening of the show. While her father attended to the business in New York, Jean was to visit her old home in Connecticut.

At first Jean was reluctant to leave the ranch—for who would keep house for Clarissa and Nat with her gone? Then she suddenly thought of Conchita, old Pedro's niece. Perhaps they could hire the girl to take her place while she was away. Conchita, when consulted, was delighted to come and it was arranged that she should be there with Jean for two weeks before the departure so that Jean could train her in the ways of American cookery.

"Else, I'm afraid," Jean told the family, "you would have nothing to eat but *frijoles* and tamales, three times a day, with *tortillas* thrown in."

Pedro promised to come up and milk Sukey and take care of Jean's chickens, twice a day. Although badly crippled, he kept his cheerful, sunny manner, and the Merryweathers loved the old fellow for the philosophical patience with which he bore his misfortunes. Jean and her father often stopped in to see him at Roberto's house, and Mr. Merryweather had insisted on paying him a small pension each month, which Pedro contributed to his niece's household. It made him feel proud that he was not a burden on his relatives, but Jean knew how hard it had been for

her father to pay even that small sum before she began her
"guest ranch business."

Mr. Merryweather began busily assembling the pictures
he had made during his sojourn in Arizona. Not only did
he have landscapes and many paintings of desert blooms,
he had a whole series of rodeo and round-up subjects—
lively action pictures of bull dogging, bronc riding and
roping. He sent a few samples of this kind to the art dealer,
asking his advice about including them in the show. The
answer came back, "By all means, do."

From the proceeds of the pictures he had sold, Mr.
Merryweather was able to buy a few heifers from the
Stevens and Lottie Dawson. Nat was very proud of these
additions to Circle M herd. He took his job as superin-
tendent very seriously, riding the range faithfully to keep
an eye on the cattle, applying all the knowledge he had to
the improvement of the ranch.

The plentiful rainfall that summer meant that the pasturage was good, and, as a result, all the cattle looked fine
and fat. In spite of the loss of such a large part of the herd,
it looked as if they would have a good number of head to
sell after the fall round-up. The young cattle, which had
survived the last summer's drought, were excellent speci-
mens now.

"I wish we could get another bull of the class of
Domingo Third," Nat said to Jean one day.

"Maybe we can," Jean answered, "if Daddy makes
enough money from his show in New York. But I'd hate
to have a bull around here with a disposition like Domingo's."

"Well, Jean," Nat said, "if we can buy a new bull, I'll

try to pick out one with a personality like Ferdinand's for you."

"Don't tease me, Nat," Jean answered. After all, she reminded herself, Nat had not been present at either of those dreadful times when Domingo Third had behaved so terribly.

On September first Joe Smith drove up to the ranch in his battered truck, bringing a message from John—a telegram which had been phoned to his store, announcing that John would arrive in Tucson at noon that day by bus. Nat and Jean hurriedly drove in to town to meet him.

Oh, it was good to see her brother again, Jean thought, as he jumped from the bus and hurled himself at her. How well and sure of himself John looked! He gave her a big hug and pumped Nat's hand exuberantly.

"Sis," he said on the way home, "I've got some stuff for your patio garden in my bags—a couple of pepper tree slips from California and a lot of colored rocks I've picked up in the mining country we've been through. Boy, I've seen big hunks of the U.S.A. on this trip, all right!"

"How nice of you to think of my garden, John," said his sister.

"I've got a real present for you, Nat," John went on. "I won it at the Fort Dodge rodeo. It's a swell saddle with silver mounting."

"Gosh!" said Nat. "You'd better keep it for yourself, fella."

"Not a chance," John replied. "If it hadn't been for you, I couldn't have gone to that or any other rodeo, don't you ever forget, Old Hoss."

That night Circle M Ranch had a real celebration. Nat

rode over to Lottie Dawson's and invited her and Jake to come over for John's welcome home supper party. Jean outdid herself preparing her brother's favorite dishes. Around a bountiful table, they listened eagerly to John's tales of his rodeo experiences.

"Bert and Sally are grand to travel with," John commented. "They will be back at the close of this season—and Sally sent you all her love."

"Whatever will Bert do when he gets too old to ride in rodeos?" asked Jean.

"I reckon he'll be an announcer," John answered. "One day at Butte, the regular announcer took sick and Bert got wind of it and asked the manager to let him try it. He sure was a whiz. Made the audience split their sides at his 'Bert-isms.' He started out by saying, 'Well, folks, here's one announcer that actually knows something about cows. Believe it or not, I know positively, absolutely and without a gilmmerin' shadow of a doubt which end of a cow gets up first.' You should have heard 'em. They gave him a big hand and all afternoon they laughed at every crack he made, no matter how feeble it was. He is going to run an ad in *Hoofs and Horns* this winter offering himself as a rodeo announcer. Maybe he will be able to pick up some work in that line. If he can, he won't have to ride unless he wants to, because announcing pays pretty well, considering he always gets his money. It doesn't have to depend on his winning anything."

"I'm awfully glad," said Jean. "I've been worrying about what Bert and Sally would have to live on when he can't ride any more."

On registration day Jean and John went into town so that he might enroll for his year's work at the University. Afterwards they picked out a room nearby where he could stay from Mondays to Fridays.

Jean tried to stamp out the little wave of envy she felt toward her brother. She had never quite reconciled herself to doing without a college education—but now, well it looked absolutely impossible. She would go on studying Spanish, of course, and with a father like hers and a person like Clarissa Hodges living in the household she surely was not deprived of intellectual stimulation. But she longed for the gay life of college, too—the fun with boys and girls of her own age. She did not guess that her father had long since sensed this longing of hers, and that he understood her far better than she ever realized.

"Well," said John to his twin as they drove home to the ranch, "this is worth all the bumps I took to get it."

When he came home for his first week-end the family listened with delight to his enthusiastic talk of his courses and teachers. Saturdays and Sundays were busy days for John. He spent most of his time on the range with Nat, taking a keener interest than ever in the work, now that he was on his way to becoming an expert cattleman. He was immensely proud of Nat's work and the good condition of the herd.

Shortly after the fall round-up Jean and her father began their preparations for the trip East. Mr. Merryweather, with Nat's help, had crated and shipped the pictures some weeks before. And Clarissa and Jean had been busily engaged in buying "city clothes" for the girl who had been spending so much of her time in levis and frontier pants. It was wonderful having a woman like Clarissa to advise about her clothes, Jean thought. She had, for one thing, come so recently from the East herself that she knew what the styles were there.

Between training Conchita, who was very willing and an apt pupil, and getting her clothes ready, Jean had a busy time. But at last the great day came when she and her father boarded the train. Jean was beside herself with happiness. John and Nat and Clarissa Hodges were all at the station to see them off.

"Don't forget to come back, Jean," said Nat, huskily, as he squeezed her hand. He hated to see her go. Would her old life appeal to her so much that she would be discontented with Arizona again? he wondered. There was a prayer in Nat's heart as he watched the train pull out of the station—a prayer that Jean would come back to him.

As the train sped on over the miles Jean was wondering how her old home would look to her. Would she, like Sally Hazelton, think that the East was crowded by too many people living in too small a space?

The first few days in New York were full of excitement while Mr. Merryweather superintended the hanging of his pictures. The art dealer was enthusiastic about the work—and apparently the art critics only disagreed enough to make it interesting. Prior to the opening several pictures were marked "Sold" and at the opening the red star with "Sold" inscribed upon it appeared on many more.

Jean found herself thinking of these sales as steps toward buying a bull. She and her father made a little joke about it. "I arranged to get Domingo's two front feet," he would say, or, "I got one of Domingo's horns all lined up," and Jean would know by that how many pictures had been sold since the last report. Jean did not know it, but her father's eagerness to sell many pictures was not entirely in order to build up a herd of cattle. Mr. Merryweather had a secret plan which he was determined to put through, but he told Jean no word of this, yet.

The first week-end after the opening, they boarded a train for Connecticut where they were to be the guests of Dr. and Mrs. Braman. Jean looked at her old home with mingled feelings. It *did* look cluttered and squeezed together, she thought, like a pretty toy village. Her eyes had grown accustomed to great open spaces, vast skies and far horizons.

It was fun, great fun, seeing old friends, going to parties and dances, running in and out of neighbors' houses. She liked it all, of course—and yet—"What's happened to me?" she asked herself when she awoke early one morning. "For two solid years I've been longing to be here, and now— oh, darn it all, I'm homesick for Circle M Ranch, and for John and Lottie and Clarissa—and—and Nat," she finished, blushing furiously.

One day her father came to her with some news.

"Darling," he said, "I want to have a serious talk with you. Our tenants have made a very good offer to buy our house. I told them I wouldn't be able to give them an answer until I had talked with the other members of Merryweather, Incorporated. Now, my dear, I know you've always wanted to come back here to live—how lonely and unhappy you've been out West."

"Me, Daddy?" said Jean in great surprise. "Me lonely

and unhappy in the West? Why Daddy, I love it out there. I'm homesick to go back—really. Why, I—" She broke off as she saw the twinkle in her father's eyes and they both burst out laughing.

"Well," said Mr. Merryweather, "as Nat would say, 'who'd a-thought it?' Here I've been thinking, and so has John, for the last two years, that we were being selfish keeping you in that great lonesome place against your desires to be home in Connecticut . . ."

"It's sweet here, Dad," Jean told him. "I do love Connecticut and all my old friends—but there's so much to do out there—and life seems so—so worth while," she finished.

"Then shall we sell them the house, dear?" he asked.

"Sure, let's sell 'em the house," the girl answered in a perfect imitation of John's tone and manner. "We won't even have to consult John. He'll be tickled to death because you'll have more money to put into more land and cattle and a couple of Domingos, maybe."

"There will be more than enough for that," her father assured her. "Enough for a plan I've had in mind a long time—for you to stay in the East and go to college here, if you want to. How about it? Miss Hodges writes that Conchita is doing very well with the household and becoming a good cook, too. The girl is willing to stay on there and keep house for us. I had Clarissa sound her out when I found how well my pictures were selling, you see. You could stay on here and enter college at Vassar where your friend, Dorothy is, next term. Would you like that?"

Jean drew a long breath. Here it was—the chance she'd longed for—but now?

"College, Daddy," she cried eagerly, throwing her arms

around his neck. "Why can't I got to the University of Arizona along with John? Then I could be home week-ends."

"Is that what you really want, Jean?" her father asked.

"Yes, Daddy," Jean said, solemnly, "that's what I really want—to be home on the ranch with you."

Back in New York they wired the family at the ranch, "Home soon. With the wherewithal for a brace of Domingos. Love. Dad and Jean," a wire which sent John and Nat scouring the countryside to find a suitable successor to Domingo Third.

As the train got closer and closer to Tucson, Jean was beside herself with excitement. Ever since they had left El Paso, she had sat at the window drinking in the vast beauty of the great open desert—loving every inch of it. She could scarcely wait to get home. "Home" nowadays meant Circle M Ranch, she thought to herself, not the tight little New England town—mighty pretty, she admitted—but still, not a patch on Circle M.

How good it would be to see John and Clarissa—and—and Nat! At the thought of Nat she felt herself blushing, as she had done that morning not so long before, in Connecticut.

A rousing welcome awaited them, as they got off the train. She and John hugged each other, unashamedly, before a whole platform full of strangers. Clarissa gathered her in her arms and kissed her heartily—but Nat held back. Finally Jean went up to him and shyly put out her hand.

"Welcome home, Ma'am," he said, in the tone and manner with which he had addressed her long ago when they first met. But Jean was not disappointed, for she saw that Nat's dark eyes were bright with joy.

One Sunday, soon after their return to the ranch, Jean and John and Nat and Clarissa and Mr. Merryweather took a long horseback ride to call upon their good neighbors, the Stevens, Lottie Dawson, Roberto and Yolanda and Pedro. As the sun was setting, they turned their horses homeward. A molten glory radiated upward from behind the dark, sharp-edged peaks, filling the sky with gold and crimson light.

Instinctively the party stopped their horses, hushed by the beauty of the heavens. All around the horizon the wonder spread, staining the sky with matchless hues. Beyond the indigo valley hung dream-like mountains of rosy violet touched with sharp purple shadows.

"Do you remember that poem of Arthur Hugh Clough's that we've always liked?" asked the twins' father. And he quoted softly:

> "And not by Eastern windows only
> When daylight comes, comes in the light;
> In front the sun climbs slow, how slowly!
> But Westward, look, the land is bright."

"Westward the land is bright," murmured Jean.

John shook himself free of their mood of wonder. "Clough was an Englishman, wasn't he? How did he know what Arizona is like?"

"That is just what it is—big bright land," said Jean.

Without quite knowing how it happened, Jean and Nat lingered behind the others on their way back to the house. They walked their horses slowly, side by side, each filled

They walked their horses side by side

with awareness of the other. Finally Nat put his hand over Jean's where it rested on the saddle horn. Jean turned to look deep into his eyes.

Then, their hearts filled with new happiness, they rode on slowly, side by side, while the glory faded from the sky and the desert grew dim and mysterious in the twilight.

THE END